NOHAR HADN'T RUN FROM THE COPS SINCE HE WAS FOURTEEN. . . .

But the cops here seemed hell-bent on killing him.

There were two cars in the garage, a Jaguar air-car and a sleek black BMW with tinted windows. Neither looked bulletproof. But the tinted windows gave him an idea.

It took Nohar a few agonizing minutes to short out the lock and get into the BMW. Once in, he hacked into the auto-navigation feature and jacked up the minimum speed to sixty klicks an hour.

Thanks to the gas the cops had released, Nohar could barely see through his stinging and watering eyes as he got the Jaguar opened. Then he ducked back into the BMW, engaged it in drive, and let the navigation computer take over. Nohar took cover in the Jaguar as the garage door began opening.

The cops began strafing the garage. Nohar could hear the Jaguar taking hits. But he also heard the BMW's engine rev up. Heard it accelerate out toward the cops. The gunfire got a little more frantic.

While he heard all this going on, Nohar desperately worked on the dash, trying to get the Jaguar moving. It took him five tries with his claws fully extended to get the jumper engaged.

The sound of something going smash out in the street made him risk a look out the windshield. The BMW had taken a full header into one of the cars. The police were pouri

He had a chance to get o
tracted. Nohar maxed out th

D0448711

FEARFUL SYMMETRIES

THE RETURN OF NOHAR RAJASTHAN

S. ANDREW SWANN

DAW BOOKS, INC.
DONALD A. WOLLHEIM, FOUNDER
375 Hudson Street, New York, NY 10014

ELIZABETH R. WOLLHEIM
SHEILA E. GILBERT
PUBLISHERS

First Printing, April 1999
1 2 3 4 5 6 7 8 9

This book is dedicated
to the Cajun Sushi Hamsters,
who saw the first one.

ACKNOWLEDGMENTS

I would like to thank the members of the Cleveland SF Writer's workshop who looked over this: John; Jerry; Geoff; Maureen; Charlie; Becky; Mary. I would like to stress that nothing in this book is their fault.

CHAPTER 1

Nohar Rajasthan stood still, the stand of pines giving him partial cover from the clearing about thirty meters away. His breathing was slow and deep despite the adrenaline that was tightening his perception. He could smell the musk of the deer in the clearing, and from the way the deer stood—taut, alert—Nohar could tell that the animal was beginning to smell a predator in the vicinity.

The bewildered animal had not yet figured out where the smell was coming from. Nohar moved deliberately so that when it knew, the knowledge would be too late to help it.

The wind was in Nohar's face, bringing a light dust of February snow to his fur. He could feel his age in his joints as he raised the bow to be level with his shoulder. His arm was steady despite the ache that shot through his right knee and his left shoulder.

He could feel his pulse, as his aging metabolism sensed the proximity of combat and blood. He sighted through the bow, focusing on the unmoving buck. The scene through the eyepiece had the contrast artificially heightened to compensate for his poor day vision. Nohar placed the crosshairs over a vital spot, and drew back on the bow. A small digital readout in the corner of the eyepiece started reading off the kilos of tension he put on the composite bowstring.

The small green numbers had just crossed three

hundred when the buck moved. The movement snapped the animal into focus and Nohar loosed the arrow slightly early.

The shaft plunged deep into the front of the buck's chest. The impact dropped it to its knees and nearly knocked it over. It let out a bellow and struggled to its feet. The wind carried the ferric scent of blood to Nohar.

The smell lit up his nerves like a high-tension wire. The universe shrank down to just him, his prey, and the thirty meters between them. The buck struggled to run, even with its mortal injury. Nohar dropped the bow, springing after the animal.

Nohar's adrenaline-fueled attack closed with the buck before it had reached the edge of the clearing. Like his genetic ancestors, he attacked the neck. He sank his fangs into the soft flesh of the throat, his powerful arms—claws fully extended—crushed the vertebrae, and his one fully functional leg kicked at the buck's abdomen, slicing it open from sternum to groin.

It was dead in less than a minute.

When the buck ceased moving, Nohar rolled off of it, exhausted. He lay next to the body, sucking in breath after burning breath while snow swirled in the pines above him.

In every part of his body, he felt his age. His fifteen-year-old knee injury flared as if he'd just recently torn apart every tendon and ligament. His hands ached with arthritis as the claws slowly tried to retract. The small of his back ached, as if someone was trying to knee him in the spine, right above his tail.

Beneath him, pine needles itched, and were sticking to the blood in his fur.

Over and over, in his mind ran the words, *Too old, way too old.*

When he'd retired to the woods, escaping human and morey alike, hunting wasn't a difficulty. Back then, he'd even occasionally hunted without a bow.

Now, with the bow, he could barely manage it. His forty-year-old body was telling him that his days as a hunter were numbered. Soon he was going to have to either go into town for his food supply or violate the local firearms restrictions.

Doing either was too much like admitting defeat. As far as he was concerned, self-sufficiency was all he had going for him. Someone whose genetic code was engineered for combat, and whose ancestors included Siberian and Bengal tigers, should certainly be able to feed himself.

Nohar winced as the claws in his hands finally retracted. *It'd be easier if the gene-techs didn't always fuck up the hands.*

Nohar's bloody confrontation had lasted less than two minutes, but he lay next to his kill for nearly half an hour. Between that, and the several hours he'd spent lying in wait, it was late afternoon before he tied up the body and started carrying it home.

A year ago he would have hung the meat out in a tree and gone for another kill. Today, though, he felt all of his forty years. Today, he would just return to his cabin, wash up, and sleep.

The mountain snow stopped as he made his way through the pine forest toward the clearing where his cabin was. As the trees thinned, Nohar could catch occasional glimpses of where the Sierra Nevadas merged with the sky. His eyes weren't keen enough to resolve details on the neighboring mountains, but they were a constant, a cloud bank that never moved.

He was so swamped in the aroma of musk, blood, and his own exertion that he was almost in sight of his cabin before he smelled the car. The scent drew him up short. There was strict regulation of vehicles this close to the park, especially in the homestead areas.

Nohar stopped at the base of a bluff that was between him and the cabin. He could smell a human now, which meant that being covered in blood and stinking to high heaven might not have betrayed his presence to the stranger.

Nohar knew it was a stranger, no one he had ever met before. That meant that it was unlikely that it was a ranger. He knew all of the humans that worked the forest around here.

Nohar had been avoiding people for so long that he seriously considered simply waiting out his visitor. Eventually the pink would leave, and he could go back to his life. When the thought made itself concrete, Nohar felt disgusted with himself.

He would deal with the stranger, whoever it was.

He tossed the buck over the bluff, ahead of him. He pulled himself up after it. His shoulder protested, but he swallowed his discomfort. He didn't know who was watching, but there was no reason for him to advertise how difficult this day felt.

The front of Nohar's cabin angled toward the bluff, and his visitor had been sitting on the cinder blocks that made the makeshift front steps. He stood up as Nohar cleared the bluff, took a step forward, and stopped.

The guy got high marks for not shying away. Nohar was old, but he still towered over the man, 260 centimeters worth, and right now his fur was matted with blood. Nohar smiled, but politely, without showing any teeth. "Can I help you?" he asked.

The man did not belong in the woods. He wore a black suit and tie, and his vehicle was a silver Jaguar aircar. The man belonged at a board meeting somewhere. In contrast, Nohar's appearance stopped just short of feral—and then only because of the bow and utility belt he wore.

"Nohar Rajasthan?" The man asked.

"You are?" Nohar asked, picking up his kill. Now that he saw the man, he didn't feel any threat from him. He'd smelled hostility off of a lot of pinks; he wasn't getting any from his man. If anything, Nohar smelled fear—which made sense considering the situation. Precious few pinks ventured into the homestead areas.

As Nohar carried his kill to the back of the cabin, his visitor followed at a careful distance. "My name's Charles Royd. I'm a lawyer from Los Angeles."

Nohar made a noise halfway between a snort and a growl. He didn't like lawyers, and he liked Los Angeles even less. It had been nearly a decade since the National Guard razed almost all the moreau neighborhoods in LA. Nohar had been there when it happened. Ten years was not enough time to wash the taste out of his mouth.

"It's been difficult finding you—"

Nohar nodded. "That's intentional." He hung up his kill on an iron hook attached to the back wall of the cabin.

"I would like to talk with you."

"Come inside, then."

Nohar's cabin was an ancient building made of local wood. There was no electricity, and water came from a rusty hand pump in the corner. The furniture was limited to a bed, a table, a few rough chairs big enough to support Nohar's 300 kilos, and a footlocker. He hung his bow on a peg in the wall and began pumping water into a plastic bucket.

As the handle made screeching protests, Nohar said, "So what does an LA lawyer want with me?"

There was a hesitation in the lawyer's voice as he looked around the sparse room. Nohar didn't prod the man, he simply finished topping off the bucket. Then he brought out a scrub brush and began attacking the blood matted in the fur of his leg. Within a few moments the water had turned the color of rust.

"You're Nohar Rajasthan, the private investigator. You do missing persons work."

From the man's expression, and his confused smell, Nohar could tell that he was having trouble reconciling the rustic surroundings with the moreau he was looking for.

Nohar scrubbed his legs and said, "No."

For a moment he thought to leave it like that and let the crestfallen lawyer leave disappointed. But Nohar knew if he did that, the man would be back. "Once, but not anymore. I'm retired."

The man stepped forward and extended his hand. "I represent a client who wishes to hire you."

Nohar looked from the hand to the man's face, then back again. He didn't take it. He returned to grooming the blood off of his other leg. "I'm retired."

After a moment, the lawyer dropped his hand and said. "Hear me out. My client was adamant that I hire you. I can offer fifty thousand for this job in advance."

Nohar looked up at the man with narrowed eyes. He was starting to distrust him. Pinks bearing large sums of money usually meant trouble. The last time anyone offered him nearly that amount, he'd been beaten, shot, had his best friend killed, and was eventually driven out of his hometown.

"I don't handle human cases."

"This isn't a human case. I'm just an intermediary.

My client desperately wants this person found." He
took a small folder from his pocket and removed a
high-res picture of a feline moreau. "His name is Manuel. He disappeared from his job a week and a half
ago." He placed the picture on the rough-hewn table.
The picture was obviously from some state or federal
ID. Manuel didn't look as if he liked having his picture
taken. Nohar didn't reach for the picture, but he did
examine it. Broad nose, broader than Nohar's in proportion to the face. The fur was glossy black for the
most part, but there were bands of russet in it, sculpt-
ing the outlines of a snarl that didn't quite show teeth.
The ears were laid back, so Nohar couldn't make out
any markings.

"Species?" Nohar asked, though he expected the
answer already.

"He's a crossbreed between two large felines."

Mule, he means. Nohar felt a wave of sympathy for
the kid in the picture. How old was he—ten, thirteen?
Physically mature, but still young enough to take the
pain of the world's prejudice personally. Bad enough
to be nonhuman and young, but to be a mule as well?
That was the worst curse Nohar could wish on anyone,
to be an outcast from both worlds, human and nonhuman. The genetics of mules were always a crap shoot.
No two moreys had their genes fiddled in quite the
same way, and with a mule the engineered and nonengineered chromosomes decided to link up mostly at
random. A mule could turn out nearly pink, or—more
likely—like a defective beast only slightly out of the
jungle. Perhaps worst were the mules that got the engineered body, and whose brain reverted to an animal
nature. Manuel looked lucky, humanoid—and the fact
he held a job somewhere meant that his intelligence
wasn't too adversely affected.

Most moreaus nowadays were born as the result of

artificial insemination. Manuel was an exception. Two feline species had merged in him—two parents who probably never expected their union might result in offspring.

In every case, a mule was a minority of one. Even Nohar had the knowledge that there were, somewhere, other tigers descended from the same genetic stock as he. Manuel was different, unique. That uniqueness would forever prevent him from being fully accepted into the moreau community, such as it was.

Almost better to be a frank.

The pink lawyer was still talking. "He was last seen at his job, at the Compton Bensheim Clinic."

There's still a Compton left? Nohar thought.

There was an irony having a mule work at a Bensheim Clinic, where the point was to allow the thousands of moreau species to breed with their own genetic material. There were so many strains that even a couple who looked exactly alike needed genetic testing to see if they could breed true. Nine times out of ten, they couldn't. Two moreaus not only had to have the same genetic ancestors, they had to've been engineered out of the same lot in the same lab. There were probably twenty-five hundred species of moreau rat alone. Add to that the fact that a lot of gene-techs had fiddled with the reproduction instinct in their creations—the idea was to keep a constant supply back during the war—a lot of moreys *had* to breed. It was a problem that the Bensheim Clinics were designed to solve.

From the folder, the lawyer brought out two ramcards and laid them on the table. The little plastic rectangles shimmered rainbow colors, masses of optically-encoded data fracturing the light. He tapped one and said, "This is your fee, to be credited to any account you prefer. The other is a comprehensive data file on Manuel."

"Did I say I'd take the case?"

"Take some time to think it over—"

"Who's trying to hire me?"

"My client has requested anonymity."

Any inclination Nohar had to get involved with the lawyer's offer evaporated at that point. He stared at the man and said quietly, "Leave."

"But—"

"I'm retired," Nohar said with a growl under his voice. "And I don't work for people who hide behind lawyers."

"My client assures me that when you hear the details you'll want to take this job—"

Nohar stood. The scrub brush in his hand sprayed droplets of bloody water across the table and Manuel's picture. "Take your money and leave. Take that sports car and find some Culver City pink who doesn't ask questions."

The man backed up and then reached over, taking the ramcard that was to be Nohar's payment. "I'll take this. But I'm leaving the picture and the file. When you read it, you might change your mind." He put the ramcard back in the folder, and put it away. He then took another shiny card, paper this time, and placed it on the table. "This is my card. Call me if you change your mind."

"I won't."

Nohar stood, towering over the man until he'd retreated from the cabin, and he didn't sit until he heard the fans of the Jaguar aircar engage. As the lawyer flew away, Nohar finally sat. He spared one ironic glance at the ramcard the man had left, the file on Manuel. The thing was worse than useless to Nohar. He didn't have a comm to read the damn thing.

He gave Manuel a last look, wondering why the curve of his dark-furred cheek seemed familiar. Then he returned to the business of washing the blood from his hands.

CHAPTER 2

Nohar woke up to monochrome night and was instantly alert. He didn't immediately know what had awakened him, but he felt an unease in his gut that he translated into threat. He tensed, unmoving, focusing on what he could perceive.

The wrongness quickly coalesced into a series of rapid realizations. He heard nothing, the forest had fallen into a silence that was unnatural. Something had startled the nearby insects and night birds into quiescence. Large predator, probably human. The second impression came rapidly upon the first, a smell that was alien to the woods. Petroleum-based, it made his nose itch.

The smell had him moving even before the final impression reached his conscious awareness. He rolled off the bed to take cover on the floor even as he realized that the shadow that the front window cast on the wall had acquired a new bulge at the base of the frame, as if someone had gently set something on the sill.

Something that contained a lot of petroleum-based hydrocarbons.

Something that exploded three seconds after Nohar hit the floor.

Nohar hugged the floor, curling up to expose as little of himself to the wash of heat as possible. He felt debris from the window scatter itself on his back like hot coals. He could smell the acrid scent of burning hair, then it became too painful to breathe through his nose.

The moment the explosion was over, he rolled, putting out half a dozen small fires on his back. Adrenaline was already coursing through his veins, awakening ancient programmed combat reflexes. The flames engulfing the ceiling took on an unnatural clarity. They seemed to roll from the front of the cabin like breakers on hell's own ocean.

Nohar heard another explosion. There was little concussion, but he could taste the chemicals in the air. Another firebomb.

The blast from the front window had knocked his bow from the wall. He rolled across the floor, not daring to stand, and grabbed it and the two arrows that hadn't spilled from its attached quiver.

Nohar's cabin had turned into an oven, and he knew that in a few seconds it would become a crematorium. The doors and windows were useless for escape, engulfed in orange fire.

Nohar slammed his fist into the floor. The blow was partly martial art, partly adrenaline, and mostly desperation. Luck was with him. The board under his fist gave with an anemic crack and a puff of dry rot. He dropped the bow and grabbed the boards to either side, pulling up and out with all the strength his aged muscles could manage.

The boards came up with a squeal of protesting nails. Even so, it was almost too late. The air was searing his lungs, and he could smell his fur burning again.

Nohar grabbed the bow and dove through the hole, landing face first in the soft earth under the cabin. There was barely room for him to roll and put out his smoldering fur.

Nohar twisted away from the hole he'd made—he could feel it sucking air from underneath the cabin. He knew he'd only gained himself a few moments. Now that the dry wood of the cabin had caught, it had become a bomb itself. In a minute or two the heat would make the whole building combust into a fireball worse than any of the arsonist's explosions.

Nohar looked around for an escape route. He didn't have much choice. The cabin sat on four cinder-block posts, but the ground was sloped so that the rear and the left sides of the building were too close to the ground for him to wiggle out from. The front of the building was a mass of fire where debris had fallen.

That left one way out. Nohar crawled toward the right side of the building. When he reached the point where he could emerge, his brain finally caught up with events and asked, *Who's done this? Why?*

And, most important to his current survival, *Are they still out there?*

Someone wanted him dead, and if they wanted it badly enough to torch his cabin, they probably wanted him dead enough to have a sniper watch the building for escapees. Luckily for him, the right side of the cabin was the route that offered the most cover. There were less than three meters between him and the lip of the bluff that curved around the clearing in front of his cabin.

It could just as well be thirty if a sniper had a bead on him.

Nohar pulled his bow out in front of him. It was awkward, but the sight had an infrared setting. He looked out at the woods, squinting through the IR noise that the fire was pumping out. Above him, the structure of the cabin groaned, as if it were in pain.

There was someone. A humanoid figure crouched on the crown of the bluff down toward the front of

the house. He had a rifle, at the ready, pointed too
close to Nohar's location.

Then, above him, Nohar heard the sound of his
cabin reaching its flashpoint, a roar that shook the
ground beneath him. Nohar had no time for planning,
his reflexes took over.

He rolled away from his house, across the three
meters of exposure, dropping over the bluff and into
the wooded area. He felt dirt spray him as shots from
the woods missed him, thudding into the ground.

Even in the woods, he was way too exposed. The
exploding fire lit everything like a spotlight and the
bluff's shadow was still rosily lit by reflected light.

He rose with an arrow fully taut in the bow. In a
single fluid motion, he raised the bow to position,
loosed the arrow, and began a scramble along the bluff
toward the sniper's position.

His action assumed that his arrow would find the
gunman.

The assumption was valid.

He heard other gunshots, but none connected with
him. They were coming from places that weren't covering his escape route, and the distraction of the cabin
blowing up gave him a little leeway as he ran along
the cover of the bluff.

He landed next to the rifleman. The man had taken
a header backward after being struck by the arrow.
An arm and a leg were bent at ugly angles. The rifle
had spilled another four or five meters down the slope.

Nohar stopped next to him. He was human, dressed
in black combat gear. He'd been wearing night-vision
equipment that the fall had knocked askew. He wore
an armored vest, from which Nohar's arrow pointed
up at the sky. While the armor might have prevented
impalement, the man didn't seem much better off. He

was gasping for breath, and his lips were flecked with blood.

Nohar bent over the man, intending to shake some answers from him, find out why this attack was happening. But a look at the man's face told Nohar it was hopeless. The man's eyes didn't track, and the pupils were fixed. There was no reaction when Nohar leaned over him.

"Shit," Nohar whispered, the first time he'd spoken since awakening. The word tasted like smoke.

Even as he bent over his would-be assassin, Nohar began sensing movement in the woods. They moved quietly, but not quietly enough. Whatever was going on wasn't over yet.

Nohar dropped his bow and sidestepped to pick up the fallen man's rifle. It wasn't designed for hands his size, but it was manageable. He kept moving, quietly and low to the ground.

They were getting too close. The first time he'd had surprise going for him. Now, if these bastards got a clean shot at him, he was dead. He could hear them in front of him, closing. Between the light coming from the fire, and these guys' night-vision equipment, Nohar gave it a minute or less before someone had that clean shot.

Nohar put a tree between him and the sounds, putting his back to it. He checked the rifle over. It was a Colt Special Operations rifle—Nohar had heard the thing called the "Black Widow." It was American military issue, designed for covert operations. It was matte black, light, fired caseless ten-millimeter rifle ammo. It was made mostly of composite carbon fiber, and carried a combination silencer/flash suppressor that was built into a barrel that was almost as thick as the body of the gun. Even with the silencer, its shots could punch through the bad guy's body armor as if it were balsa wood.

It had a digital scope with a night-vision setting. Nohar adjusted the sight, and flipped the Widow from single-shot to full auto.

He took a deep breath, and when he felt ready, he dove, flattening upon a bed of pine needles as he brought the rifle to bear.

Someone saw something, because Nohar could hear bullets whizzing through the trees above him. The silencer-muffled gunshots sounded like a fist slamming into wet concrete.

There were two of them, their motion—lit by the fire—was unmistakable to Nohar's eye. Despite the flash suppressors, to the scope, every shot was an obvious flare. Nohar let go with two bursts.

He got up and ran toward the hole he'd made in the encircling enemy. He stayed low, using as much of the cover as he could. He avoided firing again because any more shots would be a signal flare to the Bad Guys, and he could hear the others closing on his location.

The world became a blood-tinted chaos as his engineered reflexes took over. Somehow he made it through the hole before the others closed on him. He jumped over the corpse of one human in a commando outfit and didn't pause.

He could feel the presence of others in the woods around him, but he couldn't stop to determine where they were. Instinct told him that if he ever stopped moving he was dead. He dodged tree after tree as the slope steepened on its way downward.

The forest floor was covered with pine needles that slid as he ran. Soon the slope was difficult enough that every third step was a near stumble down the side of the hill. In the distance he heard the humans, their pretense at silence gone. He heard their radios, their running steps through the woods, and eventually he heard the fans and smelled the ozone exhaust of an aircar somewhere above.

The aircar was unlit, and eventually it left Nohar's hearing. If he was lucky, that meant that the canopy was too thick for whatever video equipment that was installed on it.

He ran for miles down the mountain, adrenaline fueling exertion far beyond what his body should have to endure. It was shortly after the aircar left his awareness that Nohar realized that he no longer felt the pursuit of the heavily armed humans.

He slowed, the panic fueling his muscles draining away with every step. The beast the genetic engineers had designed into him, the instinctual combat machine, confused his sense of time; minutes could be hours, or vice versa. It was sinking into him that what had seemed like a few minutes of panicked escape had been a run down the side of the mountain. The sky above him was lightening, and the slope was flattening out.

He could feel it in every muscle in his body. He looked at the weapon in his hand, the rifle he'd taken. It was empty. Somewhere during his escape he'd emptied the thing. He didn't quite remember, the whole episode was a blood-tinged blur in his memory.

Who the hell are these people? Nohar thought. *What the hell do they want with me?*

Empty, the Widow was useless to him, so when he passed a fairly deep creek, he ditched it.

Nohar stumbled down the rest of the way to the highway. He didn't leave the cover of the woods when he finally reached the roadway; a naked moreau would attract too much unwanted attention. Enough people were giving him that kind of attention.

After dawn had passed, and Nohar was walking in full daylight, he came in sight of a small rest stop off of the highway. There was little there but a scenic overlook and a set of restrooms, but what attracted Nohar's attention was a public comm box.

He crouched in the woods across the highway from the rest stop. There was one blue Plymouth Ariel minivan sitting in the parking lot. Nohar stayed crouching, fatigue dripping from every pore of his body. Every muscle ached, all the way down to the base of his tail. He felt as if all his muscles had been torn off of his body and then reattached at random.

Staying awake was a major effort, but he kept his attention focused on the little family van. Eventually its little family returned. Two adults and a pair of kids. As he watched them, Nohar felt an irrational wave of enmity toward them, the two middle-class pinks and their children. The parents were probably his age, but with nearly half their lives in front of them. Their kids, happy, smiling, safe. . . .

Nohar felt sick watching them, sicker at his own reaction.

Eventually the Plymouth and its family drove off, leaving the rest stop deserted. Once the car had disappeared around a bend in the road, Nohar dashed across the street to the comm box.

He hoped Stephie was still willing to talk to him.

CHAPTER 3

The comm box was in working order, which was a plus, It was off to the side of the rest area, boxed in what tried to look like a tiny log cabin with one side open to the outside. The roof was nearly half a meter shorter than he was. There was a bench, but it was way too narrow. Nohar had to crouch, half outside, putting more strain on his bad knee.

He spent ten minutes keying in old account numbers, hoping they were still valid. Most belched out error messages at him, and one telcomm company that he used to use seemed to have gone out of business.

In the end he had to try calling collect and hope that his ex-wife would accept the charges.

The screen fuzzed and went blank after he keyed in Stephie's old apartment. The blackness lasted a long time, and Nohar began to fear that either Stephie had seen his face on her comm and disconnected, or that she'd moved and some poor pink was looking at the ragged moreau on their screen wondering what the hell was going on.

After a few long moments, Stephie's face came on the comm. Nohar saw an office in the background, and he realized that the call had been forwarded. It must be a weekday.

"Nohar?" Her lips mouthed the words almost soundlessly. She was still the same person he remembered. The same golden skin, same lithe neck, same raven hair.

Nohar realized he must look like hell. "I've got a problem," Nohar said, "Do you still have the keys to my locker?"

Anything that might have been tenderness leaked out of Stephie's expression. "Still as curt as ever, aren't you?"

"Something happened—"

"God forbid you just want to talk to me."

"You wanted me to leave," Nohar said quietly.

They stared at each other through the video screen for a few long moments. Nohar thought he saw her green eyes moisten, but it could have been a trick of the light.

"Seven years," she said finally. "That's a long time."

"I know."

Stephie looked at him and shook her head as if she was disgusted with herself. "Of course I still have it. I still have your damn cat. What happened to you? You look like hell."

"Someone tried to kill me."

"I wonder why." After a pause, "I suppose you don't have any way back to the city . . . ?"

Standing, partially hidden at the edge of the scenic overlook, Nohar began to realize exactly how alone he was. What would he have done if Stephie hadn't been willing to help him? She had all the right in the world to tell him to fuck off.

A part of his mind, the same part that hunted in the mountains above him, told him that he would have managed, he was a survivor. There was another part of him, the part that had married a woman named Stephanie Weir, which seemed ominously silent on the subject.

It took two hours for her to arrive. There were two false alarms during that time. One when an old Antaeus started turning into the rest area, and when Nohar stepped out of the woods, it accelerated out of the lot leaving the smell of rubber behind it. The other when an old pickup truck, the back filled with morey rodents, the cab belching Spanish music, stopped by long enough for half a dozen rats to gather at the rail and piss over the side of the overlook. The truck left a dozen empty beer bulbs in its wake.

Stephie finally drove up in a metallic-gray Mercedes. The windows were tinted, so Nohar didn't know it was her until the car rolled to a stop and she opened the door.

When he saw her standing next to the new car, he felt an impulse to stay hidden. He ignored it and stepped around, in sight of the parking lot. As soon as she saw him, standing there naked, she shook her head and muttered, "I *knew* it."

As he walked up, Stephie reached in and tossed him a bundle.

Nohar caught it as Stephie said, "I don't know what it is with you and clothes, but you're going to put those on before you get in my car."

The bundle was a pair of sweat pants and a matching sweater. The sweater had the logo of the Earthquakes, the Frisco morey-league football team. Nohar was surprised to find the sweats cut for a morey, and one his size. The pants even accommodated his tail and digitigrade feet.

The clothes still had the receipt tags on them. Nohar tore them off with his index claw.

"Come on," Stephie said. She looked impatient. "I'd like to get this done and get back to work."

Nohar nodded and walked around to the other side of the Mercedes. He touched the gray surface, seeing the reflection of his hand as if it were some dim pool. "Nice car," he said.

"Yes, damn it," she said. "I did manage to get a life for myself after you left."

After you asked me to leave. Nohar resisted the urge to voice the thought.

The door opened for him and he slipped into the passenger seat. There was a hydraulic whine as built-in motors began adjusting the seat to his weight and height. It actually accommodated him without making him hunch over his knees.

Stephie slipped back into the car and slammed the door. She slid a cardkey into the dash and the windshield lit up with a soft green headsup display overlay on the scene outside.

Nohar was silent for a while as she drove the car back out on the road. It had been a long time since Nohar had been in any vehicle. He had never been claustrophobic. But there seemed to be a dull fear in his gut, now that he was thrust back into the world he left seven years ago.

He didn't know if it was the Mercedes, or the fact that Stephie's familiar smoky smell was dredging up unpleasant memories.

"What do you do now?" Nohar asked.

She stared at the windshield, avoiding any eye contact with him. "I work for Pacific Rim Media." On the windshield, lines of green light sketched their speed, the charge in the engine, and the route they were traveling. Nohar looked at Stephie's profile and realized that she didn't want to talk anymore. They fell into a sullen silence.

She pulled up next to a small warehouselike structure on the edge of what used to be an airport. She popped the locks, tossed him a cardkey, and said, "Get out."

Nohar took the key and slid out of the car. The passenger seat underwent another series of hydraulic gyrations while it settled into its default configuration.

Something made Nohar ask, "Why?"

She looked at him and he could smell a cold anger wafting up from her. "Why bother with you at all, you mean?"

Nohar nodded.

"Because I was naive enough to think seeing you might help me get over it. I was wrong." She pulled the car door shut with a slam. "I don't think we'll see each other again," Nohar heard her say though the door. He didn't know if she intended him to hear it.

The Mercedes pulled away, leaving him across the street from the dull cinder-block complex.

A dented, rusty sign stood above the front gate, saying "Saf-Stor." It sported at least five bullet holes. The gate was rusty chain-link and opened into a parking lot of cracked, weedy asphalt. A dull-gray metal box stood next to the gate, while above it a dented security camera panned across the empty driveway.

Nohar slid the cardkey into the dented box and hoped that both the reader and the card still worked. The reader made a grinding noise and spat out his card. After a few seconds, the gate began sliding aside for him.

When he stepped through, ducking under a bar that said "Clearance 2.5 Meters," a buzzer sounded. As he crossed the path of an electric eye, the gate began rattling shut behind him.

Saf-Stor wasn't the epitome of security storage lockers, but it had allowed long-term storage and had been willing to do business with him. The latter was always a rarity, no matter how enlightened things were supposed to be.

The place was fully automated, and from the empty parking lot, he was the only one here. He looked back through the chain-link and out at the decrepit turn-of-the-century neighborhood. The streets were lined with boarded-up storefronts, many with unrepaired earthquake or fire damage. The only movement came from the cars shooting by on the street between him and the buildings. The only noise was the electric whine of the motors as they passed by.

That was Los Angeles, an empty shell populated by automobiles.

Nohar passed a series of outbuildings, video cameras tracking him from every corner. The buildings were low, one-story cinder-block structures that smelled of concrete dust, stagnant water, and mildew. On each one, two opposing sides held ranks of rolling steel doors; the remaining walls were covered by huge painted letters, black against flaking yellow—A through G.

Nohar's locker was in E.

It had been dry lately, and each step Nohar took kicked dust off the broken asphalt and deposited grit under the claws of his feet. He hadn't worn shoes in ages, but the city made him want some.

Nohar stopped in front of building E, identical to its siblings except for the painted wall, and looked for his locker. It was four doors down. The seams of the steel door had rusted, little trails of rust descended from every bolt. At its base, small piles of windblown debris had gathered against the frame. It looked as if the door hadn't been opened in years.

It hadn't. Nohar had not come here since he and Stephie had separated. In here was everything else he had left behind. His entire material world.

He slid the card into a box next to the door. This one sounded worse than the one by the entrance. This time it didn't spit out Nohar's key.

Above the door, an old grime-covered light flashed red. Inside, Nohar could hear the strain of a motor, and smell electricity and burned insulation. The door began to shake as the motor tried to pull it open. Nohar could hear the tension in the mechanism, until something gave way with the sound of shearing metal. The door shot up about a meter and a half and stuck there. Nohar could hear the motor inside suddenly rev and he heard the sound of a chain striking something.

The motor stopped running, and the grime-streaked light changed from red to green. The box spat Nohar's card back.

The door stayed frozen in place. Nohar shook his head and ducked under it and into the darkness beyond.

The place smelled of rotting paper and rat droppings—thankfully, nonengineered rats. Over all was the smell of scorched machinery. Nohar could hear the ticking of overheated metal.

He fumbled around for a light switch in the dark, and after a few minutes the fluorescents above came on with a buzz. The first thing Nohar noticed was the drive-chain for the door. It dangled from the ceiling, still swinging gently back and forth. The links looked fused together, and when Nohar reached to stop its swinging, it was still warm to the touch.

Nohar shook his head again and looked over the locker. It was a near-cubical room of unpainted cinder block, a bit larger than three meters square. The ceiling was corrugated steel, from which a half-dozen unshaded, fly-specked fluorescents dangled. Half of them were lit, and half of those were flickering.

Wire shelves ran from floor to ceiling on three walls.

The shelves held stacks of boxes and a few suitcases. In the center of the floor, three filing cabinets and an old comm unit stood sentinel over a squat, black fire safe.

Neglect had taken its toll. A whole stack of boxes had collapsed off of one of the rear shelves, and rats had nested in the spilled clothes and papers. Leaks in that side of the roof had stained most of the boxes in that corner of the room, and the smell made Nohar write off that corner entirely.

Nohar felt unmoved looking at the damage. Clothing and records from his years as a PI. Nothing truly important. It was as if the things here weren't really his.

He walked over to the wall opposite the one with the leak and started peeling boxes open. He needed some changes of clothes. If he was going to deal with the pink world again, he needed some protective coloration. He found an old military surplus duffel bag and began throwing things into it. Two salvageable changes of clothes and one suit went into it.

In other boxes he dug out some old equipment. He recovered an expensive set of binoculars with a built-in digital camera. They needed recharging. He also uncovered his clunky palmtop comm, which needed recharging and its account renewed.

Then he keyed in the combination of his fire safe. It opened with a sucking sound as the air pressure equalized. He pulled out a leather wallet that lay on top of everything. He checked it. It held a half-dozen ramcards, a few that would still have money on them. There was also about three hundred in cash.

Beneath the wallet, still in its holster, was Nohar's Vindhya 12-millimeter. Nohar drew the automatic out of the holster, cleared it, and checked the action. It was metal and composite ceramics, all with a utilitarian gray finish. Deadly, efficient, and it still worked perfectly.

Nohar looked at the 70-centimeter-long barrel, and felt a premonition that something nasty was going to happen.

He made sure that the Vind was fully loaded before he put on the shoulder holster over the sweater Stephie had given him. He drew on a red windbreaker—stiff with age but baggy enough to hide the gun from casual inspection—then he filled his pockets with every magazine that was in the safe.

He put on a pair of old stale sneakers, and left, the broken door hanging open on his past.

CHAPTER 4

Nohar had to call three taxi companies before he found one that would service the neighborhood he was in. After nearly half an hour, a black-and-white van rolled to a stop next to the public comm Nohar'd been using. It was a dented Chrysler Aerobus that ran on remote.

Nohar stepped inside as the door opened for him. A camera watched him from behind a metal mesh screen. The floor was littered with disposable air-hypos, beer bulbs, and used condoms. It smelled like the lid of a garbage can.

Nohar felt claustrophobic again as the door shut on the cab.

A tinny-sounding speaker in the ceiling said, "State your destination clearly," in a half-dozen different languages.

Nohar gave it the name of an intersection in Compton. He ran one of his cards through the deposit slot before the cab could jabber any further to him. Compton was a long ride down the clogged LA freeways, but Compton was morey territory, and he knew the area. At least he *had* known it, seven years ago. He was confident enough that he could find a motel to hole up in while he tried to piece together what had happened.

The cab drove south down the Hollywood and Harbor Freeways, never managing more than forty klicks an hour for all the traffic. Nohar had a lot of time to sit in the wretched-smelling taxi and look out at the LA skyline. There wasn't much for him to see; it was all a blur of glass and concrete at the extremity of his vision. All he really could focus on was the movement of maniac-driven cars cutting off the taxi, and the debris that collected in the breakdown lanes.

He smelled Compton before he reached it. It was a smoky smell of fires long since dead. It drifted through the taxi's air filters—if it had any—as if they weren't there, overwhelming the ozone smell of the traffic around him.

Compton was in the southern portion of a swath of destruction the National Guard had cut through the second-largest Moreytown in the United States. The riots had burned through a diagonal strip of the Greater Los Angeles area, extending from Compton through to East LA. At one point the area had been devastated worse than the Bronx.

As the cab took the off ramp, the first thing that Nohar noticed were the vacant lots. There were hundreds of them. Places where the city, or the National Guard, had bulldozed the abandoned buildings and spread dirt over the rubble. Tawny grass grew high in ragged patches throughout the lots, and the ground was uneven where erosion had uncovered the remains of the buried wreckage. Each lot was littered with trash and abandoned vehicles, as if the town had become one huge landfill.

The autocab stopped at the intersection of Rosecrans and Alameda, the door opening before Nohar realized that he had reached his destination.

He stepped out on the broken concrete. Behind him, the cab raced off as if it didn't like the neighborhood. Nohar started walking south on Alameda, following the overgrown set of train tracks.

Other moreys walked by, usually on the other side of the street. Mostly young-looking rodents who talked to each other in a combined Spanish-English slang that Nohar couldn't understand. Many of them gave him looks that seemed to say, "You don't belong here."

They were the shortest lived of all the morey breeds. In the seven years Nohar had been in his self-imposed exile, two generations of rats had been born and reached maturity. They had been designed for fast reproduction, and it was only the short life span that kept the engineered *Rattis* from overwhelming every other species.

When they stared at Nohar, he felt something alien. There was a gulf behind the glossy blackness of their eyes that had more than species behind it. Most moreys had been engineered around the same time, in the decades surrounding the Pan-Asian War. Nohar himself was only a single generation removed from the labs. The rats who walked around him, staring and chattering high-speed Spanish, were generations removed from the labs in Central and South America where their kind had been born. In Nohar's lifetime, ten generations of rats had come, and mostly gone.

The rats weren't the only moreys out on the streets, though they were the most numerous. There were other South American breeds, rabbits and other rodents that were harder to identify. There were a few canines, and one or two felines, though none as large as Nohar.

In fact, Nohar stood out in Compton as badly as he would have in Culver City. He towered over everyone else, and even if that hadn't been the case, his dress marked him as an outsider. Everyone else on the street here seemed to have adopted the same dress, almost like a uniform. They wore blousy pants with large vertical slashes through the material, leaving them so much strips of cloth. If they wore anything on top, it was little more than an abbreviated vest. Maybe they would wear a silk scarf or bandanna around the neck.

The clothing was in every material Nohar could think of, from denim to polyester, but the style was almost universal. He saw a few other moreys wearing other things, but they looked as out of place as he did.

One thing made him agree with the rats' accusing stares, agree he didn't belong here anymore—he thought the clothes looked ridiculous.

Nohar found a motel. Its sign was rusted, the neon smelled of a short circuit, and the parking lot was weed-shot and had one rusted hulk of a vehicle that seemed to have been resident ever since they stopped using petroleum.

Nohar ducked in one graffiti-swathed door and stepped up to the desk. The musk smell of a dozen species layered the lobby, making it an easy guess what the rooms here were used for. There wasn't anyone there. Nohar dropped his bag and leaned on the desk. There was a button screwed to the desktop and Nohar pressed it. Deep in the bowels of the building, he heard a buzzer go off.

He scanned the place while he waited. The area behind the desk was a narrow mirror of the lobby. Rusty acoustical tile, scab-colored carpet, and plastic plants that smelled of dust. One thing on the desk caught Nohar's attention and made him feel more of an outsider than ever.

A box of condoms sat on the desk with a little sticker saying "$2.80 ea." The condoms weren't that noticeable at first, and with his bad vision he would

have missed the crucial part if he wasn't leaning
over them.

They weren't the regular pink-designed condoms,
but half a dozen varieties, each color-coded and labeled with a two-letter code. Under the box, attached
to the desk beneath a sheet of plastic, a large index
listed the species the codes went with. Blue went with
mostly canines, red went with rodents—in particular,
a "Blue AX" would fit a Qandahar Afghani, though
Nohar doubted that any of that particular attack strain
would have use for a condom.

Then again, he never had either. Almost all morey
relationships were sterile unless you found a mate of
exactly the same species. Mules, while undesirable,
were too rare for most of Nohar's contemporaries to
worry about. Looking at the box, Nohar wondered
about species-jumping diseases.

"Looking for a little party, are we, good sir?" The
voice drifted in on the odor of curry and incense.
Nohar looked up and saw a morey of a kind he'd
never seen before. That was enough to give him pause.

He had a short muzzle, and wide golden eyes. His
limbs were long and thin, the fingers even longer. He
wore a kimono that hung loosely on his body, as if he
was only a wide-eyed head propped up on a stick. His
sinuous movement and long fingers made him think
of an old friend named Manny—

Nohar pushed the thought away. "I want a room,"
he said.

"Good, yes." He hissed the words. "I can provide
you with any manner of companionship."

Nohar shook his head. "Just a room, and a bed for
the night."

The manager nodded, and it seemed that his head
nodded around those huge golden eyes, whose gaze
remained fixed on him. Nohar suspected that he was

looking at someone whose ancestors were intended for night recon work. "This is fine, and any time of night you change your mind—"

"I'll be sure to call you," Nohar said.

"Yes." the manager held out a hand that was longer than Nohar's. Nohar fished the cash out of his wallet and paid for the room. The manager did not complain about the cash, and didn't ask him for an ID.

"Room 300," he told Nohar, sliding a cardkey across the desk. Nohar turned to go and he heard the manager say, "Rajasthan?"

Nohar stopped, frozen at the mention of his name. He looked over his shoulder, suddenly nervous. "What?"

"Yes, I see, you are Rajasthan '20 or maybe '23." He held out something. Nohar took it. It was a yellow foil wrapper with the letters XT on it. "The only one of those left, you see. On the house. Don't want you contracting the Drips, do we?"

Nohar nodded. He felt more out of place than ever. Not just the condom, or the fact that he'd never heard of "The Drips," but the fact that he was one of a generation named for his species. He knew that his name, by itself, was enough to mark him as from another age.

He put the condom in his wallet and walked out to his room.

Behind him, the manager said, "You call me when you want some diversion, yes?"

Room 300 was a dull gray anonymous hole at the opposite end of the broken parking lot. When Nohar closed the door behind him, he collapsed on a bed that was much too small for him and felt fatigue and pain drip from every pore. It felt as if he had just run down a whole herd of deer by himself, without the bow.

His mind was awake and alert, but every muscle in his body screamed fatigue. He'd been able to hold off the crash long enough to get somewhere relatively safe, but now he paid for it. He stayed immobile, panting, staring at his collapsed body in the mirror on the ceiling. The reflection resembled a crime-scene holo, with him as the shooting victim.

Staring into his own green eyes, it came home to him how close to death he'd been this morning. He had been shot at before, and it wasn't even the first time he had been that close to an explosion. But something about the attack gave him a sick feeling of his own mortality.

"Age . . ." he whispered to himself between burning breaths.

Who wanted him dead? The only answers that came were that they were human, and well-equipped, and they weren't cops. Why they wanted him dead was easier—it had been triggered by the lawyer's visit. There was absolutely nothing else in his last seven years that Nohar believed could have sparked anyone's interest.

The attack had to be related to Charles Royd's visit, and the job he'd pitched. But Nohar couldn't figure out if the attack was because he'd refused the job, or because the attackers thought he'd taken it.

Nohar thought of the picture of Manuel and the ramcard that had burned in the fire. Right now he wished he knew what was on that ramcard. He was going to have to track down Royd and find out who he was working for, and why. . . .

After a half hour lying still on the bed, Nohar began to snore.

*   *   *

Nohar awoke with a start.

The light had gone from the windows, leaving the room in monochrome darkness. The room stank of his own leftover exertion. What parts of his body didn't ache, itched. Nohar sat up slowly, annoyed at himself for falling asleep. Even though his body was designed to grant him short bursts of supernormal activity, the cost was a deep lethargy. Nohar knew he must have slept for hours, and he *still* felt tired.

Old pain from his bad knee and shoulder prodded him awake the rest of the way. Sitting on the edge of the bed, he massaged his right knee and thought of exactly what it was he was going to do.

His cabin had been burned to the ground. The cabin and the small plot of land had been part of a government homestead grant, an attempt to de-urbanize the moreau population after the riots. It had cost him nothing, and he never had any insurance on the building. He'd never be able to afford to rebuild.

Even if he found out who had tried to kill him, he had nothing left. He'd been four years on the waiting list for that cabin, and he probably didn't have another four years.

Part of the cheap wooden bed frame gave under his hand. His fingers ached with his claws extending to bite the wood.

Anger began burning in his gut, all of it focused on Royd. It was the pink lawyer's fault, that was a certainty. Whatever the end reason was for the attack on him, Nohar knew that it would never have happened if that human bastard had just left him alone.

After a lifetime of dreams and desires, that was the only one that remained: to be left alone. Royd had taken that away from him.

Royd was going to pay for that.

CHAPTER 5

Nohar plugged in the palmtop comm he'd liberated from his locker, and the binocular camera, letting them charge while he washed himself off in this place's excuse for a bathroom. Nohar could only do a half-assed job of washing himself off, and when he was done, he could still smell Los Angeles in his fur.

When he came out of the bathroom, his comm was glowing at the head of the bed. The motel had a comm setup, but Nohar suspected that it charged by the minute, and probably didn't have an outside line.

His comm supposedly had a lifetime telcomm usage attached to it that billed one of his accounts monthly for the time he spent on-line. He hoped that the telcomm account was still good.

He sat on the bed, fur still drying, and picked up the little device. He hadn't touched it in years, and it showed. There was an ugly violet tint to the screen, and the letters on the boot screen carried ghosts of themselves on their backs.

He extended a claw and tapped the screen a few times, pulling down menus and finally grabbing a city directory. The lawyer had done a good job of keeping his home address unlisted, but it wasn't difficult to find his office. It was in Beverly Hills.

Nohar snorted. What was this guy doing talking to him? The guy probably made more an hour than Nohar had seen in the past three years.

Charles Royd's home address was supposed to be unlisted. All that meant was that Nohar had to spend half an hour finessing the database—and half that time was spent refamiliarizing himself with what he was doing. Royd wasn't in the public city directory, but he was in the records of every place from the FAA, for that aircar, to the Department of Water and Power. Given his name, and the make of car, it was child's play to lift his address from his vehicle registration.

Beverly Hills again.

Nohar shook his head. Even though Royd had been driving an expensive aircar, Nohar had him pegged as small-time. Mostly because Royd was dealing with moreaus, and only small-timers dealt with moreaus. Back in his cabin, Nohar had been as small-time as he could get.

Nohar keyed the screen until he got a too-purple GTE test pattern, and tried to place a call through to Royd's house. Royd's comm picked up instead, and asked for a message. Nohar disconnected before it was finished asking. He looked out the louvered windows of the motel, and saw the first rose glow of dawn filtering through the dust.

Royd might be making an early day of it. It was just after seven.

Nohar keyed in Royd's office.

Again he got the comm asking for his voice-mail.

Royd could be on the comm with someone else. Nohar didn't want to leave a message, though. Nohar wanted to see Royd's eyes when he called him. If Royd was behind the attack, he would give something away the first time he saw Nohar again. That was the theory anyway.

Nohar spent the next few minutes doing a trick that an old hacker friend had taught him. He built a little script program into his comm's memory to keep call-

ing Royd's numbers and to alert Nohar when something other than a comm answered the line.

That accomplished, he needed a car. There wasn't
any way to exist in Los Angeles without a groundcar
at the least. While he waited for contact from Royd,
he started calling rental agencies.

There weren't any rental agencies in the area, and
getting a rental car delivered to Compton was like
trying to invite some deer for dinner at his cabin.
Nohar eventually had to settle for a little no-name
rental company that charged an exorbitant delivery
fee and insisted on three times the normal liability
insurance.

Nohar figured he had to get to Royd in person. He
got himself ready, grooming himself and putting on
the old suit he had liberated from his locker. The suit
was conservative, black, and itched like hell.

He looked even more out of his element now. But
he hoped that he was ready for a trip into the pinkest
part of Los Angeles.

He was dressed by the time the car showed up. His
comm had yet to get through to Royd.

He heard the horn blare a few times. Nohar took
the gun, the comm, and the binoculars and went out
to the waiting car. He walked out and saw a nervous-
looking pink looking back and forth as he reached in
the driver's side and laid on the horn. He stopped
when he saw Nohar come out of the motel.

The guy stared at Nohar as he walked up and held
out his hand.

He kept staring.

"Keys?" Nohar asked.

The guy shook his head, as if to clear it. "Mr.
Rajasthan?"

"Who else?"

He seemed too young to Nohar, barely half his own age. That seemed even younger on a human. He was blond, tan, and smelled as if he expected to die. He handed a cardkey to Nohar. His hand was shaking.

Nohar felt sorry for the guy. "You need a ride back?"

He shook his head vigorously and pointed his thumb back to the street, where a sleek-looking Chrysler Tempest idled by the mouth of the motel's parking lot. Even the car gave the impression that it would spring into a hasty retreat at any moment.

Nohar looked at the waiting car. "Better go, then."

The kid nodded and almost ran back to the waiting Tempest.

Nohar looked at the car he had rented, and quietly sighed. A Tempest it wasn't. The car was an old GM Maduro sedan—which would have been a luxury car five years ago. But the vehicle showed its age with a dented body, threadbare interior, and the smell of decaying ceramic inductors.

Probably the worst part of it, aside from the smell, was the fact that it had been repainted a matte-finish lime green. Nohar thought it the color of dried phlegm.

Fortunately he'd called for a large car, and that's what he got. It took him a few tries to force the driver's door open, but he managed to slip inside. He pushed his seat all the way back, almost off the rails, so he could drive comfortably.

It took a few more times to close the door. And a few more to disentangle himself from the too-tight automatic safety belt that tried to strangle him. Eventually, he was on his way.

The comm in his pocket had yet to contact Royd.

Rush hour was just starting, and it took Nohar nearly an hour to drive through to Wilshire Boulevard.

All the time he had a death grip on the steering wheel. The traffic got to him, the traffic and the feeling that he was sinking in a quicksand of urban landscape. He felt trapped.

He tried to get some music on the Maduro's comm, but the speakers were shot. So he sat behind the crawling traffic in silence, the news feed scrolling across the screen between the two front seats.

The major news item was the launching of the *America*. It had spent nearly twelve months in transit past Jupiter's obit, and it had just test-fired the main drive within the past few days. In a few more weeks it would start a twenty-five-year journey to Tau Ceti. The news made a lot of the fact that the crew of the *America* had a high percentage of moreaus.

Getting their trash off the planet, Nohar thought.

The sad thing about the *America* was that the Americans had precious little to do with it. It was all a U.N. project now, and had been since the first completed ship, the *Pacific,* was taken over by Japanese Nationalist terrorists. That takeover was the last media news event that Nohar remembered being aware of, back in '63, just before he exiled himself.

Back then, the manned interstellar project was run by VanDyne International and the U.S. Government. Since then, the U.N. had taken over all seven starships, finished construction on four, and launched three. *Pacific* was halfway to Alpha Centauri, *Atlantic* was heading toward Sirius, and *Europa* was on its way to Procyon.

A lot had happened in seven years.

Nohar wondered what it would be like to be on one of those ships. Strapped in a can going half the speed of light.

The next story that Nohar noticed scrolling across the screen was about the alien containment facility on Alcatraz. It caught Nohar's eye during a spasm of paralysis in the traffic. He caught the words ". . . search for survivors . . ." and pressed the "back" button on the screen.

Nohar shook his head as the story replayed.

Someone had blown up the dome on Alcatraz. The place had been leveled, destroying the entire habitat. The explosion had killed off a good fraction of the alien population of the dome, and nearly a hundred of the scientists that studied the aliens. That had been the single repository of all the extraterrestrials on the planet, if the government and the U.N. were to be believed.

A car honked at him, and Nohar shut the news feed off.

He had met an alien once—soft and blubbery, like half-formed, bad-smelling, white Jello. They didn't think like humans, and they were inscrutably hostile. They'd been at war with Earth, on this planet, for years before anyone caught on. Nohar had been one of the first few to catch on, but it got him precious little.

Nohar suspected that the starships were military missions, whatever the U.N. said about exploration and the broadening of humanity's horizons.

Probably some moreau infantry would have their horizons broadened, too—just like their ancestors had in Asia, getting their guts blown out in a war the humans were running.

Nohar followed Wilshire up to a point just a few blocks short of Santa Monica, then turned north. In a few blocks he came to Royd's office, a new polished building set back from the street. The place was gated, but the gate hung open on a driveway that tried to look like gravel.

The Asian influence on the structure wasn't subtle at all. The drive was flanked by statues of Oriental lions—or dragons, they were too stylized for Nohar to tell—and the small grounds were landscaped into stasis, as if every plant was as much inanimate sculpture as the lions.

The building itself was a set of green marble cubes, the roof turned up at the corners to suggest a pagoda. Nohar pulled the Maduro into the parking lot. It looked out of place between a BMW and a Mercedes. The cars were all late-model luxury cars, and all of them seemed to be pastel shades of red, green, or blue. Nohar felt the same way looking at the cars as he did when he looked at the clothing on the streets in Compton—here was the style for this year, and he felt it looked ridiculous.

The place even smells contrived, Nohar thought as he stepped out of the car. He stood there a moment, looking at the building, noticing the too-heavy scent of flowers, and thought of security that was in place. There had to be cameras around here, and the garden smell could be covering the more subtle smells of the guards themselves.

No reason to make anyone more nervous than they had to be. Nohar leaned back into the Maduro, slipped the Vind out of its holster, and slid it under the passenger seat.

Nohar straightened his tie and walked up to the front of the building. He noticed a metal detector set into the door. It was well-hidden, but his natural paranoia was returning, helping him pick up details like that.

The door fed into a lobby that was wrapped in another Asian-themed mosaic. Nohar walked across a giant wheel filled with figures that appeared vaguely Tibetan. At the top of the wheel sat a round desk behind which sat a human who fulfilled all the connotations of the slang term "pink." The moreys used the term referring to humans' general hairlessness. This human was bald, soft, and white. He *looked* pink.

"Can I help you?" he said as Nohar walked up. The guard didn't look up from the screen he was watching, and Nohar didn't smell any nervousness on the man. In fact, he didn't smell much of anything from him.

"Here to see Charles Royd," Nohar prepared himself to do some convincing to get himself in to see Royd. He didn't have any proof that Royd had even come to see him, and if Royd had anything to do with the attack he doubted that the lawyer'd admit to being there.

To his surprise, the guard punched a button, said, "Visitor for Royd," hooked a thumb at one of the corridors out of the lobby, and told Nohar, "Down there, up the stairs, first door on your right."

Nohar stared at the guard a moment.

The guard finally raised his head and looked at Nohar. "Anything else?"

The guard's expression didn't change. Nohar, however, was startled and hid it by shaking his head and heading for the corridor. The guard's face remained etched in Nohar's mind. The eyes had been gloss-black, the nose hadn't existed except for two vertical slits that had flexed when the guard breathed.

The guard was a gene-engineered human, a frank.

Nohar didn't know what to make of that. Whatever the pink world felt about moreaus, they were an order of magnitude more twitchy about people messing with the human genome. U.N. treaties had banned human genetic engineering for decades. Which was why the moreaus existed—since it was fine with the U.N. if you gene-engineered a soldier, as long as it wasn't human.

Of course, there were a lot of leftovers when the wars were over.

Nohar walked into the outer office where Royd worked. He got another subtle shock. Royd had plastered the walls with etchings of newsfaxes and static holos that apparently showed high points of his career.

The first holo that grabbed Nohar's attention was a picture of Charles Royd with Father Alvarez de Collor. The spotted Brazilian feline was half a head taller than Royd. Nohar knew the jaguar because he was the only ordained Catholic priest on the West Coast who also happened to be a moreau.

Letting the moreaus into the Church had caused a near schism back when Nohar was ten years old. Father Collor was one of the first morey priests in the States. What was Royd doing with him?

A newsfax nearby had the headline, "Beverly Hills Lawyer Aids Homesteaders," and was all about a fight Royd had with the government to allow a number of nonhumans—franks in fact, not moreaus—to take advantage of the homestead project.

There were other stories lining the walls—Royd defending moreys arrested during the explosive riots a decade ago. Royd bring class-action suits against a number of employers for awful working conditions. Royd fighting against the continued separation of hospital facilities between human and nonhuman. Royd had even once represented the aliens held at Alcatraz.

Royd was neither small-time, nor a typical pink lawyer. Looking at all the stories lining the walls, Nohar felt that he would have known who Royd was if he had watched anything on the comm in the past seven years.

Now it made sense that Royd was hiring someone to find a lost morey. The guy made a living out of morey cases. He was high-profile enough that any non-human with a problem would come to him.

The question wasn't why Royd was looking for a morey named Manuel—the question was why Royd had sought Nohar out to look for him.

"Can I help you?" came a voice from behind him. From the husky overtone of the voice, and from the scent, Nohar knew that it was a vulpine moreau before he turned around.

He turned around and looked down on the up-turned muzzle of a short female fox.

"My name's Nohar Rajasthan, I'm here to see Charles Royd."

"Of course you are," she said. She extended a black-furred arm. "My name's Sara Henderson, I'm one of Mr. Royd's assistants. Maybe I can help you?"

It was odd hearing a Southern California accent coming from a vulpine mouth. This was the first fox he'd ever met who bore no trace of the ancestral English accent. It was also odd seeing a moreau in a dress. Female moreaus weren't built like human women, and human-designed clothing would hang wrong. All the females Nohar knew had worn male clothing, and as little as possible.

Sara wore a dress, though, and one that seemed to be designed for her frame. It was black, businesslike, and most of all, it fit—even around the problem areas for human clothing on a moreau, the chest, where a moreau didn't have breasts to speak of, and the rear where the large human ass was replaced by a tail.

While he'd been gone, someone had started manufacturing moreau clothing.

"Mr. Rajasthan?" Sara Henderson repeated.

Nohar shook the offered hand and said, "I'm afraid I really need to see Mr. Royd himself."

The corners of Sara's mouth turned in a frown. A

lot of moreaus couldn't do facial expressions very well, but this one carried just the right amount of annoyance.

"He is very busy. Do you have an appointment?"

You know damn well I don't. Nohar shook his head. "I don't think so. Mr. Royd visited me and made a business proposition. I want to talk to him about it."

Sara stared at him, her black nose pointing at the knot of his tie.

"I was—am—a private investigator."

The fur fluffed out a little on her face when she smiled. Nohar saw a brief flash of a canine tooth. "That's where I've heard that name before." She shook her head. "You were, like, the only mo—" she caught herself as Southern California was on the verge of completely taking over her voice, "—Nonhuman detective in LA for the longest time. Weren't you?"

"A dubious distinction."

"Didn't you retire?"

"Apparently not."

Sara nodded, as if everything made perfect sense now. "Well, I'm sorry but Mr. Royd was called out of town on an emergency."

You have to be kidding. "Do you know how to get a hold of him?"

Sara shook her head, "I wish I did." She looked back toward the office. "All we received was a short memo from his comm saying he'd be gone for a week. We have to shuffle his caseload onto an already over-worked staff— In fact, I really should get back to work myself."

"How do I get hold of Royd?"

"Wait till he comes back," Sara said, taking his arm and gently maneuvering him toward the door.

As the door shut behind him, Nohar couldn't help

thinking, *What kind of lawyer leaves town without telling the firm how to contact him?*

Nohar answered himself, *Maybe a very scared lawyer.*

CHAPTER 6

Against his better judgment, Nohar found himself driving farther west, across Santa Monica, into the residential area of Beverly Hills. He drove the green Maduro past twenty-million-dollar homes, feeling as if a signal flare followed him down the street.

Pedestrians, joggers, dogwalkers—all turned to look. Nohar couldn't tell if the stares were for him, or for the car. He passed a number of walled estates that didn't even have access to the street, aircars were the only way in or out.

Royd wasn't in a mansion, for which Nohar was thankful. He lived in a more subdued neo-Tudor building whose most ostentatious feature was the oval driveway and the multicar garage.

Even so, the location probably cost him five mil.

Nohar pulled straight into the driveway. He had thought about this on the way here and had decided he was going to go through with it, despite the fact that this was probably the pinkest neighborhood on the planet. Nohar was gambling that with Royd's association with moreaus, the neighbors wouldn't have the automatic reflex reaction and call the cops because a morey was in the driveway.

If anyone was watching him—and he was certain they were—the suit probably bought him some slack. Since he had no hope of going unnoticed, his only possible tack was to be unashamedly blatant and look as if he knew exactly what he was doing here.

He killed the engine and felt a sudden unease that was more than just the neighborhood. He tried to shake it, but he had a sick feeling in the pit of his stomach. Nohar felt the urge to gun the engine and head for Mexico.

Instead, he quietly took the Vind from under the seat and slipped it back into his holster. Then he stepped out of the car and strode up to the front door.

Nohar could feel all the houses watching him.

His first thought was to try the call button, and if that failed, do a survey of the security on the door and try forcing it as quickly and quietly as possible.

He didn't have to.

The call button was on the door, and when Nohar reached up to press it, the door swung open. The bad feeling came back, magnified.

Beyond the door was a small foyer. A draft came past Nohar carrying the scent of blood. Human blood.

Nohar stepped in, drawing his gun, letting the door swing shut behind him.

The house was thick with blood smell. Nohar ran through the rooms in the house, tracking down the carnage he smelled. He passed through a living room, a den, a dining room. . . .

They had done him in the kitchen.

Nohar lowered the gun and stared through the door into Royd's kitchen. Royd was taped into an antique chair someone had dragged in from the dining room. Nohar could see the scuffs on the kitchen tile. They had propped him up against the wall next to a huge stainless-steel cooktop. More than the blood now, Nohar smelled burned flesh.

Who did you piss off?

Nohar took a few tentative steps into the kitchen.

The sink was filled with expensive cutlery, most showing rainbow-burnished edges where someone had heated them red hot. A few dish towels sat in the sink too, stained red. The water in the bottom of the sink was colored a translucent pink.

Nohar looked at Royd. He hadn't seen anything as bad since the last time he had seen a victim of "shaving," a nasty ritual practiced by morey gangs when they thought one of their fellows was getting too close to the pinks. . . .

When they shaved someone, they took off most of the top layer of skin. Only most, since the victim usually died halfway through the procedure.

What had been done to Royd was worse. They— whoever *they* were—had systematically removed bits of flesh from Royd's arms, torso, and face, cauterizing the wounds so they wouldn't bleed. When they were finished, they had just slit his throat and let his life drain away.

From the smell, Royd had been here since before the attack on Nohar. The poor bastard hadn't called out the hit. Which begged the question, who did?

It was beginning to look like the only answers he would get would be from this missing kid, Manuel, and the person who hired Royd to find him.

Nohar backed up and holstered his weapon. He had no desire to contaminate a crime scene with his DNA.

As if the thought were a premonition, outside he began to hear sirens.

He backed out of the kitchen. *This was great.* Someone *did* call the cops on him, and with a body in the house. He wasn't worried so much as annoyed. Dealing with the police was one huge waste of time. He knew that he could look forward to a few hours of interrogation until they discovered that his gun hadn't been fired, and that Royd had died long before he showed up, then he'd face a few more hours as they grilled him about the arson of his cabin and why he didn't call it in to anyone. . . .

Nohar really disliked cops. The only species of pink he disliked worse were Fed agents.

He let his breath out in a sigh that was more like a growl. There was no way around it at this point. He headed toward the front door. The sirens were almost on him when he stepped into the foyer. He could hear car doors slamming as he stepped outside.

Nohar began spreading his arms as he stepped outside, showing he was unarmed.

Someone fired.

Instinct had Nohar diving back through the open doorway before it fully registered that the cops were shooting at him. Above him, chunks of Royd's front door began splintering as slugs tore through the even, vat-grown wood.

When did cops start blowing away unarmed moreys on a disturbance call?

Nohar scrambled backward along the floor as he heard glass breaking inside the house. Adrenaline began pushing him, and he felt the urge to draw his gun and return fire. He suppressed the urge. Escape was his only real option. Escape, and figure out what triggered the goddamn cops.

More glass broke to either side of him. Then, for the moment, the cops stopped shooting. Nohar took the opportunity to get to his feet and head toward the rear of Royd's house. He ran back toward the dining room.

He smelled the ozone before he saw it, and was diving for cover before it started firing. Thirty-two caliber slugs tore into the walls of the dining room, blowing a china cabinet into shards of glass and porcelain. Hovering above the table was a police drone. It was a tiny remote-controlled helicopter that carried a multispectrum video camera and a built-in submachine gun. With its ovoid body, and dual offset rotors, it looked like a flying rat face, the camera one eye, the gun the other, the rotors its ears.

It didn't stop firing, and the gun was swinging back toward Nohar.

He did the only thing he could, diving under the dining room table, directly beneath it. He heard it buzz as it tried to reacquire him. He rolled on his back, drew the Vind, and fired three shots—a quarter of the clip—through the table, straight up. The room echoed with the triple explosion from the twelve-millimeter handgun, and the smell of powder-burned wood drifted down from the holes punched through the table.

Nohar also smelled the odor of fried electronics.

That's it, then. Nohar thought. *I've nuked one of their toys, there's no talking to them now.*

He rolled out from under the table, and he heard more gunfire from the police. He had really pissed them off.

On the dining room table, the drone had fallen cockeyed, dormant, pointing toward the windows it had crashed through. Ozone smoke leaked from the shattered camera, and its twin counter-rotating rotors were still slowly turning.

Nohar heard the buzz of another drone under the sound of gunfire. It was coming from the den and the living room, toward him.

Nohar kept his gun out as he dove through the kitchen door. The second drone banked into the dining room after him. Nohar dove around the door for cover. He heard it closing on him as he hugged the wall.

The thing was less than a meter square and cleared

the doorframe as it entered the kitchen. It started to sweep the room, looking for him, but it stopped when its camera locked on Royd's body. Nohar was hoping for that. There was still a human operating the thing, as susceptible to surprise as anyone.

Nohar leveled the Vind at the backside of the drone's chassis and let go with two more shots. The camera exploded and the thing tumbled, slamming into the side of the sink and falling upended at Royd's feet.

The firing outside stopped again.

Nohar heard the sound of something whistling through the air— Multiple somethings. Either tear gas, trying to drive him out, or concussion grenades to stun him while they took the building. Neither one was something he wanted to stick around for.

The kitchen had a doorway into the garage. He made for it, past Royd, little worried about stray hairs or DNA at this point. He reached the door as he heard multiple hissing explosions throughout the house, and the first acid touch of the gas hit his eyes and nose.

He made it into the garage and slammed the door.

He hadn't run from the cops since he was fourteen. It always caused more trouble than it solved. But the cops here seemed hell-bent on killing him. Cooperating with authority only went so far.

It was getting hard to see, even in the garage. His eyes watered, and he began coughing. The gas was leaking from the house, through the cracks around the door. Inside it had to be intolerable.

He held a hand over his nose and mouth and looked around the garage. There was only one other way out, the doors pointed out on the driveway, straight at the cops. There wasn't anywhere else to go.

There were two cars here, the Jaguar aircar and a

sleek back BMW with tinted windows. Neither looked bulletproof. . . .

But the tinted windows gave him an idea.

It took Nohar a few agonizing minutes to short out the lock and get into the BMW. By that time the alarms were going off and the car's computer was already calling the police—as if that mattered. Once in, he hacked the auto-navigation feature and jacked up the minimum speed to sixty klicks an hour.

Nohar could barely see through his stinging and watering eyes as he got the Jaguar open. By then, he felt he didn't have much time left. He ducked into the BMW, engaged it in drive, and let the navigation computer take over. Nohar took cover in the Jaguar as the garage door began opening.

The cops began strafing the garage, Nohar could hear the Jaguar taking hits. He could smell melted composites. But he also heard the BMW's engine rev up. Heard it accelerate out toward the cops. The gunfire got a little more frantic.

While he heard all this going on, Nohar desperately worked on the dash, trying to get the Jaguar moving. He ripped panels covering the control circuits, found the security system, and pulled that card out. He tore a wire from the comm to jump the power connection that had run through the card. With his big hands it took him five times with his claws fully extended to get the jumper in place.

When he did, he heard the flywheel engage and the fans start up.

About then he also heard the sound of something going smash out in the street. Nohar risked a look out the windshield. The Jaguar's windshield was pockmarked with bulletholes, and through the spider cracks he saw that the BMW had taken a full header into one of the copcars. The Patrol cars were the traditional Dodge Haviers, but the BMW was a luxury car, heavier, and probably had twice as much metal in it. The nav computer was still driving, pushing the T-boned Havier slowly down the street with it. The police were pouring lead into it as if they were the Islamic Axis and the BMW was the entire state of Israel.

He had a chance to get out while the cops were distracted. Nohar set the attitude on the fans near forty-five degrees, and maxed the accelerator.

The Jaguar shot out of the garage like it was a ballistic shuttle on too low an arc. It skimmed over the driveway, barely gaining enough altitude to clear the flashers on top of the cop cars. Gunfire followed the aircar, but most of the shots went wild.

Nohar didn't have any attention to spare for the cops anyway. He was shooting straight at an old ranch house across the street, and not gaining enough altitude to clear it. He banked, barely clearing the right side of the roof. The sound of breaking glass followed the whine of the aircar's engines. Nohar didn't know if it'd been a wild shot from the cops, or if he had hit something.

He shot out from between a pair of houses, over a swimming pool. The backwash from the Jaguar's fans splashed chlorinated water through someone's garden.

Nohar hit the headsup, and the windscreen lit with fragmented navigation displays. The one thing that showed clearly on the shattered windscreen was the speedometer. With the aircar's thrust mostly going forward, he was topping one-forty klicks an hour.

He started dodging palms as he sped over someone's estate.

The headsup display flashed facets of red at him. It was a warning, probably that he was flying illegally low over Beverly Hills. Nohar checked the rear video and saw two police helicopters on his tail.

Two?

The Beverly cops probably only *had* two helicopters. Ten to one that the copters meant that it was the LAPD after him. . . .

Which meant that this was some sort of special operation, not just a neighbor calling the cops.

There was little chance he could escape the airborne pursuit. The Jaguar's computers were screaming for the cops, its transponder a gigantic red flare on LA's air traffic control screens. He couldn't gain any altitude, because as soon as he was clear of civilians, the copters riding his ass would probably frag him.

Pretty damn soon he'd be surrounded by police aircars. He had to ditch this thing quickly, somewhere he could get out from under the copters' eyes.

He began to turn west toward the mountains, away from where most of the cops would be coming. He was inviting fire from the bastards tailing him, but he was going to have to risk it. He hugged the hillside as he followed the slope of the Santa Monica Mountains. The copters didn't shoot.

Nohar hoped that meant they were unarmed. What it *probably* meant was that they didn't want to start a brush fire.

The aircar cleared a line of trees, and he saw what he was looking for. The algae-slick surface of a reservoir glistened in the midst of the woods.

Nohar aimed the Jaguar straight for it.

CHAPTER 7

The Jaguar sliced into the water like an arrow. It slammed to a stop under the surface, blowing an air bag across Nohar's face. The inductors blew with a hydraulic explosion that twisted the Jaguar on its side as water shot into the cabin from the bullet holes in the windshield.

Nohar tore the air bag from in front of him.

The aircar was tumbling, the air in the cabin not anywhere near enough to keep the fans afloat. Nohar scrambled as the aircar turned completely upside down, the cabin already half-filled with water. He took a few deep gasps of what remained of the air, and kicked at the windshield.

With the car upside down, the windshield was already completely underwater, and it gave with a single kick. Nohar ducked and pushed himself out the window just as the Jaguar nosed into the mud at the bottom of the reservoir.

Nohar swam blindly, the water dark and blurred with sediment. His head throbbed with the dull sound of machinery. He pushed himself to clear as much distance between him and the wreck as possible. He stayed under until his lungs burned with lack of air, then he pushed through the inch-thick scum of algae on the surface.

When his head hit the air, he sucked in several deep breaths as he spun around to see the nearest harvesting pylon. He dove under again, heading for the pylon. He had to break the surface twice more before he reached it. The second time he broke the surface right in the path of one of the pylon's three-meter-wide skimming arms; he had to dive under as the rotating boom swept over his head.

Then he made it to the side of the pylon and held himself against it, his head barely above the surface. The shafts of the swimming arms didn't descend below the surface this close to the pylon, but they swept by only centimeters above him. He sucked in deep breaths and watched the sky.

The copters ran a search pattern over the water. They hadn't seen him yet. Nohar hoped that they wouldn't. The machinery running the pylon he clung to should hide his own heat, as should the water and the algae. He held on, his arms going numb and his head throbbing with the rhythm of the pylon as the twenty-meter arms swept a circle in the algae.

They flew low enough for the rotors to ripple holes in the algae, incidentally hiding the scars he'd made when he'd broken the surface. One buzzed the harvesting pylons, the rotor's backwash spilling green water over him. He was sure that they had him then, but the copter kept flying down the line of pylons, oblivious.

The helicopters searched for what seemed like hours. Long enough for Nohar to get a good look at both of them. One was an LAPD chopper, the other was completely unmarked.

Little question it was a Fed helicopter.

Fed involvement meant the situation was screwed beyond belief. It could have been a Fed black-ops unit that attacked him in the cabin. The whole scene at Royd's could have been a setup. They knew he wasn't taken at the cabin, all they'd need to do was stake out Royd's corpse and wait for their lost morey to show. . . .

What had Royd stepped in?

Both copters eventually stopped the search pattern and hovered over opposite ends of the reservoir. They were waiting for a search party. They weren't about to give him any breaks. He was going to have to get to shore under the cover of the harvesting pylons.

Nohar unclenched his arms from the side of the pylon and reached up, grabbing the swimming boom as it passed overhead. As it spun, pulling him in circles around the pylon, he pulled himself hand over hand through the foaming muck the arm pushed ahead of itself. The handholds were slick, and once he was a few meters away from the pylon itself, the arm's mechanism opened up a gaping maw in front of him. Algae foam rose above his head, and slipped past his body into the screens built into the harvesting arm. He tried to get a foothold on the underwater portion of the arm. He had to kick off his shoes, so he could grip with his claws.

It would be easier, and safer, if he grabbed on the trailing end. But the froth on the leading edge offered more cover than the arm's wake.

Nohar made it all the way to the edge of the arm, three meters away from the arc of the neighboring pylon. Then he let go, dived, and came up in front of the rushing wall of foam at the edge of the next pylon. The impact stunned him, and he had to grip for two rotations before he felt up to doing it again. Then he had to spin around once more so he could pick out the pylon closest to shore and farthest from the helicopters.

Somehow he managed to make it all the way to the shoreline without alerting the helicopters. He had hitched a ride on three or four of the skimming booms, and his nose had gone numb from the smell of engineered algae. He had turned a color somewhere between shit brown and bile green from the algae stuck to him and his suit. During his ride to shore, some government boys had shown up. He saw them working the shoreline near where the Jaguar had gone down.

He ducked into the woods in the opposite direction. Once out of sight he ran, getting himself as deep in the woods as he could. Living in this kind of terrain for the past seven years made it easy. He kept moving until the sun had gone out of the sky and his body refused to go on anymore.

Sometime after dark he collapsed against a tree and went through his pockets. The Vind had survived. He did his best to clean it. Out of the extra magazines he carried, he was able to find five shells that were dry enough to be trusted to reload the thing. When he was done, he set it down next to him.

His portable comm was a total loss, which didn't really matter, since the Fed could trace his movements using that comm's account. It was better off fried.

The binocular camera came with its own case, and seemed to have fared better. He set it aside with his wallet to dry.

He had no clue what the hell he was going to do now.

As he stared at his algae-sodden wallet, fatigue claimed him with iron claws, dragging him into unconsciousness.

The itch of algae being sun-dried onto his body finally woke him up. Nohar could feel the dried slime caking his fur in clumps all over his body. His tail had fallen asleep and had stuck to the outside of his right thigh. He had to reach up and help his eyelids to open against the gunk holding them together. Even that little movement sent aches up and down his arm.

He wiped his nose as his eyes focused, trying to get the smell of algae out of it. He stopped because he realized he was being watched. Nohar saw the dog before he heard or smelled it, and that made it sink in exactly how close he'd been driving himself. It stood about four meters away, a gray mutt that looked for all the world like a natural unengineered canine. It sat on its haunches, looking at Nohar and panting.

The fact that it could get that close without waking him made Nohar very nervous.

The dog noticed Nohar move, and it let loose an odd staccato yip. When Nohar had been an LA native, he had heard stories about the feral dogs that populated the Hollywood hills, especially around the old reservoirs. He'd never really thought that much about it, until now—

He never thought of a dog as a potential threat. But as he stared at the gray dog, he realized that dogs were naturally pack hunters, and in his state he'd probably have trouble with *one* fifty-kilo animal. He couldn't even tell how many were out there. His sense of smell was still overwhelmed by algae.

He did his best not to make any sudden moves.

From the woods around him, he heard more staccato barking. Two, three, four, five others at least. Nohar nodded, doing his best not to show teeth as he forced his engineered lips into a facsimile of a smile.

"Nice dog," Nohar said as he slowly reached over to where he had placed the Vind.

It wasn't there.

Nohar heard a low growl next to him. He turned to face it and saw a black dog, somewhere between a Doberman and a Rottweiler, about three meters away from his outstretched arm. Its forepaws were placed squarely on top of Nohar's gun.

Nohar looked from Blackie to Gray, and back again. Gray was still yipping, the rhythm of it much more complex than normal. Nohar began to look at the structure of the dogs' skulls. It was hard to notice at first, since the proportions were similar to any other dog's skull, but the forehead was slightly higher, the skull slightly wider, and the whole head larger in proportion to the body.

These weren't natural specimens of *canis familiaris*.

The first moreaus, the first examples of macro gene-engineering that were used for warfare, were a species of dogs with enhanced intelligence designed by the South during the war of Korean unification. Almost all of the moreaus since were based in part from those Korean Dogs. Since the U.N. banned the use of the human genome after the Korean Dogs were designed, the countries that built intelligent moreaus all started with the specs from those enhanced dog brains rather than the human—

Which was a bit of hypocrisy, since the Koreans unabashedly used human genes in the creation of their dogs.

That was all history to Nohar. As far as he knew, all those first efforts were destroyed in the labs of the gene-techs or died in the war once the Chinese-backed North overwhelmed the South.

Nohar stared at Blackie and felt as if he was staring into the eyes of his own past.

"Your move," Nohar said.

Blackie kept growling, but didn't move.

The tableau remained like that as Nohar tried to get an impression of how many canines were out in the woods beyond where he sat. His senses were too entml:

dull at the moment to give a specific number, but he
began to realize that there were a lot of them.

From beyond a tree a few meters in front of him,
Nohar heard an electronic monotone ask, "what is
your name."

Nohar sat up, causing Gray to retreat and Blackie
to growl louder. He hadn't expected a response.

As he sat up, a large brown dog walked out of the
woods and cocked its head at him. Around its neck it
wore a collar, and an electronic device was attached
to the collar with silvery-gray duct tape. The electronic
voice came from the device. "who are you. why are
you here."

"My aircar crashed," Nohar said.

The brown dog paced in front of him, close enough
that Nohar could finally make out the smell of agitation and fear off of him. The box spoke without emotion, but everything in the dog's posture carried
tension that the words didn't contain. "men follow you
here. men look for you. why."

Nohar looked around him. He was surrounded. Canine eyes seemed to peer from around every tree,
every rock, every bush. He could sense that he was
just one move shy of a deadly confrontation. He
couldn't do anything to spook them.

Nohar decided to rein in his own tension, and tell
the truth, If they sensed him relaxing, the whole situation might calm down a few notches. . . .

If his story didn't fire them up.

Nohar sucked in a breath and said, "They think I
killed someone."

Brown stopped pacing and looked at him. One eye
was clouded, and Nohar finally realized how old
Brown was. He could see scars on his side, and one
of his ears was ragged.

"Did you kill someone," Brown's electronic box asked as he stared at Nohar with his one good eye.

Nohar shook his head. "No."

"why do you carry a weapon."

"Someone is trying to kill me."

"who."

"I don't know."

The pack around him erupted in a chorus of the odd staccato barking. Nohar realized that they had to be talking to each other. He was at a disadvantage. They could understand him, but the only one he could understand was the one-eyed leader with the salvaged electronic voicebox.

Even without understanding them, Nohar could pretty much figure out what they were debating. They were arguing whether or not to kill him.

Of all the groups to have a run-in with after the cops.

Nohar looked at the barking crowd and had an uncomfortable realization. Most of these dogs were sick. Many had crusts around their eyes and noses, many seemed unsteady on their feet.

"we should give you to the men. you are a man problem."

Slightly better than voting to kill him off and bury him in the woods, but not by much. "I could help you out."

"why would you help us." The old dog with the electronic voicebox stared at him. When he blinked, Nohar noticed with a little unease that the eyelid on the leader's clouded eye traveled more slowly than the other.

Nohar slowly pushed himself to his feet. There were a chorus of barks. This time Nohar noticed that a few seemed weak. Blackie growled at him and pulled the

Vind farther away. "I don't want to see those pink bastards again."

The old dog's gaze followed him. When Nohar was fully upright, the old dog was dwarfed, despite being large for his species. The dog's posture didn't change, even as he tilted up so his good eye could follow Nohar's movement. "a deal."

"A deal," Nohar said. He turned around slowly. A fine dust of dried algae drifted off of him as he moved. It made him want to sneeze. "How many of you are sick? Half?"

Around him came a chorus of agitated barking. It was as if the woods around him had suddenly come alive. From the sound, he had struck a nerve. The barking went on while the canines debated. Nohar kept moving slowly, trying to look nonthreatening. He stretched overused muscles, and tried to work the stiffness out of his bad knee and shoulder.

"what do our problems matter." For once, the old dog's posture matched the fatalism of the electronic monotone.

"I could bring back a doctor—"

The barking became loud, aggressive. Nohar stopped moving. He had struck another nerve. "no men. no doctors. if that is the help you offer, it is no help."

Nohar swore quietly under his breath. He had no love of doctors and hospitals himself, but the canine pack around him looked at him as if he had suggested mass euthanasia.

"Okay, no doctors. but I could bring you medicine."

"what kind of medicine."

Nohar was tempted to say he'd cure all of them if they let him go. But he doubted they were that gullible, or that he could pull off that kind of fabrication. "I'm not a doctor," he said. "I don't know what's the matter. But I could bring back antibiotics, antivirals, at the very least something to help with the symptoms—decongestants, aspirin."

Nohar spread his arms and tried to look friendly.

More barking, subdued this time. Nohar hoped that they were considering this seriously. Looking at them, he could tell that they did a lot of scavenging. Some of them wore jury-rigged backpacks across their backs. A few wore collars with items hooked or taped to them. Nohar even saw a watch strapped to a dog's foreleg.

But pharmaceuticals weren't things you could easily scavenge.

"what is your name."

Nohar realized he had never answered the first question.

"Nohar."

"no-har." The hesitation over the syllable was the first time there'd been a disruption in the voicebox's smooth monotone. "we survive here because men do not know of us. if we make this deal with you, you must tell no one of us, of where we live. no men. no doctors."

Nohar nodded.

"i am elijah. we will accept your help."

Nohar felt a weight lift from his chest. He looked down at himself and said, "Can I clean up somewhere?" Walking into a pharmacy covered in algae was probably going to attract attention.

Elijah stepped in front of Nohar and said, "you will help. you will be followed. do not betray the trust we give you."

Nohar nodded.

"we will return your possessions when you do what you've said."

As Elijah's voicebox spoke, Blackie picked up the

Vind in his mouth and slipped it into a neighboring canine's backpack. That answered a nagging question that had been bothering Nohar, how these dogs could get along without hands. He supposed it was only natural, especially in a pack, for the dogs to team together to do things like loading a backpack, or even putting one on.

The busted comm and the camera followed the Vind.

They were about to do the same to his wallet. "Wait, I'll need that to get your medicine."

Elijah shook his head in a gesture the humans seemed to have bequeathed on all their engineered brethren. "we will return your possessions when you do what you've said."

The dogs began to leave him in twos and threes. In a few moments only Elijah was left facing him.

"prepare as you wish. but return with what you've gathered before the sky darkens. you will be watched. you will be followed." Somehow, the one-eyed pack leader managed to instill the toneless voice with a sense of threat.

With that, Elijah left him as well.

Fuck.

Nohar walked down out of the hills.

He wasn't alone. A fluctuating number of canines paced him on the way out of the woods. They stayed out of sight, but Nohar could smell them, and occasionally hear them.

He did get his chance to clean up. He passed a small creek on his way down toward Hollywood where he managed to wash most of the algae out of his fur and out of his clothes. He continued the remainder of his journey toward Hollywood dripping wet.

He was still trying to figure out how he was going

to keep his promise to the dogs. He was tempted just to skip, letting them keep his gun and his wallet—

Nohar doubted he'd get far pulling that. However he matched up one on one, he wasn't about to win a fight with a whole pack of angry, engineered canines. And when it came down to it, they could have overpowered him, could have fed him to the cops and whatever Fed agency wanted his hide. He was going to keep his promise.

Besides, he couldn't get into any *more* trouble than he was in already.

He got his bearings when he saw the Hollywood Freeway. He stopped next to it, standing amidst the trash that heaped next to the road. He hunted in the midst of car parts and rubbish until he found what he was looking for, a length of old blackened PVC pipe about one-and-a-half meters long.

Carrying the pipe, dripping wet, his suit wrinkled, streaked with green, and smelling of dead plants, Nohar walked into Hollywood.

The dirty streets had a few moreys in the midst of the prostitutes and hustlers, but even they stepped aside to let Nohar by. The pinks turned away from him and tried to fade into doorways or behind lampposts. Nohar didn't pay much attention. He was keeping his eyes out for cops.

He stopped at the first pharmacy he came to. It was an automated storefront, open twenty-four hours a day. Behind a thick window, a large holo displayed an image of a smiling, white-coated druggist, and in front stood a small kiosk where someone could place an order for whatever they needed.

Nohar ducked into a trash-strewn alley next to the store. The drugstore had a few windows back here, set into the looming brick wall. They were small and covered by a steel latticework set into the wall as a security measure. There also was a side door to the pharmacy, armored, flat, featureless, and locked with a cardkey panel.

Nohar was looking for a weak point, and after a moment of looking, he found it. The doorframe was old, contemporary with the century-old building. Above the new armored door was a flat panel where an old-fashioned air-conditioning unit would have fitted. That area was only so much plywood.

Nohar rammed his pipe at the flat space above the door. The plywood splintered, bowing inward. Nohar withdrew the pipe and rammed the panel again. The pipe hit with a crack, breaking the plywood almost in half. When he withdrew the pipe this time, he had to step back as the panel fell from the wall, revealing a small opening above the door.

Nohar could see another security grate over the hole, on the other side. He rammed it with the pipe a few times, and it clattered to the floor inside the building.

Nohar looked around a few times, and when he was sure no one was watching from the street, he tossed the pipe through the hole and heaved himself up and through. His suit caught and tore on splintered wood, but Nohar didn't pay it much attention.

He fell to the floor on top of the bent security grate.

The rear hallway was dark, but he was almost certain to be on someone's security video. All sorts of alarms were going off right now. He had five minutes, ten at the most.

He raced through the narrow hallway until he found a storage area. It was through an open doorway at the end of the hall. Motion sensors turned on the lights as soon as he stepped through the threshold. In the cavernous room, boxes sat on plastic shipping pallets, waiting for the owners to come feed the items into the automated bowels of the store.

A rancid chemical smell permeated the place. It reminded Nohar uncomfortably of a hospital.

He stripped off his jacket and started going from pallet to pallet, looking for what he needed. When he saw a label that indicated an antibiotic or antiviral drug, he tore into the top with his claws and grabbed two handfuls, tossing them into his jacket.

He went from pallet to pallet, tearing open boxes until he felt he had pushed the limit of his time here. He ran back to the rear door as he began hearing sirens in the distance. He tied his jacket in a bundle and tossed it through the opening above the door. Then he raised his foot and kicked at the crash bar on the door, twice. It didn't want to give, but on the second kick something in the mechanism gave and the door swung outward into the alley.

Nohar ducked through the broken door to retrieve his jacket and his booty—

The jacket wasn't there. Instead, lying on the ground in front of the door, was his wallet, the comm, the camera, and his Vind. Elijah had been as good as his word, the dogs had followed him all the way, watching his every move. Nohar found it disconcerting that he didn't know where the dogs were, worse was the thought that he had missed them when they were right outside the door. He never knew how close they'd been.

He must be getting old.

Nohar gathered his possessions and ran to find the other end of the alley before the cops arrived.

CHAPTER 8

Nohar waited in the dark, a few blocks north of Wilshire and a few blocks east of Santa Monica, trying to figure out another option. There was no way he should be here. He was too exposed. It was only a matter of time before the Beverly cops found him. He didn't dare get within a block of Royd's offices; they were almost certainly watched. Just like Royd's house had to have been watched.

Evening had fallen, and Nohar was crouched in the cover provided by a small park that nestled at one end of the street that held Royd's offices. The other end of the street was a cul-de-sac, so all traffic from Royd's building would pass through the intersection in front of Nohar.

Like when he hunted, he was crouched, absolutely still. He held the binocular camera. He watched through it, looking at a night-enhanced monochrome view of the entrance to the parking lot of Royd's building.

Occasionally, he would hit the zoom button to get a close-up view of a car leaving, and its occupants.

By now he had gotten a pretty good idea where the watchers were. A Chrysler Mirador with tinted windows hadn't moved from its parking spot since Nohar had found his hiding space. It was a luxury sedan, but in Beverly Hills it was anonymous enough to be unnoticed, where an unmarked police car would draw attention to itself.

Though Nohar wondered if they were police.

After waiting for two hours, he started to wonder if he had missed her. Just as he was about to give up and consider what the hell he'd do next, Sara Henderson walked out of Royd's building.

He watched her slim vulpine form walk through the parking lot, through the too-manicured garden. Now was the hard part. He needed her to help him discover what Royd had been up to with him and the missing morey, Manuel—but he doubted that convincing her would be easy.

Nohar took a few deep breaths and prepared to move. He was going to have to catch her car as it stopped at the intersection in front of him. He was only going to have a few minutes to get down there, and somehow get into her car. He was still trying to figure out how to do that without making it look like an attempted kidnapping.

Henderson got into a jet-black BMW and pulled out of the parking lot. Just before Nohar lowered the camera, the Mirador started up. It pulled out just as Henderson's BMW reached the first statue lining the drive.

The Mirador never turned on its headlamps.

Nohar didn't know what to make of what was going on, but he headed toward the intersection anyway, a heavy feeling in his gut. He reached the edge of the park just as Henderson's BMW came to a stop at the intersection.

The Mirador didn't.

It screeched past the BMW and angled itself across the BMW's path. Nohar's instincts told him that Henderson had to peel out in reverse, *now*.

Henderson didn't have his instincts. Three humans

erupted from the Mirador before it had come to a complete stop. Nohar had a horrid sense of dejá vù. They wore the same black paramilitary gear as the men who had attacked his cabin. Two of them carried Black Widows. The third was already smashing in the window of Henderson's car.

Nohar whipped the Vind out of his holster before he heard Henderson scream.

Twenty meters separated him from the Mirador. He started running to clear the distance before the combat team knew he was there. The unarmed pink was dragging Henderson from behind the wheel, while the two gunmen were turning, realizing something was wrong.

Nohar's nerves sang with the high-tension hum of genes primed for combat. The night snapped into monochrome clarity, and everything slowed to the rhythm of a ballet.

His pulse thudded in his ears as he ran, and he hesitated to aim, almost too long. He could smell the adrenaline of the men, and the fear of Henderson. The first gunman had started firing, the silencer thudding on his weapon, before Nohar got off his first shot.

He was halfway there, and the Vind spoke in a resonating explosion that shook Nohar's jawbone. The shot landed in the gunman's upper chest. The armor he wore didn't slow the twelve millimeter slug much. Nohar saw blood as the man folded backward over the hood of the Mirador

Gunman Two saw his partner go down and started firing as he tried to dive for cover behind the Mirador. At the same time, the third pink had pulled Henderson out the broken window and was raising his head at the sound of the gunshot.

Nohar was only five meters away when the Vind spoke again.

Glass exploded as the shot blew through the Mirador's rear passenger window, through the Mirador's rear window, and finally through the right shoulder of Gunman Number Two. He spilled to the ground behind the Mirador, his gun flying from his grasp.

The Mirador's driver gunned the engine, jerking the car forward so Gunman One rolled off of the hood.

The guy with Henderson was reaching for a holster. By now everything was razor-sharp. The gene-engineered beast had taken over. Nohar's instincts had overrun his thoughts by about five times, and he had taken the shot before he could think if it was worth the risk.

The bullet landed in the center of the pink's face, spraying Henderson with blood and clumps of brain tissue. She scrambled away, her look of horror unmistakable.

The Mirador pulled out, aiming for him. Nohar ducked aside, but the car still clipped the side of his leg, knocking him spinning. He landed in a crouch as the Mirador turfed the lawn of the neighboring park in an effort to come around at him again.

Nohar leveled the Vind at the car and pumped five shots into the windshield. At least one hit the driver. The car stopped accelerating, slid by Nohar, and crashed into a light pole by the side of the road.

"What's happening?" Henderson pleaded. She was looking down at the guy who'd dragged her out of the car. His face had been obliterated. In his hand he held a Baretta nine-millimeter halfway out of its holster.

Nohar ran to the BMW, reached in the broken window, and unlocked the car. It was still running.

He pulled Henderson into the car and got into the driver's seat. It wasn't until then he holstered his weapon. He put the BMW in drive and pulled away from the intersection. A navigation display rolled by the windshield, one corner flashing red, telling him that one of the windows had been broken.

He kept accelerating until he hit Wilshire, then he turned left, away from Beverly Hills.

"You killed them." There was a hollow sound in Henderson's voice. For a moment she sounded as emotionless as Elijah's voicebox.

"Two of them," Nohar corrected automatically. The Beast was still running his neurochemistry. He was holding on to the knife-edge of battle with ragged mental claws—he couldn't let himself crash now, not when he was going a hundred klicks an hour down Wilshire Boulevard, not in Beverly Hills, not within a few miles of the commandos who had tried to take Henderson.

Henderson was looking down at her dress. It was another black one, with a slightly different cut. She was staring at the flecks of skull and brain that still adhered to it. "I never saw someone die before."

Nohar didn't have a response for that. He maneuvered the car left, to start heading for the Santa Monica Freeway. He felt as if every cop in Beverly Hills was about to appear behind him and start shooting.

Henderson turned to look at Nohar. "Are you going to kill me?"

"What a stu—" Nohar shook his head. "I just saved you life."

She shook her head, and Nohar saw her fatalistic expression out of the corner of his eye. "You killed him."

Nohar was about to say something about nuts with guns when he realized she was talking about Royd. "No," Nohar said, "I didn't."

"The police came to the office, and it's been on the news."

Wonderful, let's try and keep a low profile now; when half the city thinks you killed Royd. . . .

Nohar shook his head. "You work for a law firm. You think the cops are always right? They never jump to conclusions when a morey's involved?"

Nohar looked across at Henderson and saw her eyes glisten. He turned away. His own tear ducts weren't engineered to be triggered emotionally. Like facial expression, it was something the gene-techs often left out when they were building their warriors. He couldn't stand to see moreaus cry. It brought back a memory of something he didn't want to relive. Especially now, when he had a lot of other problems he needed to deal with, in the present.

"He was the best man I ever knew. He was putting me through law school—" She sniffed, wrinkling her muzzle, and looked at Nohar accusingly. "You didn't kill him, like they said?"

"No," Nohar said flatly.

"Why should I believe you?"

"Because I saved you?"

She looked out the front windshield. The reflection of the headsup brought out odd highlights in her fur, making it look like slightly tarnished copper. "What from?" She was staring at the gore on her dress again.

"From the same guys who killed your boss."

"Who are they? What's going on?"

"I'm trying to answer both." Nohar pulled the BMW on to the Santa Monica Freeway. As soon as he merged with the nighttime traffic, he began to relax a little. He also began to feel the crushing aftereffects of what he'd just gone through. They sat in silence as the BMW carried them into the heart of downtown Los Angeles.

"I want to go home." Henderson's voice sounded weak.

"Not a good idea."

She turned to look at him, but Nohar kept his eyes fixed on the road ahead. "They're probably watching your place."

"They?"

"They're heavily armed and know what they're doing." Nohar looked down at the dash of the BMW. "We've got to ditch this car—"

"What?"

"Tracking devices. Too small for us to find."

"This is insane."

"Do you have a change of clothes in this car?"

She looked at him, his green-stained shirt and torn pants, and said, "For you?"

"No. You."

"Maybe in the trunk."

Nohar pulled the BMW into the first parking garage he came to. He parked the car in a spot as far from the entrance as he could. He stepped out and stripped off his shoulder holster and his shirt. "Find something to change into. We can get lost on the subway."

In a few hours, Nohar found himself and Henderson at an all-night Mexican diner on the fringes of East LA. The moreys here were of South or Central American stock, mostly rodents of various types, with the occasional Brazilian oddity.

He and Henderson stood out even without the way they were dressed. Henderson wore a blue sweater, faded and with grease stains, over a pair of ragged cutoff jeans that looked as if they had never really fit. Nohar still wore his suit pants, and the stained shirt which he now wore billowing open so he could hide the holster, somewhat, underneath it. It didn't really work, but they hadn't run into any cops, and no one else bothered them about it.

Nohar had blown most of his remaining cash on dinner. He hadn't eaten in a long time, and his body was screaming for food. He ordered three carnivore burritos—mostly raw ground meat wrapped in a warm tortilla.

Henderson just had a glass of water, which she spent most of her time staring into.

"I should go to the police."

Nohar bit into his burrito and nodded. "That may be an option for you. Not me."

"Why not?"

"Ask the cops who tried to blow me away." Between bites, Nohar told Henderson what had happened, from Royd's visit, until he had come gunning down her assailants.

"These guys figured I'd head for Royd, and set themselves up for me. They were watching for me when I entered the house, then called in the Beverly cops—probably with some story about moreau terrorism, something to push their buttons—prime them to shoot at anything."

"But why?" Henderson shook her head. "Charles Royd was a good man. Why would someone do this to him?"

Nohar shook his head. Henderson seemed awfully naive for someone who worked in the legal profession. "I doubt they were pissed at him personally. They were trying to get information." Nohar picked up a burrito. "Something they didn't expect me to know, something they didn't get."

"How do you know that?"

"If they thought I had what they wanted, they wouldn't have tried to barbecue me. If they'd gotten what they wanted from Royd, they wouldn't come after you." Nohar shook his head slowly. He felt a nagging frustration because he couldn't put a finger on exactly what was happening. "This all stemmed from Royd trying to hire me. This all has some connection to a missing crossbreed named Manuel."

Henderson looked up and said, "What has that got to do with anything?"

"That's the only connection I have with Royd. His anonymous client insisted that he hire me to find this Manuel. He apparently worked at—"

"The Compton Bendsheim Clinic." Henderson finished for him. She was staring at him, and he smelled something like terror coming off of her. "No, this can't be Manuel— Oh, God," Henderson buried her face in her hands.

Nohar bent over and placed a hand on Henderson's shoulder. She was shaking.

He heard her whisper, "It's all my fault. God, I didn't know he was hiring *you* . . . !"

"You're Royd's client?"

She shook her head and stood up. "No. No. But it's all my fault. Christ, do you think they've killed Manuel, too?"

Nohar just stared at her, trying to read her shifting emotions, fear, anger, agitation, confusion—a lot of the latter mirroring his own. "If you didn't—"

"I have to call someone. God, I hope she's all right." She ran off to the front of the restaurant, where a public comm stood.

Maybe the Bad Guys were looking for the same thing he was, the identity of Royd's client. Nohar watched Henderson at the comm. She obviously knew about Manuel.

When Henderson got a connection and started nodding, Nohar stood up and started walking to the comm. It was a good bet that the person Henderson was talking to was Royd's client. The pieces began fitting together. Henderson knew Manuel, his family, friends, or maybe his wife. When Manuel turns up missing, Henderson introduces those loved ones to Royd—everyone blithely ignorant of "them," the commando goons that Manuel had stirred up.

That still left the questions of what exactly Manuel had gotten involved in, and why Royd's client had insisted on hiring Nohar, and remaining anonymous.

"No," Henderson was saying, "something Manuel must have been involved in. They tried to kidnap *me* less than an hour ago, but he—"

She got quiet when Nohar stepped up next to her at the comm. The party on the other end began to say, "Sara?"

Then she got quiet as well.

Nohar looked at the screen, not quite believing. Now he knew why Royd's client had asked for him, and why she had required anonymity.

"Maria," Nohar whispered. All the breath had gone out of his body, as if he'd just taken a blow to the kidneys.

"Raj," she replied, using a nickname no one had used for nearly seventeen years. She hadn't changed, she had the exact same Jaguar face he remembered. Nohar began to realize why Manuel had looked familiar.

Maria had been on the cusp of Nohar's memory ever since he had seen Henderson crying. No matter how much time had passed, moreau tears always reminded him of Maria Limón. He always thought of her the way she'd been the second-to-last time he had ever seen her. It was on a battered comm screen like this.

Then she'd been at a public phone, streetlights behind her. Nohar could still remember a shimmer where the lights reflected off the black fur under her whiskers. He remembered the look of accusation in her golden eyes. He could still remember how the unnatural white of the streetlight refracted through a tear caught between the hook of her claw and the pad on her index finger—causing rainbow arcs across the screen.

He didn't remember the words. But he remembered the pain. He remembered her leaving. And he remembered the last time he'd been happy in a relationship with his own kind.

That had been seventeen years ago. But seeing her face again made it feel as if she had left him yesterday.

Seeing the curve of her black-furred cheek he could see echoes of Manuel's unhappy scowl. As he looked at her, a dread certainty began growing in the pit of Nohar's stomach.

He stared at Maria's face on the comm and could barely bring his voice above a whisper. "How old is Manuel?"

Maria looked pained. Her voice was tinny through the comm's speakers, as if she was talking down through all the years that separated them. "I'm so sorry, Raj."

"God *damn!*" Nohar yelled. The voice tore through his throat as if it was barbed and tore the flesh away as it escaped. Nohar slammed a fist into the wall next to the comm. It went through the drywall like it was air, and there was the sound of protesting metal as his hand struck a support. He felt the skin spilt open, and as he pulled his hand away, blood spilled from his knuckles, splattering on the ground.

The whole restaurant was staring at them now. A crop of beady little rat eyes and, close by, the smell of fear. The manager came forward, started to say, "Hey—" then either noticed Nohar's gun or his size, and backed off.

Henderson was backing away, too. "What's wrong?"

Nohar backed away from the wall, looking at his bleeding hand. "What's wrong?" He started laughing. *"What's wrong!"* Once he started laughing, he couldn't stop. It was like a stuttering roar that shook his whole body, belting out the frustration of not just the last few days, but the last decade, the last seventeen years.

He stood there gasping for breath, clasping his bleeding hand, and said, "He's my son." He stared at Maria's image through blurred eyes and said, *"He's my fucking son!"*

CHAPTER 9

"You should come here," Maria said. "I shouldn't say all this over the comm."

"Okay," Henderson told her. She was staring at Nohar wide eyed, with a barely concealed fear. He was leaning against the wounded wall, his whole body tensed, claws extending and retracting, tearing at the drywall.

Can't say it over the comm, he thought. *You* left *me over the fucking comm.*

Something was torn apart inside him. Somehow this was a worse blow than any pink bastard with a gun could deliver. Nothing he had felt in the past few days could compare with the wound this made inside him.

He kept telling himself that nothing had changed. He was the same person who had walked into the restaurant, and it was the same world outside it. But something drastic had changed. When he had come in here, he was alone by choice, someone who had decided to have no close connections whatever void it left inside him. Now, he was someone who *had* a family, had a connection to someone, and who had had it stolen from him.

It was as if all the emptiness of the last seventeen years was focused on that single moment. Compared to that, the fact that someone tried to burn down his house and kill him seemed minor.

"We'd better go." Henderson put a hand on his arm.

Nohar shrugged away from the touch, but he looked around the restaurant. People had shied away from the comm, and rats were standing up to move away from their tables. The manger had retreated to the back somewhere—probably calling the cops.

Nohar pushed past Henderson and headed for the door.

Maria Limón lived deeper in East LA, in a neighborhood of Hispanic moreaus. The place was better than Compton, the buildings newer. Here they'd actually rebuilt after the riots.

Most of the street signs were in Spanish, which left Nohar lost. Henderson, however, seemed to know where she was going.

They were as out of place walking down the nighttime streets of East LA as they'd been in the restaurant. It was another thing that made Nohar feel misplaced, alien. He was decades out of place here. He came from a time when moreaus were a single people. The idea of moreaus segregating themselves seemed sick and self-destructive. It was Moreys and the pinks; it didn't matter what nationality bred you, or what species. Those were dividing lines drawn up by humans. . . .

As he followed Henderson, he wanted to see some other moreaus, something other than the lab-animal descendants that the quantity-driven Central-American gene-techs had engineered forty years ago. He wanted to see something from Asia, a Chinese ursine, a Vietnamese canine, an African feline, even a frank from some long-lost black projects lab.

But the streets here were as racially pure as a moreau society could achieve. Enough that even Maria, a Brazilian jaguar, would seem as out of place as Sara Henderson.

Maria lived in a housing project that rose three or four dozen stories above the highway and surrounding shops. It was a modern building of flat white concrete. The windows were strips cutting deep black grooves through the floodlit walls. It had been built after the riots, but already looked heavy with age. Henderson led Nohar through a gate in the chain-link fence, and through an abandoned playground stranded in weed-shot asphalt.

The setting reminded Nohar of Saf-Stor. A concrete block where you stored stuff you didn't want anymore. The sight of the building shook him with a sense of claustrophobia.

They stopped in the playground. Henderson had led him in silence through the long walk. Now she looked up at him and asked, "What happened?"

"I knew Maria. She left me." Nohar shook his head. It was still hard for him to accept.

She walked up to him and put a hand on his arm. This time he didn't shrug away from the touch. "Is that it?"

"Yes."

No.

That wasn't it. But Nohar didn't know how to say it. He had been the product of two expatriate moreaus from the Indian Special Forces that escaped to the U.S. right as their homeland was collapsing near the end of the Pan-Asian War. He had probably been conceived on the airlift over the Atlantic.

His mother had died early, and he hadn't found his father until he was fifteen. That meeting with Datia Rajasthan left him despising his father.

Nohar had made a lifetime promise to himself that he would never be responsible for a fatherless child.

He had never told himself that in so many words, not until now. He had never donated sperm to a Bensheim Clinic, even though every male moreau he'd known growing up had used it as a source of ready cash.

Nohar's greatest fear was that he would somehow become his father.

"Did you know your father?" Nohar asked Henderson.

"My mom went to a Clinic, like everyone else."

Like almost *everyone else.*

Nohar wondered what Maria had told Manuel about his father. Did she tell him that the Clinic had screwed up? That he was dead? That he just wasn't worth knowing?

Nohar stared up at the light-washed concrete. The sky beyond was dead black, as if the only things here were the building and the void.

"Let's get this over with," Nohar said.

The outside of the building was wrapped in graffiti that extended over Nohar's head. It poured inside, into the lobby, as if it were some fluorescent fungus infecting the building. Nohar looked at it as they entered the building, until he realized that he was looking for his son's name.

They took an elevator thirty stories up to reach Maria's floor. Her apartment was at the end of a graffiti-swathed hallway, the last of a long line of armored doorways. Above every door, cameras peered at them from behind their scratched shields of bulletproof polymer.

It took a long time for Maria to answer the call button. Nohar spent the time building up his anger, rehearsing in his mind what he was going to say.

How dare she keep this from him: How could she deny him that part of his life? They'd even been living in the same city. She should have told him. . . .

When she finally opened the door, all the words left him. The last time he had seen her, she'd been barely twenty years old. She was younger than he was, but right now she looked much older. She sat in a wheel-chair, and the short blanket she wore across her knees didn't hide the fact that her legs were oddly twisted. Her free hand rested on her lap, open, claws partially extended. He saw the joints swollen with arthritis.

Her face, however, was the same. She looked up with a weak smile that turned up her feline cheeks, but didn't seem to reach her eyes. "Come in, old friend."

Henderson walked in, but Nohar stood outside, still staring, speechless.

Maria shook her head. "Come on, Raj."

"What happened?" The words came out in a whisper.

Maria's golden eyes turned down toward her legs and the hand in her lap. "Age, Raj. That's all." She lowered her other hand, which had been holding onto the door. It was as bad as the one in her lap.

Age? Your fur hasn't even grayed.

She rested her hand on a large shelflike brace set in the armrest of her wheelchair. She pulled her arm slightly back, the shelf rocked, and the whole chair moved backward to give Nohar room to pass.

Nohar walked in and closed the door behind him. As he did, he saw that the normal keypad had been replaced with an oversized handle. Seeing Maria like this made him angry, this time at the whole process of their creation.

The gene-techs had been making weapons, not peo-ple, and a long life was not part of the design criteria. Any problems that occurred outside a ten-year design window wasn't their concern. That meant that once moreys aged a little past their prime, they were prone to arthritis, degenerative hip dysplasia, multiple sclerosis, muscular dystrophy, Huntington's disease, a thousand flavors of cancer, and almost every other degenerative ailment that existed—including a few that were only native to some badly engineered species.

Nohar was lucky. His engineered joints were only slightly arthritic. Maria was only in her thirties. She might never reach Nohar's age.

He felt sick.

Maria rolled into the living room. "I'm sorry I don't have much in the way of chairs here. They're sort of a luxury for me."

There were two old wooden chars that seemed to have been refugees from an old dinette set. Nohar doubted the chairs could take his weight, so instead he walked to the window and stared at the blurry nighttime sprawl of Los Angeles.

The silence stretched uncomfortably until Nohar finally said it.

"Why didn't you tell me?"

He could hear her chair whir, smell her familiar musky scent. In his mind he could still feel the way she was then. Her lithe muscular body—

"I was going to tell you . . ." Her voice was soft, but Nohar could hear a painfully hard undertone to it.

"When?" Nohar's own voice was hard. "Seventeen years? Long enough for him to grow up. When were you going to tell me?"

"When I found out I was pregnant, Raj."

Nohar turned slowly around to face her.

"You stood me up that last time, and I just couldn't take it anymore."

Nohar remembered the call. He remembered Maria's tear-streaked face on his comm, telling him it was over. It had been the last in a long string of dates that had been sacrificed for his work. He couldn't even remember why he had missed it.

"You didn't have the right to keep it from me." In his own ears, Nohar's voice sounded weak and pathetic—the voice of a whining cub.

"Would you have changed, Raj?" Maria wheeled the chair up to him. "You were married to that pink twitch before he was even born. Why *should* I have told you?"

"I'm his father."

"I'm sorry, Raj, but when did you ever have room in your life for that kind of responsibility?"

"I was never given the opportunity, was I?"

Henderson stepped between them. "*Please.* Manuel is the important thing here. Isn't he?"

Manuel. The reason his life was turned inside out. Nohar turned away from both of them and tried to calm his anger. "What happened?" His voice was quiet, almost a whisper. He felt that if he raised his voice, he would start yelling and clawing the walls.

"Manuel disappeared," Henderson said, "Two weeks ago now."

"I know." Nohar waked up to the window and leaned his head against the top of the frame, staring down into the darkness. "What I need is details. All the things that might be relevant. Where he disappeared from, where he worked, who his friends were, how you and Royd became involved, his habits, if he was involved in any illegal activity—"

Maria snorted.

Nohar shook his head. "You know the questions, and the answers. To get to the bottom of this mess, I need them, too."

For nearly an hour, he questioned both of them about his son. The questions were the sterile antiseptic details that he always ended up asking when he was a PI. Somehow, though, there seemed a desperate urgency to the routine questions now that it was his own flesh and blood involved.

One of the most basic details was the name. The last name was a slight detail that Royd had left out of their meeting. Something as simple as that began painting a picture of his son in Nohar's head. The kid kept an unfashionable surname, perhaps as a way to distance himself from a moreau culture that would never fully accept him, the mule. It was an impulse Nohar could identify with.

Maria and Royd had expected him to take the case as soon as he looked in the little information file that Royd had left him. All it would have taken was the last name and the date of birth for him to have put it together. Of course, they hadn't figured that he didn't have a working comm out in the woods with him. *Everyone* had a comm. Why the anonymity? Maria thought that it was more likely that he'd look for his son if he didn't know who was hiring him.

Where did the fifty-grand offer come from? It's not like Maria could afford it.

They both looked surprised at that. Maria had only managed to scrape together five grand. It must have been Royd's money. When Henderson realized that, she broke down into tears. . . .

Nohar began to feel a little guilty about how he'd treated the late Charles Royd. He'd never thought he'd ever meet a rich pink who could turn out to be a decent person.

He drilled them about everything he could think of about Manuel's life. None of the answers seemed to lead to the Bad Guys. Manuel seemed pretty typical, if isolated. He'd gone through the accelerated moreau educational system, and had been working with a high school equivalency for the past three years. Maria said she had some hopes for college, but the way she said it made Nohar wonder if Manuel had the same hopes.

Manuel worked at the Compton Bensheim Clinic, mostly as a shipping clerk, not working with the patients. Nohar wondered if that was a bit of morey prejudice, *let's not have the mule working the desk where prospective mothers might see him.*

The only real friends Manuel had—that Maria knew about—were his coworkers. No school friends—Manuel's time in the morey excuse for a school system seemed predictably awful.

He'd left home at twelve. Though, despite that, he had come to visit Maria faithfully every Friday.

In fact, Manuel hadn't missed a single Friday until two weeks ago. When Maria called to find out what happened, no one had seen him since the Tuesday before. She had called the police and had gotten a sympathetic but nonproductive response.

When Maria was trying to discover where Manuel had gotten to, she discovered Sara Henderson looking for him as well. When Nohar turned around to look at Henderson, she said, "Me and Manuel, we—like—"

"I have the picture," Nohar said. Henderson and his son. He wondered what had brought the two together. How old was Henderson? She was in law school, that put her at least a couple of years older than Manuel, and only if she started college right after the morey public schools spit her out. It seemed an odd match, but Nohar had seen odder.

"Royd did some legal work for the Clinic," Henderson said by way of explanation. "I made a lot of trips there. That's how we met."

"It was Sara's idea that we get Mr. Royd to help us." Maria looked up at Nohar. "It was my idea we try and hire you."

"Why? It's been ten years since I had a case—"

Maria looked up into Nohar's eyes. "Because you'd take it, Raj. No one else would care."

"So what was Manuel involved in?" Nohar asked.

Both females stared blankly at him.

Nohar felt the edge of a growl creep into his voice. "I've been going over this for an hour. Neither of you have told me anything that might have dredged up an army of human commandos who've tried to kidnap or kill anyone who might be looking for him."

Maria looked at Henderson. "*I've* been looking for him."

Nohar was about to respond with a sudden realization struck him. Why wouldn't these people come after Maria? What were they after? If they were trying to cover up something that happened to Manuel, they were doing a shit-poor job of it. Just killing Royd increased the risk that someone would connect the whole thing to Manuel's disappearance.

What if Manuel was running from something?

What if he was running from the Bad Guys, and they didn't want someone else finding him? That almost made sense. . . .

"Does anyone else know I'm Manuel's father? Any records?"

"Only Manuel," Maria said. "And he only knows a little of what you were like in Cleveland—"

"What about Royd?" Nohar asked.

Maria shook her head. Henderson looked Nohar up and down. "I didn't even know. Not until an hour ago."

"I was afraid he might not hire you if he knew," Maria said.

Nohar tried to construct a sequence of events in his head. Manuel disappears. The Bad Guys start looking for him—probably the first to start looking. Then Maria and Henderson work out a deal with Royd. At some point after Royd makes his pitch to Nohar, the Bad Guys come in and torture the poor bastard. Probably still looking for Manuel. They don't find what they want, but they do they find out Royd had come to Nohar, and they decide they don't want any competition.

If the Bad Guys were looking for Manuel, their attempt to grab Henderson meant they hadn't found him yet.

That brought the question back to why they hadn't grabbed Maria. Nohar had an uneasy feeling that he knew the reason.

Bait.

If the whole point of all this was to find Manuel, you wouldn't strong-arm the kid's mother. You'd watch her apartment, bug the place, tap her comm, and wait for the kid to make some sort of showing.

Worse, that meant that where he had thought that he and Henderson had slipped away from these people, they had really stepped up under their noses.

Nohar walked past the two women and hit the light switch, plunging the room into darkness. He heard Maria's wheelchair spin around. "What are you—?"

Nohar raised a hand. Her eyes had adjusted, and she responded to his quieting gesture. He pulled his binocular camera out of his pocket and shifted its spectrum toward the infrared as he raised it.

He looked toward the window and saw what he had been afraid of. A small shimmering spot of infrared light sparkled on the edge of Maria's window. Nohar had a good idea what it was.

Someone had pointed a laser mike at the window, picking up every vibration their voices made in the glass. Nohar edged around until he could get a bead on where the listener was stationed.

He narrowed the source down to a window on a

black van parked in the project's weed-shot parking
lot. Nohar cursed himself for not noticing the out-of-
place van earlier.

Nohar took a picture of the van and slipped the
camera back into his pocket. He flipped the light back
on. "Oops, sorry about that." his back was to the window, and he held a finger up to his lips.

Maria's voice was uncertain, but she went with Nohar's lead. "No, it's all right. . . ." She looked at Henderson, but Sara seemed just as confused.

"It's been a long day." Nohar walked through a
short hall and found Maria's bathroom. Nohar noticed
the long padded handles on the fixtures and felt an
irrational wave of anger at all pinks, especially the
ones in the van. "Do you mind if I spend a little time
to clean up?" He turned on the faucets in the sink
without asking.

"That's fine." Maria's voice hovered close to a question as Nohar slipped out of the bathroom and headed
for the front door. Maria and Henderson followed
him.

He opened the door and faced both of them. He
pointed at both of them and then pointed at his
mouth, then made yakking gestures with his hand.
Henderson stared at him blankly, but Maria got the
point. She reached over and tapped Henderson with
the back of her hand. "Do you think these people got
to Manuel?"

Henderson looked flustered. Still staring at Nohar
she said, "I don't know. Why are they doing this to
us?"

Nohar nodded encouragement, tapping the wall
with his finger and pointing to his ear. *They're
listening..*

Before he closed the door on their strained conversation, he pointed to his wrist and flashed them the fingers on his left hand twice. *Ten minutes.*

If he took longer than that to come back, he probably wasn't coming back.

He closed the door and began running for the elevator.

CHAPTER 10

It had to be sheer luck, but the bastards in the van weren't on to him as he reached the ground floor. He was hoping—counting on—the fact that they were listening, not watching, and they'd been doing it long enough to become complacent.

What really worried Nohar was who the men in the van might have called in when they heard him and Henderson arrive. The Bad Guys must have decided to let the pot stir to see if the three of them came up with what they wanted. But by now there had been enough talk for the Bad Guys to piece a lot together. It was only a matter of time before they made the decision to come down on them.

He had seven minutes.

Nohar left the side of the lobby opposite the parking lot that held the van. He headed straight out, keeping the floodlit bulk of the building between him and the watchers. He reached the fence ringing the grounds and didn't bother following it to a gate. He grabbed the fence, pulling himself up on top in a crouch that set off flares of pain in his bad knee. He stayed there as long as he could stand it, staring at the barbed wire angling away from him, over the outside of the fence.

Then he grabbed a strut holding the barbed wire in place, and vaulted over the wire.

He hit the ground in a stumble that fired pain off

in his knee and his shoulder. He could taste his own exertion like copper in his mouth.

Six minutes.

He backed into the darkness and circled the property around toward the van. He could smell them before he reached the driveway that led to the project's parking lot. Three pinks had been here; their distinctive odor was as obvious as a neon sign. How the hell had he missed it before?

Nohar drew his gun and wondered if he was still capable of going through all this shit.

He edged up the driveway, sticking to the shadows on the upwind shoulder of the road. The van was twenty meters into the parking lot, on the edge farthest from Maria's building. The van was a modern Electrostar that looked out of place on the broken asphalt, in the midst of cars that were either headed for the junk heap, or customized beyond recognition. It was parked next to an old Ford Jerboa with a gold paint job, jacked-up rear, and a purple-fringed interior.

Five minutes.

Nohar was running on instinct. He wasn't sure what he was going to do, even when he started running up on the van. He held a dim hope that he wasn't going to shoot anyone. Knowing who he was dealing with, that seemed unlikely.

He closed the distance with the van in a matter of seconds. He landed between the van and the Jerboa, his back against the van's cold composite wall. He edged up on the passenger-side door. It had tinted windows that reflected the sodium lights of the parking lot.

Nohar sucked in a breath.

Four minutes.

He spun around before the men in the van would

have time to react, bringing the butt of his gun down on the passenger window. There was a tense moment when the thought of armored polymer crossed Nohar's mind, but the window was just plain safety glass and exploded inward when the blow hit.

Nohar pointed the Vind in toward the driver's seat, yelling, "Nobody move."

Nobody did.

Nobody was there.

Nohar was pointing his gun at an empty driver's seat. He ducked his head in to look in the back. That was equally empty. There wasn't anyone in the van. The smell of the pink owners was strong, but ghostly. They hadn't been in the van for a while.

Nohar shook his head and lowered his gun. He did have the right van; he could see a portable comm unit in back, what looked like a satellite uplink, and what had to be the laser mike on a tripod, pointing toward the driver's side window, which was open a crack to let the beam reach Maria's window.

Chalk one up for the Bad Guys. Wherever they were watching, it was from a distance.

Nohar reached in and opened the passenger door. As he did, he heard the whine of the flywheel as the Electrostar's inductors were engaged.

"Shit!"

Nohar had a choice of backing up or diving in before the van pulled out. He dove into the passenger seat, broken glass digging into his knee as the van's autopilot engaged.

Nohar held on as the van accelerated over the parking lot's broken pavement. He could see a red light on the dash flashing the alarm he'd triggered when he busted the window.

There was little point to subtlety now. The Bad Guys had a live uplink to what was going on. They knew their van was compromised, and they probably had a video feed of him right now. He reached over to the dash and began flipping up the nav display. Security measures kept him from reprogramming the comm, but the Bad Guys left the display functions alone, so as the van tore out of the lot, swinging the passenger door shut on a sharp turn, Nohar managed to call up a map on the headsup with the van's programmed route flashing in red.

It was going for the freeway, then north to an address in Pasadena. That was all Nohar needed. He didn't want to follow the van into an ambush. He slipped into the back of the van, bracing himself in a crouch behind the driver's seat. Then he lowered his Vind and aimed at the nav computer.

The Vind exploded in the enclosed space, and a nasty hole opened up in the dashboard. The headsup winked out and the van rolled to a stop as the governors kicked in.

Three minutes.

Nohar backed into the van, checking over the equipment they'd been using to eavesdrop on Maria. It was sophisticated stuff. Nohar figured that the uplink alone cost a bit shy of ten grand. There was a set of numbers on an LCD set into the base of the uplink. Nohar noted them.

He probably only had a few more minutes before the Bad Guys descended on Maria's apartment complex. He had to get back and get both of them out of there.

"Is there a friend's place you can stay at?" Nohar ran into the apartment, gun still drawn, killing lights and going toward the windows. He looked out and cursed his bad vision. It had never been great for distance, but age seemed to have begun eating at his once-excellent night vision. He had to put the gun away and pull out his camera to make sense of the parking lot.

The van was still on the driveway, stalled, hazards blinking. No sign of the Bad Guys yet.

"What's going on?" Maria voice was strained.

"Like, what happened out there?" Stress brought out the Southern California in Henderson's voice.

"We don't have much time." Nohar kept scanning the parking lot, shifting through the spectrum on his camera. "They were watching this apartment. They know I'm here with Henderson. If they're true to form, they'll fall on this place like a tac-nuke."

"But—" Maria began.

"They were watching here, waiting for Manuel to show, I think." Nohar lowered the camera and waved both of them into the bedroom. "Grab what you need. You help her. We have to get out of here before—"

They must have heard it about the same time he did. Nohar turned back to the window. When he placed a hand on the glass, he could feel the vibration caused by the rotors.

A black helicopter hovered over the parking lot, close enough for Nohar to make it out without the camera. It was heavy, armored, and three times as wide and twice as deep as a civilian aircar. The thing was matte black, and an even blacker hole was opening in its side as it descended.

Nohar raised the camera and saw it barely kiss the parking lot's surface. The camera was still set for IR, so the hole in the black helicopter's side was suddenly the brightest thing in the lot. The pit in its belly glowed, and Nohar saw the IR shadows of a dozen men spill out toward the building.

"Shit. We're moving *now!* Get out the door." They

should have all been gone by now, before these guys showed up.

Nohar put away the camera and drew the Vind. How the hell were the three of them going to get out of here? He pushed through the door after Henderson and Maria. He felt a sinking feeling as he looked at her wheelchair. They couldn't get her down the stairs, and the elevators in the lobby would be the first thing the Bad Guys would secure.

"No chance of an aircar lot on the roof?"

"In this neighborhood you're lucky you have the roof."

"How do we get out of here, past them—" Nohar was at a loss, swinging his gun up and down the hallway, expecting commandos to storm them at any moment.

"Maria?" Henderson spoke up.

Maria and Nohar turned to face her.

"You have, like, a friend in this building, maybe upstairs?"

"I know a lot of people here."

"Come on, then."

Nohar followed, willing to try anything.

Maria had a friend on the forty-third floor. They were lucky on two counts. First, the Bad Guys hadn't seized control of the elevators yet, and second, the elevators only had up-or-down indicators on the outside, nothing to tell bystanders what floors the elevators were on.

When they reached the door to the friend's apartment, Henderson began pounding on it. Nohar nervously stashed the Vind in the holster under his shirt.

After a while the external camera swiveled to cover them and a whispery voice buzzed through the

speaker next to it, "Ungodly hour, what is this—
Maria, is that you?"

"Let us in, Sam," Maria said.

"We need to use your comm," Henderson said.

The camera moved toward Henderson, and the
voice said, "Well, ain't you the pretty one? I guess for
you, Maria—" The door slid open on a gray lepus in
a ragged bathrobe. "Who's your friend?" the rabbit
stared at Henderson.

Nohar pushed through the door, leading the other
two in. "Where's the comm?" Nohar asked.

"If you're going to be like that," the rabbit said.

Maria wheeled up next to the rabbit and said,
"Now, Sam. We need your help." She raised the back
of her hand and patted his cheek with it.

Sam sighed and waved them into the living room.

Nohar led Henderson into the room, feeling time
pressing on his back.

The living room was a wash of colored lights and
incense. A black velvet couch faced a yellow comm
that was two decades out of date. Above the couch
hung a giant holo of "The Last Supper," the principals
played by various moreys. Christ was an angelic canine, while Judas was some sort of ferret.

Henderson stepped in front of the comm and
started to make a call. Nohar split his attention between her, the window at the end of the living room,
and the door where Maria and Sam were talking. He
expected to be on the wrong end of an assault at
any minute.

"*Eye on LA,* Enrique Bartolo speaking. How can I
help you— Sara? Is that you?" On the other end of
the line was a fuzzy picture of a human. Nohar
couldn't tell if the fuzziness was due to the connection,
or because the pink had just woke up.

"Hi, Rick—"

"Christ, lady, where're you calling from? What happened?" The pink's face began to show some interest. Nohar could tell he was looking past Henderson at the rest of the apartment. Nohar stepped aside, out of view of the comm. He didn't know how much publicity there was connecting him to Royd's death, but he didn't want to test this guy.

"—this is hot, Rick. There's a SWAT team going into Pastoria Towers in East LA. Guns, armored helicopter, the works."

"No, shit, when?"

"Five minutes ago. They're running through the building right now."

"Christ! Then we've got to get a team moving *now*. Thanks. Where're you?"

"Where do you think?"

The pink's face went a little blank. "No shit? Well, we're—"

Enrique Bartolo never finished the comment, because the line went dead. A few minutes later the lights flickered and went out. "Just in time," Henderson said.

"What was all that?" Nohar asked, edging up to the window and looking at the helicopter in the parking lot. By now the commandos had found Maria's apartment empty, and were probably doing a systematic sweep through the building. Cutting the comm lines and the power would be the start of that.

"Rick's an old friend. Royd's office used to feed him stories all the time about folks screwing us—nonhumans—over."

"A reporter—" The more Nohar thought about it, the more it made sense. The Bad Guys weren't cops. They didn't like the daylight. Unless they were part of the Fed, the presence of cameras might scare them off. Even if they were Fed agents, cameras might keep them from summarily shooting someone.

With Maria in a wheelchair there was nothing more they could do but wait.

Nohar stayed by the window and pulled out his camera. It seemed that the commandos were everywhere out there, ringing the parking lot. He could hear noises through the skeleton of the building now. Odd thumping sounds through the air vents. Occasionally, Nohar thought he heard something that might have been muffled gunfire.

"What's going on?" Sam asked. For the first time Nohar heard in his voice how old he must be. His voice had become high and papery, the lisp much more pronounced.

Maria, sitting, was at eye-level with him. "Some people have broken into the building."

"Who? What people?" Sam walked into the living room. He moved slowly, limping on a bad leg. He walked up to Nohar and looked him up and down. "Oh, this is bad. It's you, isn't it?"

Nohar didn't know what to say, so he returned to watching out the window.

"You, you're the one who killed that lawyer." Nohar felt something soft strike his hip. *"Bastard."*

Nohar looked down and saw Sam pounding on him with both fists. Nohar barely felt the blows. Looking down at Sam, the only emotion Nohar could dredge up was a feeling of pity.

Henderson stepped up and pulled Sam away from him. "Calm down."

"Calm down? That cat's a terrorist. He's likely to kill everyone in this building. I saw it on the comm."

"You don't believe everything you see on the comm." Henderson led him back into another room. "Do you?"

"Why shouldn't I?" Nohar heard Sam reply.

Nohar shook his head slowly and raised his camera again.

"Do they want to kill us?" Maria's voice sounded small and weak. The words tore at his heart. Her voice hadn't changed at all from what he remembered.

"I don't know." Nohar shook his head. "I think they want Manuel, and they don't know where to find him."

"But why?"

"That's the big question." Nohar lowered the binocular camera and turned around. "Every time they show up, they seem more blatant. More desperate . . ."

Maria looked away from Nohar, toward the bedroom where Henderson had led Sam. Whispered parts of their conversation drifted toward them. Henderson seemed to be explaining the last few hours to the rabbit.

Maria looked back at Nohar. Her eyes were moist. "I saw about Royd on the comm, too."

"About me?"

"Don't worry, I know you didn't." She wiped her eye with the back of a twisted hand. "But were they right about what they did to him?"

All Nohar could do was nod.

"Could that happen to us?" Maria asked him.

Nohar walked up, knelt, and wrapped his arms around her. She rested her head against Nohar's shoulder and started shaking. "I keep telling myself I have to be strong for Manuel—but I couldn't take that. I can't take any more pain."

Nohar ran his hand over her head and whispered, "Shh."

"I don't have the right to ask you anything—"

"We'll get through this."

"—but don't let them do that to me."

"I won't."

Maria pushed him weakly, and Nohar let go of her. She was looking at him with a grave expression. "I mean this, Raj. If they're going to torture me to get information about my son, I want you to kill me."

Nohar looked into her eyes and couldn't find any words.

"Promise me." Maria held up her hands in a pleading gesture. They were cupped, as if to catch Nohar's nonexistent tears.

Nohar was about to respond when a wash of white light flooded the living room. Nohar spun around to face the window, where the light was coming from.

He headed toward the window, and behind him he heard Henderson rush out from the bedroom asking, "What's happening?"

When Nohar reached the window, he announced, "I think your friends are here."

He didn't need his enhanced camera to make out what was going on. Even his rotten vision could make out the two aircars shining floodlights on the scene around the building. The aircars looked like huge flying beetles with two huge fans in place of wings. On the sides, twinned pylons carried spotlights and video equipment that was probably more sophisticated than any recon unit had during the Pan-Asian War.

When the spotlight swept by their window, Nohar caught sight of the side of one of the copters. It was painted in fluorescent colors so that no one could miss the screaming red logo of *Eye on LA*.

Nohar raised his camera so he could focus on the parking lot and what was going on.

Henderson had called it right. The Bad Guys were in retreat. Nohar could see two on either side of the hatch in the helicopter, weapons raised as if they expected someone to fire on their retreat.

More of them poured from the entrance of the building, running for the helicopter. In a few moments the helicopter had lifted off—just in time for the groundcars of another half-dozen news crews to arrive.

"You did good, Henderson."

"Sara," she said. She had edged up to the other side of the window to see what was going on. One of the *Eye on LA* aircars was trying to follow the unmarked helicopter; the other still hovered over the building.

"Sara," Nohar repeated.

"So," she asked, "are you going to find Manuel?"

He nodded.

CHAPTER 11

They had to wait until the power returned before they could leave. By then dawn was breaking and about half the news crews had left. They managed to slip out from under the cameras. The reporters had their hands full with all the morey residents who wanted everyone to know how their rights were violated by these pink commandos—who everyone assumed were cops.

The Bad Guys had found Maria's apartment empty, then had begun systematically breaking into every apartment in the building. As Nohar escorted Maria and Henderson through the crowded lobby, he heard at least two stories about gunfire being exchanged.

They had to make their way outside the parking lot to meet their taxi, because the police—real ones this time—had dressed up in riot gear and set up barricades around the building to keep people and vehicles out. Nohar worried about the three of them looking obvious in the sea of Hispanic rodents, but the cops were as overwhelmed as the reporters.

The cops had it worse than the reporters, the residents at least *liked* the reporters. Nohar had the feeling that if the cops weren't armed, they might not have survived being this close to Pastoria Towers.

They passed through the confusion, and to the taxi, without much difficulty. It was another automated cab, and Nohar let Maria direct it while he fell into an exhausted slumber.

Nohar dreamed of his father. They weren't pleasant dreams.

Nohar had been sired by Datia Rajasthan, commander of the mutinous airlift that brought almost all of Nohar's species into the U.S. just as the Indian military began collapsing. His mother had never told him who his father was. That was something he had to unearth himself, after she was gone.

He was only fifteen, still part of a street gang, when he'd found Datia. At first the discovery had impressed him. Datia had become, by then, a national figure advocating moreau rights. It wasn't until Nohar had met him that he'd discovered that Datia was a fanatic, more interested in controlling the destiny of the non-human population than he was in any family he might have had.

Datia couldn't have given a shit for Nohar.

They had only met once, and shortly after that the country erupted into riots—which many blamed on Datia Rajasthan. Datia was gunned down by the National Guard only a few dozen blocks from where Nohar was living. The only thing Nohar had ever gotten from his father was the gun he carried—something he received after Datia's death.

Datia Rajasthan hadn't even acknowledged Nohar as his son until he was dying in a burned-out building in Cleveland's Moreytown. There he mentioned his son to an audience of police, paramedics, and National Guardsmen. Nohar hadn't even been there.

In his dream, Nohar walks through the ruins of the building where his father had been killed. He looks for his father's body. He finally finds a corpse, high up in the building, where no roof lies between him and a black rolling sky.

Nohar turns the corpse over. Manuel's face stares up at him.

Someone laughs behind him, and Nohar spins around to confront whoever it is.

Datia Rajasthan is laughing at him. In his arms he holds a young Maria Limón. She laughs at him, too.

"Now," his father says, "you know how it feels."

Nohar crouches and growls. "Lying bastard. You're the one who died."

Datia shakes his head. "No. You died."

Datia points the Vind at Nohar and fires.

Maria's friend was an old canine named Beverly who lived on the fringes of Compton. Her eyes were clouded over, and Nohar thought she was nearly blind. Her eyes reminded him of Elijah, the half-blind dog in the hills.

But she walked with her nose forward, and it was hard to tell she couldn't see.

"Come on in, Maria. Introduce your friends." Beverly ushered them all into a two-room apartment. The inside was better kept than the hallway, which was wrapped in stains, trash, and graffiti. Beverly lived in a neat pair of whitewashed rooms. The apartment was in the basement, so there weren't many windows. Beverly compensated by having plants hanging from the pipes that ran across the ceiling.

The apartment smelled like a garden.

Maria rolled in first and said, "Sara, and Nohar."

"Pleased to meet both of you." She extended a hand and patted Nohar's forearm. "I'm afraid you'll have to duck a little. The ceiling's a bit low in here."

Nohar let Henderson go in first, then he ducked inside himself. He had to bend over more than a little.

Not only was the ceiling low, but there were pipes, and below them the plants. He had to bend almost double, and he still set one begonia swinging.

Beverly shut the door and faced them. Her ears perked up, and Nohar saw her tail wag, a smile in compensation for her lack of facial expression. "Can I get anyone some tea?"

"I think we can all use something to settle our nerves," Henderson said.

"Sure, my dear." Beverly turned around and began opening cabinets in the other side of the living room. Nohar realized now that there was a kitchen hidden in that wall. As she filled a pot at a sink hidden behind a cabinet door, she asked, "Maria, what brings you here? The room's thick with worry."

Nohar could smell it himself. He just hadn't been noticing it since he'd been living with it for the past twelve hours.

"I'm sorry," Maria said, "I don't want to bring trouble to your doorstep, Bev."

"Shush. I'll take trouble to have some visitors. Tell me about it." She fiddled a few more minutes, then put the pot into another cabinet that apparently doubled as a microwave. "You aren't going to scare me after living in this neighborhood for twenty-five years."

"It's about Manuel," Maria began.

"Our son," Nohar said, almost involuntarily.

"Oh, dear," Beverly said. "This *is* going to be interesting."

Beverly fed them on Chinese green tea and a package of processed meat that Nohar supposed once bore some relationship to a pig or a cow. It was what passed for carnivore food in Compton. After all his years away from processed food, Nohar was glad that the strongest taste it had was the salt.

Maria gave Beverly an abbreviated version of what happened. At the end of it, Beverly shook her head and said, "Isn't this exciting?"

"That's one word for it," Henderson said. Her voice was weak and frustrated. Nohar looked down at her and saw how fatigued she looked. Her fur was sticking out at odd angles, and she seemed to have shrunk within her ill-fitting clothes. Looking at her, Nohar realized how bad off he must look. His fur was matted and still smelled weakly of algae. His shirt was an opaque gray, and his pants were torn badly enough to see his leg all the way up to the hip.

"Well, you all need some rest." Beverly said. "And to clean yourselves up. You're all welcome to my bathroom." She walked past Nohar and into the bedroom. "I'll find some comforters for all of you."

Her nose wrinkled as she passed Nohar.

"Did you fall in a sewer, my friend?"

"Reservoir," Nohar said.

Beverly shook her head. "Those clothes go in a disposal chute. And you get the shower first." she patted his shoulder. Even sitting, it was about even with her own. "I don't want to sound ungracious, but I don't want that smell sinking into my furniture."

Nohar chuckled a bit. It was the first time he had felt any real lightness since before this had all started. "Yes, ma'am."

Beverly chuckled herself. "I'll get you something else to wear," she said as she walked on into the bedroom.

Nohar pulled off his shoes and began making a compact pile of his wasted clothes. He emptied his pockets onto the coffee table. He used coasters to rest his possessions on, since most were still streaked with algae.

When he peeled off his shirt, Henderson looked across at him and said, "What are you doing?"

"You heard her. And I've wanted this pink crap off for days." He could feel the fabric adhering to his fur as he pulled off his shirt and stuffed it in one shoe. He began unhooking his holster, was stymied for a place to put it, then finally he hooked it on an over-head pipe next to a spider plant.

"But you're, you're . . ." Henderson seemed unnaturally flustered, and when Nohar started undoing his belt she just turned away from him. Maria was looking at her oddly, as if she was surprised at the way Henderson was acting, too.

It took a few long moments for Nohar to realize what was the matter. And realizing it made him feel all the more alien.

Henderson had inherited the human neurosis about clothing. To Nohar's generation, clothing was a contrivance used solely to appease the humans that most moreys had to deal with. To someone whose body was covered in fur, pink clothing was often useless and annoying, something to be used only when necessary.

To his generation, Maria's, too, stripping in front of someone meant as little as a pink taking off his hat.

Now, however, it was sinking in that, in his first foray into Compton, a place almost completely absent of pinks, he hadn't seen one morey going without the human-mandated clothing. When he was living back in Cleveland's Moreytown, half of the moreys he'd see would be going around with as little as possible.

Henderson's embarrassment made him want to cover himself up.

He sighed and shoved his pants into his other shoe.

"I better go and shower off—" He glanced at Henderson, who still wasn't looking at him.

Maria looked at Henderson and nodded, as if she had just realized what was bothering her.

Nohar sighed and ducked into a bathroom that was much too small for him.

It took him nearly an hour to clean himself and dry out his fur. He could only fit part of his body in the shower at a time. He borrowed way too much of Beverly's soap. And he almost clogged the john with the clumps of fur he brushed off his body. He spent another fifteen minutes returning the bathroom to the shape he'd found it in.

He left feeling better now that the algae was out of his fur. He used the wall-mounted body dryer, but before he left, he grabbed one of the towels and wrapped it around his waist for Henderson's benefit.

When he left, Henderson wasn't there anymore. The only one in the living room was Beverly, who sat in a small easy chair in the corner of the room. She didn't look at him when he entered the room, but her ears perked up.

She held a canine finger to the tip of her muzzle, telling him to be quiet. Nohar nodded, even though he didn't think she could see him. He ducked into the living room, dropped the towel on the couch, and sat down next to it. It felt good to have his body relax for once, even in a space this small. The few snatches of rest he had gotten up to now didn't really count. He'd been too exhausted to receive any comfort. Even in the taxi coming here, his body wasn't so much resting as refusing to function.

Beverly spoke quietly. "I put Maria and her friend in my bedroom. They needed to get some rest." She raised a cup of tea to her muzzle and delicately lapped at it.

"That's good," Nohar's voice rumbled deep in his chest. "I wish they weren't involved—"

"From the sound of it, they involved you." She cocked her head as if daring him to tell her different.

"The Bad Guys involved me." Nohar sighed and reached for his own tea. The cup was small and nearly hidden in his hands. "They tried to kill me before I even knew Manuel had anything to do with me."

"You didn't know you had a son?"

Nohar stared into the cup he held in his hand, at the dark swirling liquid, and felt the knot of anger again. "How could you keep that from anyone?"

"I don't know, my friend. I won't condone it. But I've known Maria for years, and I knew she loves Manuel. Maybe she thought she was protecting him."

"We have it all mapped out." Nohar kept staring into the tea, the words pouring out uncontrolled. "We make kids at a Bensheim Clinic. It's so fucking common that fatherhood is reduced to a couple of sperm cells, even when—" The words choked off, and Nohar sipped his tea. He didn't know why he was babbling to this old canine. He was tried.

He shook his head. "It's as if it's abnormal to *care* about it."

"We're caught," Beverly said, "between nature, culture, and engineering." She made a small sound that was between a muffled bark and a sad laugh. "The balance we've struck seems equally unworkable on all three levels."

"I shouldn't unload on you." Nohar finished off his tea.

Beverly stood up and picked up the teapot. She managed to find his cup and refill it by touch. "Nonsense. You've had a trial. You can't bury feelings. . . ."

Nohar shook his head. "I've been doing fine till now."

How could someone do that?

How could a mother deny her child his father?

Why didn't she tell him?

When Nohar had that thought, he wasn't sure if he was thinking of Maria, or his mother.

CHAPTER 12

Nohar talked to Beverly longer than he expected. After sidestepping his personal life, they managed a few hours discussing the way things were twenty years ago, and how the changes since then weren't all for the best. It was the first real conversation he'd had with anyone in the past ten years. It made him fell a little less alien.

He could identify with Beverly. He had gone off into the woods, but she'd been as much in exile in this apartment, just as isolated, just as alone. Just as lonely.

Unfortunately, he wasn't free to converse. There was still Bad Guys out there, and there was still Manuel, somewhere.

Beverly had a comm and after they had finished their second teapot, Nohar planted himself behind it and began working on digging out of the hole they had all fallen in.

His first call was to a place in Cleveland that he hoped was still in business.

The line flashed a few times; the screen was distorted and out of focus. Nohar doubted that Beverly had ever gotten the picture properly aligned.

The blue AT&T test pattern dissolved into a shot of an office. Nohar saw the paneled walls and decided that Budget Surplus and his old friend Bobby were both long gone. He was about to cut the connection when he heard a familiar voice say, "Coming . . ."

The voice's owner walked in front of the screen, "International Systems and Surplus—"

The man on the other end of the comm stopped talking and just stared at the screen.

Nohar was equally speechless. The last time he'd seen Robert Dittrich, his old friend had been confined to a wheelchair—like he'd been since childhood. But there was no question that the man staring blankly at him was the same person, and he was *standing*.

"Good God!" Bobby exclaimed "Is that you, Nohar?"

Nohar shook his head and said, "Bobby?"

Bobby pulled up a chair and sat down in front of the comm and shook his head. "And you still don't put on clothes to talk on the comm. Christ, what've you been doing with yourself? What, five, ten years?"

"Well, haven't been doing as well as you. What happened to 'Budget Surplus'?"

Bobby shrugged. "Got in on the ground floor of a good deal—passed someone on to a hacker acquaintance on the West Coast, and the deal was rich enough for the finder's fee to set me up for life. Managed to jack the place up a few notches on the respectability scale."

Nothing remains the same, Nohar thought. "Your legs—" He didn't quite know how to finish the question.

Not that Bobby needed him to. "Oh, I was still in the chair last we talked." He stood and slapped his thigh. "Good old American cybernetics—remember when there wasn't such a thing? But we actually managed to get a project going at the Cleveland Clinic a few years ago, reverse-engineering some old Japanese prewar technology. Finally got it working."

Nohar shook his head. He had known Bobby since they'd been kids. And even though Bobby had been wheelchair-bound, he'd always been the one who was going to take on the world. Nohar had never thought Bobby might actually win. . . .

"Hey, enough about me. What can I do for you, old friend? He glanced at the bottom of the screen, where the transmit information usually scrolled by. "You're still in La-la land, I see."

Nohar swallowed. He didn't feel quite right about dropping stuff into Bobby's lap after so long. But there wasn't anyone else he knew to call. "This wasn't a social call, Bobby."

Bobby sat down, and there was a grave expression on his face. Of all the pinks that he had ever known, Bobby had always been the best at reading Nohar's facial expression. Right now it was obvious that Bobby could still read him like a book. "What's the matter, old friend?"

"Do you still do miracles on the net?"

Bobby smiled weakly and shook his head. "You're talking to someone ten years behind the curve. That's a young man's game. I do software, but I'm mostly a manger now."

"Oh . . ." Nohar frowned, wondering where he would go next.

Bobby smiled. "But there're perks to managing. I have a half-dozen bright young hackers on my payroll. What do you need?"

"I just have a number off the display from a satellite uplink. I don't know if it's an access code, a location, or what—but I want to know who was on the other end of the satellite."

"You don't go for simple, do you?" Bobby was smiling. "Give me the number, and the location of the uplink—I might be able to get the skunk works to pull something up for you."

Nohar passed on the information, and added, "Thanks for helping me out, after all this time."

"You're still a friend. And you have no idea how much I owe you. Now, where do I get hold of you?"

"I'll get hold of you."

Bobby frowned slightly. "Okay. Are you in some sort of trouble?"

"You don't want to know."

"That bad?"

Nohar nodded.

"Well, I hope I can help you with this. When will I hear from you?"

"I don't know. Next couple of days."

"Good luck."

"Thanks." Nohar shut off the connection.

Nohar spent another few hours on the comm searching through every local news provider he could access. He started with the story of Royd's death and worked from there.

It wasn't encouraging. Not only did the stories have video of him, big as life, taken from the little cop drones. But they had his name, too. "Nohar Rajasthan, ex-Private Investigator" was attached to every story in connection with Royd's death.

Somehow, the death of Charles Royd was linked to a shadowy moreau terrorist group that someone had labeled "The Outsiders." These "Outsiders" had apparently taken credit for Royd, and the bombing at Alcatraz. The attack on Pastoria Towers was being billed as an antiterrorist raid to uncover a cabal of these "Outsiders—" That's how the press played it, even though no Fed agency was admitting anything to do with the raid, and a few said they were investigating it.

Most of the news seemed to have made up its mind.

Most.

A small news agency out of San Francisco, the Non-human News Network, had a different slant on things. They took the tack that the "Outsiders" didn't exist, and were a cover for covert actions by the Federal Government against the moreau community. The news was paranoid, involving everything from death squads to biological warfare. It seemed all too plausible from Nohar's vantage point.

He agreed with the NNN story: it was unlikely that any morey group would choose to target Royd.

Nohar couldn't find anything about Manuel in the public corners of the net. That didn't surprise him. If his theory was right, and the Bad Guys were looking for Manuel, they would have been watching the comm for him, too. They probably were a lot more sophisticated about it, too, judging by the hardware their grunts carried. There wasn't even so much as an acknowledgment that the cops were looking for a missing person of his description.

He also couldn't find any news about a shootout in Beverly Hills last night, or even something about a Mirador crashing to a halt. However, there *were* reports about Henderson's disappearance. Nohar wondered who had reported it, since the story'd come out about an hour before Henderson was due back at work.

Whatever the reason, the police wanted her for questioning in relation to Royd's murder. Strangely, Nohar didn't find any equivalent stories about Maria. Nohar wondered about that. The Bad Guys weren't cops—at least they weren't *the* cops—but they were certainly able to *use* the cops. Why not have them looking for Maria as well as Henderson and him?

Unless they were trying to keep the whole thing

with Manuel under wraps. They didn't want the cops looking for Maria or Manuel, at least not publicly.

The last thing he did at the comm was patch in his old digital camera so he could get hard copies of what he'd been looking at the past twenty-four hours. He slowly managed to enhance a picture of the Mirador that had ambushed Henderson, but that was little use other than to see how they'd managed to obscure the ID tags on the car. He didn't even have a clean shot of the attackers' faces. That was a dead end.

There were a few other pictures. The only one that had much promise was a wide shot of the copter that had landed in the Pastoria Towers parking lot. The copter was unmarked, but he had a good shot of what the machine looked like, and it might give him a lead on who might own some. He also had a good shot of a few faces. The most promising one was the face of the first man out the door, apparently the leader of the raid.

He was a standout. Even with the glow of the IR view, Nohar could make out his face. He was tall, with Negroid features and a long jagged scar across his cheek that showed on the display as a cold spot. There was something deep and painful in that face, even at that distance and with the distortion of the heat patterns. Nohar thought he saw the eyes of a hunter there. . . .

Nohar spent an hour studying Scar and the rest of his boys—the ones whose features he could make out. He wanted to be sure he could pick these guys out of a crowd if he came across them. He would have felt better if he could catch their scent and the sound of their footsteps as well. Then he'd feel as if he knew these men. Just by sight, he'd only be good within a few dozen meters.

Beverly brought him lunch as he worked on the

comm. This time it was an actual piece of meat, not something that had been mechanically processed into something the consistency of gelatin packing material.

"Are you finding everything you need?" she asked him.

Nohar stretched. The comm was in a corner of the living room, and all he had to sit on was a small stool. He had been bent over it, and all his muscles ached. "Everything I expected to find." Nohar stood and slipped over to the couch, taking Beverly's offered lunch. His head knocked a dangling fern, setting it swinging.

"Only so much I can do over the comm."

Beverly nodded.

"I need to see this clinic Manuel worked at, talk to his coworkers." Nohar looked down at himself. He suddenly found the whole idea of clothing an annoyance.

"I took some liberties," Beverly said and walked over to the door and picked up a package and handed it to Nohar. Nohar put down the plate he'd been eating from and opened the worn plastic. Inside was a whole new outfit.

Nohar looked up.

"I slipped out while you were working. There's an ursine I buy my tea from, and he had some old clothes I borrowed."

"Thanks," Nohar said as he pulled out the shirt. It was a giant tank top with an embroidered yin-yang symbol on it. With it was a pair for running shorts. He had to manhandle his tail through one of the leg holes. Not something your average ursine had to worry about.

It was enough for him to go out in public in. He

took the old plastic box and put what was left of his possessions in it. "Thanks."

"It was nice to have your company."

Nohar glanced toward the bedroom. "Tell them I'll be back by evening."

CHAPTER 13

The clothing had Nohar thinking about protective coloring. His problem was his inability to blend into the surroundings. The cops and the Bad Guys were both looking for a tiger, and his species just wasn't that common. In fact, it was rare enough that the cops could claim probable cause on rousting any tiger they saw. It wasn't like pinks could manage to tell moreys of the same species apart—

Even moreys seeing the video the cops took would see little more than a tiger in an out-of-style suit packing a big gun. Most wouldn't be sure about an ID without some nonvisual cues. Scent mostly.

He needed to poke around the life Manuel left behind, but he also needed to disappear.

He had an idea how to do it. But first he needed some untraceable cash. Most of his cash cards had his name attached to them. Using them would be a dangerous prospect if the Bad Guys had any technical aptitude. And after the room, the car, and a Mexican dinner, he had about five dollars in cash left.

But he knew a quick and dirty way to get more cash, as long as his urban instincts held. Clothing styles had changed. He hoped certain other things hadn't.

He walked down the streets until he found a likely prospect. It was a hole-in-the-wall store at the base of an aging strip of concrete storefronts. The window was opaque with advertisements, and above it was a cracked yellow sign that read, "Beer, Wine, Liquor, Ganja." Three rats stood in front of the store passing a plastic liter bottle between them chattering in high-pitched rodent-accented Spanish.

This was what he was looking for.

He hugged the dirty plastic package to his chest as he ducked in past the steel door.

The cashier, a canine with the high narrow muzzle and gray coloring of central Asia, watched him enter from behind a wall of bullet-proof glass. There was suspicion in the dog's eyes, probably because the metal detector set in the door had set off a warning behind his desk.

Nohar didn't much care. He walked up to the counter, peered through the graffiti scratched in the manager's shield. "I found a live cash card on the street. It has a two thousand balance. I was hoping there was a reward for returning it." Nohar didn't try to make the story sound legit. He was better off if the cashier believed that he rolled some drunk pink for the card.

The dog cocked his head. "Slide it through the reader."

Nohar smiled to himself. He had a sale; all that was left was haggling. He pulled one of his cards out of the plastic case and slid it thought the reader on his side of the bullet-proof glass. The cashier looked at the readout on his side of the glass and gave a jaded nod.

Nohar eventually left with seven hundred and fifty in cash.

He visited an overpriced convenience store and a second hand clothing shop in quick succession. Both were in the same building, with the upper stories abandoned and boarded up. After he left the clothing store, with all his new purchases in a battered engineered-leather backpack, he slipped behind the building and made his way to a fire escape.

He managed to kick his way through the plastic sheathing covering one of the busted windows, and slipped inside.

There was almost no light inside, but Nohar's eyes quickly adjusted to the darkness. Worse was the smell of mildew, which made him want to sneeze.

Nohar wandered through what used to be set of apartments until he came to what was left of the kitchen. Here, it smelled more of sex and beer than mildew, and the floor was littered with the trash of innumerable predecessors. The walls were wrapped in arcane graffiti. Nohar noticed a lot of used condoms, which still struck him as odd in a morey neighborhood.

Across the wall, above the counter that used to hold a sink—before someone had scavenged it—someone had spray-painted on the wall the word, *Genocide.*

A not so nice word, Nohar thought. It matched a not so nice world.

Nohar set his backpack on the counter and walked to the other side of the room, where sheathing covered the window. Sinking his claws into the plastic, he pulled the sheet back into the room, flooding the place with sunlight. Noise from the street below filtered in, but he ignored it.

He needed the light for what he was doing.

Nohar went back to the sink and took out a pair of four-liter bottles of "spring water." The labels were homemade, and he suspected that the bottles were filled from a still—if not a tap—in the back of the convenience store. Nohar didn't care. He didn't buy the stuff to drink.

He stripped off the clothes that Beverly had given him and put them on the counter next to the backpack. From the backpack he retrieved two small hand mirrors and a bar of soap wrapped in heavy foil. It wasn't ordinary soap— The foil bore warnings not to open except immediately before use, not to leave it exposed to direct sunlight, and not to use after the expiration date stamped in its side.

It had cost Nohar twelve dollars a bar, and he had bought three. It was a cosmetic beauty soap that had a special coloring agent in it. It wasn't a dye—which he could have gotten cheap, would have been hideously messy, and in the end would have *looked* like a dye job—the soap was doped with engineered enzymes that penetrated fur and chemically altered the pigmentation. It was a one-use thing that would last until the fur grew back its natural color.

Nohar had never tried it himself. But back when he was a part of the rest of the world, he knew moreys who swore by the stuff, people who preferred black to brown, or brown to russet. Nohar picked it because he had rarely been able to tell when someone had used it.

He didn't have the features of a black jaguar, and he was too big, but it would be enough for him to pass as a mule.

He uncapped one of the bottles and tore open the foil on the soap. He started with his left forearm, wetting it, lathering the fur, working the enzymed soap into it.

When he rinsed it off the fur on his forearm and on his right hand had turned a solid glossy black. Just like Maria's fur.

Nohar worked his whole body over. After getting the broad areas of his arms legs and torso, he used the two hand mirrors to locate hard to reach spots on his back. In the space of an hour, his russet stripes were completely gone.

He stood there, legs and arms spread, letting the afternoon sun shine through and dry his fur. He felt oddly different from himself, as if he'd done more than just color his fur. He felt as if someone other than Nohar stood here, a different feline, darker, colder.

He stretched, reaching, extending the claws on his hands and feet until he felt the joints pop.

Looking up, he saw more graffiti on the ceiling. *Shiva,* it said.

". . . destroyer of worlds," Nohar whispered. His voice seemed to have changed as well, lowered in pitch, more dangerous. He knew it was only psychological, but he felt more threatening.

There was one thing left before he went out in public. He rummaged in the backpack until he found a small makeup case. He opened it and began applying the contents to his nose, darkening it until the skin color matched his new fur.

It smelled dry and made him want to sneeze, but like the soap, it sank in and disappeared into the pigment.

Nohar had vanished.

When he returned to the streets, he was a different person. He could tell by the way the other people moved around him. He could smell tension precede him in a wave, and he noticed that everyone—even the hard cases—made sure they weren't standing anywhere that could be in his way.

His clothing still didn't match the current fashion, but that seemed to matter less now. He wore khaki pants and a matching shirt, the only ones he'd found that had fit him—well enough that they might have been military surplus from India. Over it he wore a black long coat that was sized for an ursine or something bigger. It hid the holster and his gun well enough.

The backpack he'd left in the kitchen, with his old clothes. The makeup he'd ditched several blocks away, in case anyone traced him to that point. He didn't want them to discover signs of his change in appearance.

It was a five-mile walk to the Bensheim Clinic. Nohar walked the distance without stopping. For once in a long while he wasn't feeling his age. The few times he caught his reflection in an unbroken window, it was a different person. Not just the fur, which lacked the gray streaks, and even seemed better groomed. His movements seemed younger, more fluid.

The Clinic stood out from the rest of the depressed architecture, a small white building squatting behind a wide well-kept lawn. The Clinic must have had the grounds regularly maintained, because none of the garbage that littered the sidewalks and the gutters made its way onto the Clinic's small greenery.

In front of the Clinic was a bronze statute of Doctor Otto Bensheim. They posed him with a canine, shaking hands. Around the doctor's neck was his Nobel Prize. It was the kind of thing that the Bensheim Foundation never would have permitted while he was alive. Dr. Bensheim never even wanted his name on the Foundation, or its Clinics.

He'd been one of the thousands of gene-techs who'd helped create the moreaus. Unlike all the other gene-techs, Bensheim had a conscience. He had created the Foundation and the Clinics to atone for his part in creating a new underclass for society. Reproduction, he had thought, was a fundamental right. The Clinics were there to assure that every female who wanted offspring would have the opportunity, whatever her species.

Of the thousands of species of moreaus that were created, each small genetic variation was listed somewhere in the Bensheim Foundation's confidential files. For a nominal fee, any female could walk in, get genetic testing, and be inseminated with the matching species of sperm. Any male could come in and receive a nominal fee for donating his own seed. The Clinics had gradually expanded their mission, to include neonatal and other aspects of reproductive health.

Nohar had never been inside one of the Clinics. He disliked hospitals in general, and something about the Bensheim Clinics had always made him uneasy.

He walked up the footpath, past the statue. It had the obligatory plaque, dedicating it on the occasion of the fifth anniversary of Doctor Otto Bensheim's death. That would make it nearly ten years old.

Nohar stopped and studied the doctor's face. He had seen Bensheim in news stories before the man had died. There seemed something oddly fake about the expression on the statue, as if the sculptor had never seen Bensheim smile. The look gave Bensheim the appearance of biting back some obscenity.

Nohar pretended to read the plaque while he covertly studied his surroundings. He didn't have to take his gaze off the plaque to realize that there were pinks around, ones more alive than the good doctor. The wind carried their scent along with the ozone exhaust of the passing traffic.

He wondered where the best place to hide them would be. They had to be watching the Clinic, since he couldn't think of any other good reason for humans to be in the neighborhood. Even the LAPD now hired moreys to patrol the Moreytowns, and Compton was about as nonhuman as you could get without leaving the planet.

So the pinks he scented, at least three, were almost certainly the Bad Guys. Watching Manuel's old workplace. Probably watching for him.

He was going to get to see how well his new disguise worked. Either the Bad Guys were going to fall on him like a ton of bricks, or he was going to walk right in.

An apartment across the street, Nohar finally decided. There was a restaurant across the street, and above it were a line of apartment windows. The windows were broken and dark, but they had the only view of the front of the Clinic—and the wind was from that direction.

"We'll see," Nohar whispered to himself. He walked up the path to the Clinic door. The lobby was sparse and utilitarian. There weren't even fake plants to clutter the scenery. The lights were brilliant fluorescents that set off the blazing holo posters on the walls. The mylar holos were the only decor. He read one as he passed.

"Get the drop on the Drips!," it told him. *"A properly sized condom is your only effective protection from sexually transmitted diseases, including Herpes Rangoon."* There was a picture as well, of a peeved-looking rat who stared at an oversized condom covering his groin like a sheet, and of a smiling canine pulling one on that fit just right.

Nohar shook his head and walked up to the reception desk. A bored-looking lepus sat behind it watching some sort of comedy program on the comm set into the desk. Nohar noticed at least three security cameras as he walked up.

"What can I do you for?" the rabbit said without moving his gaze from the screen. He pulled a stalk of celery from a bowl on the desk and began chewing.

Nohar didn't want to attract any attention. "I'm here to pick up some extra money." *Just the regular crap that they get here every day,* Nohar thought. *Give them that, and they won't notice you.*

Lepus didn't even turn his head. He just kept eating his celery and said, "Donation? Fill this out." With his free hand the rabbit handed Nohar an electronic clipboard with an attached stylus. "You can go to the waiting room."

That was it. Having done his duty, the lepus ceased paying attention to him. Lepus could have looked up, seen a black-furred feline that was way too big to be a jaguar—or anything else with that kind of coloring—made the decision that his visitor was a mule, and saved the bureaucracy some effort by saying that they didn't want any from him. But the wonderful thing about bureaucracy was that no one was willing to spend the effort. Lepus would perform his job description even if a pink walked through the door.

Nohar took the clipboard and walked into the waiting room. There were more holo posters here, many warning of the dangers of Herpes Rangoon, a.k.a. the Drips. There were other posters that told people that every donation to the Bensheim Foundation was thoroughly screened for disease, and that no one could catch anything by donating.

Nohar settled into one of the larger chairs and rested the clipboard on his lap. He glanced at the glowing liquid-crystal page and read the first few questions;

"Have you ever been tested for Herpes Rangoon?"

"If so, what was the result of that test?"

"When were you last tested?"

"Have any of your sexual partners been tested for Herpes Rangoon?"

"Have you ever experienced nonhealing genital sores, itching, or difficulty urinating?"

Nohar read the list with a growing incredulity. It seemed to border on obsessive, especially if they were going to test the donors themselves. Nohar looked up from the clipboard's display. He began noticing how empty the waiting room seemed. He knew that was somehow wrong. The Clinic wasn't just for insemination, but it was a clearing house for all sorts of genetically related medical help, and it was all pretty much free. This was one of two Clinics in all of LA. The place should be packed, all the time.

There were maybe half a dozen seats taken, less than

half the waiting room. Nohar noticed that they were all male, and most filling out clipboards like his.

Nohar looked at the person closest to him, a huge ursine who'd taken one of the five oversized chairs along the far wall of the waiting room. He wore what Nohar was thinking of as the Compton uniform, the pants mostly blousy strips, the vest little more substantial than Nohar's shoulder holster.

The bear was staring at the clipboard, puzzling over the form.

Nohar cleared his throat. "Ask you something?"

Ursine eyes moved slightly in Nohar's direction. There was a hint of menace in the bear's expression. However, it was undirected menace. It only took Nohar a few moments to see that this guy was just a kid, probably just hitting puberty for his species.

It was somewhat scary to think that this kid was going to get bigger with age. He was already bigger than Nohar.

"What you want?"

"Know why this place is so empty?"

"Why the fuck ask me?" The bear turned back to the clipboard.

Nohar sighed inwardly, but he decided that the angle was worth pursuing. He didn't know what had happened to Manuel, but his son's job was the one lead he had at the moment. If there was something odd going on with the clinic, he wanted to know—and he couldn't go harassing the staff here, not right under the Bad Guys' noses.

"Thought you looked like someone who knows what's what." Nohar did his best to stroke the ursine's ego; the kid was young enough that ego was probably the most important thing in his life. "Want to know if I'm stepping into something here." Nohar waved in the direction of the poster that proclaimed that no one could catch a virus by donating to the Foundation.

The bear looked across at him again. "So you asking me?"

"See someone better?"

That won the kid over. "Fuck no, got me there." He laughed and put down the stylus that he'd been filling out his form with. His voice took on a tone as if he was talking to his little brother. Nohar didn't mind. Even though he was probably thirty years this kid's senior, he didn't look it anymore.

"You don't got no worries. They only stick you to take blood to check if you're infected."

"What about . . . ?" Nohar made some stroking motions with his hand—

"Don't you know anything?"

"First time I've been here." That was the truth. But he said it in a way to sound lost. He figured that the easiest way to ingratiate himself into Bear-Boy's confidence was to act more naive than Bear-Boy was.

"You thought they let you baste some flesh here or something?"

"Well . . ."

Bear-Boy laughed. "Look, it's just you and a little plastic cup."

Nohar did his best to look disappointed. Bear-Boy laughed all the harder and slapped him on the back. The blow ignited pain in the old shoulder injury, but he bore it with good grace. It took him a moment to think of something adequately stupid to say.

Nohar shook his head and asked Bear-Boy, "So that's why there ain't no females here?"

"Oh, fuck, are you lost! You never hear about the Drips?"

"You just told me—"

Bear-Boy shook his head at his new friend's ignorance, and it was all Nohar could do to suppress a smile. "Look, you'll be fucking plastic 'cause you're a guy. Female's got to have the wad of some stranger shot up her quim. Got me?"

Nohar paused a moment and then said, "Oh—"

"See my point?" Bear-Boy lowered his voice a bit and spoke conspiratorially. "Broad gets knocked up here with some hot juice, puts a damper on things."

"They say they test their donors." Nohar said, lowering his voice to be even with Bear-Boy's.

"Like they check them all? Fuck, boy, where you living? They got samples frozen from years before they named the Drips. Word is, females break out with this crap all the goddamn time." Bear-Boy winked at him. "Not that they admit it, or that their money's not as good as anyone else's."

"Thanks."

Bear-Boy straightened up, leaned over the clipboard, and said, "By the way, you ain't a mule, are you?"

"What's that matter?"

" 'Cause your come's dead if you are. *They* can't use it. Ain't going to pay for dead come."

Nohar put his head in his hands. "Where's the bathroom?"

"Down that hall, to the right."

Nohar nodded and went in the direction indicated. He was thankful that Bear-Boy was leaning over his clipboard chuckling. That meant he didn't notice that Nohar was just on the edge of busting out laughing himself.

CHAPTER 14

Nohar stayed at the Clinic for a little less than half an hour, filling out the form and surreptitiously watching the employees, looking for possible coworkers of Manuel. Staying longer would seem to be pushing things.

He went to the bathroom a couple of times. It gave him a view into the closed-off part of the building through an open door at the end of the hall. He could catch a glimpse of part of a storage area without being obvious about it. He could smell an odd scent or two from there, moreau types he couldn't quite identify.

It wasn't until the third trip that he caught sight of someone back there. The guy was in overalls and work gloves, and for a moment Nohar thought that somehow a dog and a rabbit had done the impossible and made a mule kid. Then, when the guy moved, he saw the broad tail and the barely engineered legs—

A kangaroo.

The guy moved so Nohar could glimpse his ID tag. The name was bold enough for him to read, "Oxford."

Not a difficult character to find again.

After that, Nohar sat and quietly filled out his form. He was especially careful to tell the Clinic people that he was a mule. Just as he wanted, once he handed in the form, they took a few minutes to say to him thanks but no thanks. He managed to get out of there without a single test.

And the Bad Guys hadn't budged.

*   *   *

It took Nohar less than fifteen minutes at a public comm to find out where Oxford the Roo lived. There were only so many Oxfords in the public database for Compton and vicinity. He kept connecting to each Oxford's comm until he came up with one whose recorded message was left by a person of the right species.

His quarry was Nathan Oxford of Lynwood.

Nohar walked away from the comm, and the clinic, and made sure he wasn't being followed. Only when he was sure that he was out of sight of any pinks did he find another comm and call a taxi to take him to Lynwood.

Nathan Oxford lived in a ranch-style housing project that was in bad shape. The lawns were dead, and the old brick residential buildings were covered in spray paint. Half the units had windows boarded over, and one set of units at the far end of the complex had been burned out, leaving nothing but a shell.

Nohar spent his first hour at Willow Estates looking for pink surveillance. He watched for a long time at a distance with his camera before he was certain that there wasn't any physical surveillance of the premises. That was good. If the Bad Guys were watching one random member of the Clinic's staff, they would be watching everyone.

Even for these people, *that* seemed a stretch. Nohar still wasn't sure that the Clinic had anything to do with Manuel's disappearance. All he was sure of was that the Bad Guys were set upon nailing anyone caught looking for him.

That might mean the Bad Guys were hunting down Manuel themselves, or it might mean that they had gotten him, killed him, and were trying to cover it up.

Nohar's anger flared when he thought of that. If they had harmed his son—

God help anyone who had touched Manuel then.

Nohar had Oxford's unit number from the comm, so it wasn't difficult to head straight there. He walked through the courtyards, listening to the yips of children playing and adults yelling. It was still daylight, late afternoon, and he had about an hour before Oxford would come home from work. More, if he did any overtime.

This place had had security at one point. Nohar counted a half-dozen brackets that used to hold cameras. The one that still held a camera was bent sidewise and dangled a severed power cord.

Oxford's unit faced the parking lot rather than one of the courtyards. The door was a security model, steel with an electronic dead bolt.

There was little chance of him breaking into the place by brute force. That didn't concern Nohar much. While the place had once been secure, it had since passed into the bottom tier of such places. Where the buildings were this far gone, the corruption rarely confined itself to the physical structure.

Nohar walked around until he found what passed for the main office. It was two buildings down from Oxford, behind a door that was exactly the same except for the words "Rental Office" stenciled on it. Nohar leaned on the call button until someone answered.

The door was answered by a shabby-looking rat who smelled of beer. "What'cha want? Damn it." As the rat spoke, his triangular head looked at Nohar's feet and started traveling up. His gaze never passed above Nohar's waist, where Nohar held a c-note at the rat's eye level.

The c-note disappeared and the rat asked, "What you need, my friend?"

"You need to let me into an apartment."

The rat didn't even hesitate. "Which one?"

*　　*　　*

After two hours, and after Nohar had the chance to go over every inch of the apartment, Nathan Oxford threw the bolts on his front door and walked in. The door was closing as Oxford's odd, not-quite-canine muzzle sniffed the air. He knew something was wrong before Nohar ever spoke.

Nohar stood at the end of the hall opposite the front door shrouded in the gloom of the windowless kitchen. He held the Vind trained on the roo.

"Don't turn on the lights. Don't look at me. Don't move."

The door clunked home. Oxford stopped moving. He had stopped while facing the living room, in the act of turning around. Nohar could smell his fear. After what Nohar had seen in the kitchen and bathroom, he didn't really care what Oxford felt.

"What is it you want, governor? You can have it." The roo had an accent that had to be feigned.

"Living room, face the wall."

Oxford nodded and did what he was told. Nohar stood in the entranceway and faced Oxford, well out of range of his powerful hind legs.

"Who are you?" Oxford asked. "What the fuck do you want?"

"I have the gun, Nathan. I ask the questions."

Oxford nodded.

"You're a dealer, aren't you?"

"You want my stash, take it. More where that came from."

Nohar nodded. "The Clinic's well stocked."

"Yeah, sure. Anything you want, we can even special order it—"

What a scam, Nohar thought in disgust. This guy was working in shipping and receiving, and skimming a prime supply of any sort of medication you could name. His kitchen was stocked with everything from methadone to synthetic morphine. He'd been doing it long enough that he could make bookshelves out of crates addressed to the Compton Bensheim Clinic.

Oxford made Nohar sick. Not only was he a dealer, but he was ripping off a charity to keep himself stocked. And he had just as much as admitted that he could falsify orders to bring in whatever he needed.

Something grew cold inside him as he thought that Manuel was involved in this sort of crap. He had to suppress an urge to shoot Oxford. The only good thing about this situation was that there were few guys less likely to call the cops.

"I don't want your drugs." The assertion made Oxford smell of more fear.

"Look, you work for Sammy. Look, I'll quit selling across—"

"Shut up, Slimeball."

Oxford shut up.

"Say anything more that isn't a direct answer to a question, and I'm going to give you a twelve-millimeter gelding."

Oxford shook, and his tail twitched, its mass giving the impression of a coiled spring.

"Understand?" Nohar asked.

"Y–yes."

"Manuel Limón. You know him?"

Oxford nodded. "Yes." His accent had slipped almost completely away.

"Last time you saw him?"

"Two weeks ago last Wednesday."

"At the Clinic?"

"Yes." Oxford's voice was becoming shrill.

"I want a straight answer here. Was he ripping off the Clinic, too?"

Oxford hesitated a moment.

"Well?"

"Yes, damn it, everyone does it. It's not such a fucking big deal."

Nohar's disgust sank into his stomach. His voice lowered to a growl as he asked, "Drugs?" If this trash in front of him had gotten his son into drug-dealing, he was going to personally remove his liver and feed it to him.

"No, he never had the connections for that."

"What, then?"

"Hospital equipment, electronics, ramcards—"

Nohar didn't know if he was relieved to hear that or not. "Did he take anything the day you saw him last?"

"I don't know. That was a while ago."

Nohar cocked the action on the Vind so it made an ominous click. He could hear the echo from the kitchen. "I want you to think harder."

"Fuck, okay. I don't know what it was. Something came in that was supposed to go to the office in Pasadena. It was marked confidential, and he thought he had a gold mine."

Pasadena. That struck a nerve. The automated van was heading for Pasadena, and the Bensheim Foundation had offices there. Nohar didn't like the way this was going.

"How big was this package?" Nohar asked.

"It was a security envelope, for ramcards—stuff too sensitive for the net. Courier delivered. Marked confidential. Manuel thought it was corporate stuff that he thought some hacker friend of his could sell."

Hacking the Bensheim Foundation, Nohar thought. *How noble.* Though Nohar was beginning to wonder about Doctor Bensheim's charity.

"Did he?"

"What?"

"Have his hacker friend sell it?"

Oxford shook his head. "He vanished after that. I

don't know. Maybe he did and bought a ticket out of LA."

Nohar doubted it. "Two more things and you might live through this."

"What?"

CHAPTER 15

Oxford's car was little better than his apartment. Nohar would've thought a dealer might have had something a little better than an aging Dodge Python. The oversized red car's fiberglass shell had been cracked in several places, and fixed with tape. Nohar could fit in it, at least from the legs down, but he had to hunch over to drive.

Still, he wasn't in a position to be choosy. He pulled out of the lot and hoped that Oxford wasn't the type to go making a police report about his stolen vehicle. Besides, he could probably trade some of his hoard on the street for something as good, if not better. The way the car smelled, Nohar suspected that was how he got this one.

The car's comm had been ripped out and sold a long time ago, so Nohar stopped at a public comm on the way back to Beverly's building. It was just as well. With all the attention focused on Manuel, he didn't want to risk anyone tracing the search he was about to make back to a comm anywhere near him.

He pulled over on a street that was mostly empty, flanked by boarded-up shops and a vacant lot. There was a kiosk with a public comm, wrapped in graffiti that looked like psychedelic urban camouflage. The only people around were a trio of rodents sitting in the doorway of the building across the street. They were passing something around between them. At this distance Nohar couldn't tell if it was alcohol or drugs.

Nohar left the car and walked up to the comm. He left the flywheel running in the Python in case he needed to make a quick exit.

He wasn't a hacker, and he was never much of anything with computers, but his job as a private eye had given him the opportunity to pick up a few tricks from Bobby. One of those tricks was picking up people from their aliases—the handle they used on the net.

· He was looking for someone named "The Necron Avenger."

Necron was the name Oxford had given him, the only way Manuel had ever referred to his hacker friend. In his mind, Nohar was already thinking of Necron as a young version of Bobby. He couldn't help but wonder if Manuel had met Necron under similar circumstances. Were they drawn together because they were both outcasts? Nohar had been raised in a human neighborhood, and the only friend he had was the weak little kid in the wheelchair. A mule in a moreau community was in almost the same position.

Nohar told himself to stop speculating about the kid and started the comm cycling into the public news databases. Unlike the commercial news databases, where Nohar usually did his research, anyone and their second cousin could post an article on the public database. Even with the rough indexing the database provided, there was so much information—most of it trash—that any given article was lucky to receive a single reader from the millions accessing the net every day.

To find anything in that morass of home-produced programming, Nohar needed a series of very specific filters to weed out everything he didn't want. He had one very basic filter—Necron's handle.

In a few moments he indexed every article The Necron Avenger had made in the last month. He was in a hurry, so he put a few extra dollars into the comm to download the articles to a ramcard, which the machine spat out at him.

He wasn't after what Necron was saying right now. He was after where Necron *was.*

Even though the net was a high-tech colossus connecting every comm and most of the full-fledged computers on the planet, the way it propagated information hadn't changed much since the turn of the century. Everything, from phoned messages to news broadcasts, flowed along the optic cables from node to node, winding its way to whatever destination. Each node along the way left its signature on the transmission, and even at a public comm, it was possible to filter the headers on any particular message to find out where it originated.

In a few moments Nohar had isolated a set of arcane strings of characters. Each string pointed to a node somewhere that had received the article and passed it on, all the way back to the node that had first received Necron's messages.

The first thing Nohar did was check the first node for each of the messages he had for Necron, about two dozen. All originated from the same node.

That was promising. Almost everyone with a computer or a comm that wasn't in a high security situation left their access to the net on permanently. However, hackers were different. Many of them left their computers and comms isolated from the net, only connecting when they were doing something specific. A lot of them, especially those who skirted the law like Bobby used to, would manufacture their own temporary node on the net, complete with faux IDs. They would then use their temporary nodes to connect to whatever they were doing anonymously, then disconnect their computers from the net.

The fact that Necron's originating address was constant meant that he was using the same server each time he posted an article to the database. That meant either he wasn't a professional like Bobby, or he was sophisticated enough to manufacture a permanent bogus address to block tracers. Nohar doubted the latter; pros like that dealt in the shadows, and generally didn't post to the public databases.

Necron was probably just an amateur with a talent with computers. It also meant he probably didn't do anything much illegal. It was possible to do a business in data trafficking without necessarily skirting the law.

Nohar logged on to the server, and like most servers, it wasn't too protective of its user list. He managed to feed in Necron's handle and it spat back Necron's given name—or at least an alias that he was more likely to use in the world off of the net.

Oswald Samson.

It was another name that was easy to trace. There was only one Oswald Samson in the whole Compton area as far as the city directory was concerned. Nohar left the comm with Necron's address.

Oswald Samson lived in a little white one-family ranch house on the edge of where Compton began to bleed into the other southeastern LA suburbs. The yard was wrapped in chain-link, and the windows had the curtains drawn against the darkness outside. The sky was dark, and the streetlights lit the area like a stage set.

Nohar wasn't certain that this was Necron's residence. There was a good chance that Necron picked "Oswald Samson" out of the directory, just as Nohar had. There was also a chance that this wasn't the right

Oswald Samson. However the fact that he was a resident in Compton made Nohar think that there was a good chance that Oswald was Manuel's hacker.

Nohar parked on the street and stepped out of the car. In the distance, music was blaring, and he heard the sounds of laughter and partying. Someone was having fun a few houses down. Nohar could smell the beer from here.

Oswald's house was quiet and dark.

Just looking at it made Nohar's hackles rise. He felt his adrenaline kicking in even before he realized why. He smelled humans. The scent was faint, but at one point there were enough standing around here to saturate the air with the odor of their sweat.

Nohar let himself through the gate and drew the Vind as soon as he was out of direct line of sight of the street. Now he was paying attention to everything. The lawn had been crushed. He could still see signs of footprints treading the weeds into the soil.

When he got to the front door, it was obvious that the doorjamb had been splintered by someone forcing the door. It was just closed now for appearances.

He began to feel ugly flashbacks of his visit to Royd's house. He was too late again; he could feel it. He was certain that he would find Oswald Samson's body somewhere inside the house.

He wanted to leave right now. A sudden certainty that the LAPD would descend on this place overwhelmed him. But he didn't really have an option. He had to follow any lead that might help him reach his son.

Nohar pushed the door open, keeping the place covered with his gun.

Streetlights filtered through the door and illuminated what was left of Oswald Samson's house. Some-

one had been looking for something, and the way
things looked, they hadn't found it.

Not only had they shredded the carpet, eviscerated
the furniture, they had even gone so far as to tear the
drywall out, exposing the wood frame of the building
and the wiring. The lights were out because they'd
been dismantled and were lying on the floor. The
comm had been taken apart, and the electronics were
scattered throughout the room.

Nohar wandered through the house. Floorboards
had been taken up, pipes had been pulled from the
wall and opened. The lining of the refrigerator had
been torn out. The sheet-metal ducts for the air-conditioning had been slit open and peeled back. No object
in the house had been left intact.

But there was no body. Oswald Samson hadn't
shared Royd's fate.

By now, Nohar didn't need to ask what everyone
was looking for. It wasn't Manuel, it was in that package he swiped, the one delivered to the Compton
Clinic by mistake. From the look of the disassembled
comm, Nohar suspected that it was a ramcard that was
in that package.

He spent about half an hour sifting through the
wreckage. There wasn't much here that told him what
he wanted to know. He did manage to find fragments
of Oswald's personal life. The guy was human, and
had a teenage kid. He found holos of both of them,
tossed in with piles of other junk. He didn't find signs
of Oswald's wife, or signs that he'd ever had one. He
did, however, find the kid's room. It was as trashed as
the rest of the house, the comm just as disassembled.

It also didn't take long for Nohar to find something
that didn't sync with the Necron he was looking for.
He found a plaque honoring Oswald Samson for
twenty-five years of service with the INS. That didn't

make sense. First off, Oswald had a job working for
the Fed. Nohar couldn't see Manuel palling around
with a government agent, even if he was just an immigration officer. Second, that plaque put Oswald in his
mid-forties at least, as old as Nohar. As Bobby had
said, hacking was a young man's game. Lastly, Oswald
was a pink. . . .

All of this made Nohar start wondering about Oswald's kid. The kid must've been around Manuel's
age. . . .

Nohar walked around to the living room and picked
up the broken holo of Oswald and son. He studied it,
hunting for some clue to what had happened to his
own son.

When he stepped out the door of Oswald's ranch,
he was hit by a chlorine smell that made his nose itch.
It was powerful enough that it overwhelmed anything
subtler. Nohar froze in the doorway, looking around,
searching for movement.

He could almost see the fumes hovering over the
lawn.

Someone had tried to cover their scent, and had
done a good job of it. He knew the smell; it was chlorine bleach. Nohar's hand hovered near the holster as
he slowly made his way down the walk toward his
commandeered car. At each step, he looked away into
the darkness, down both sides of the street, checking
for an ambush.

The only signs of life were from the party that was
still going on down the street.

He reached his car without any incident. By now
the bleach had numbed his nose to the point where
the car could have been doused in it and he wouldn't
be able to tell.

CHAPTER 16

"Nohar, what have you done to yourself?" Maria stared at him as if she couldn't quite believe what she was seeing.

"Is that you?" Henderson asked. Both of them were wearing blousy shirts and pants that were a decade away from any style. Nohar presumed the clothes belonged to Beverly. Maria was wearing green and Henderson was wearing navy. Nohar thought they should swap colors.

He stood in the doorway and said, "Can I come in?"

Beverly's voice came from back in the apartment. "He can't fit through with you both clogging the doorway."

The other two stared at him, as if they didn't quite trust his new appearance. But they moved aside so Nohar could duck inside the apartment.

Nohar ducked plants as he moved to the cramped corner where Beverly's comm sat. As the door shut, Maria swiveled her chair around to face him. "What have you been doing all afternoon?"

Nohar sat and took out the ramcard he'd minted at the public comm. "Checking out Manuel's acquaintances." He slipped the ramcard into Beverly's comm. "They're watching the Clinic."

Henderson sat down next to him. A ghost of chlorine still haunted his nose, but he could just make out

the odor of her musk next to him. She touched his
arm and asked, "You went to the Clinic? Wasn't
that dangerous?"

The touch may have been innocent, but Nohar
didn't feel it that way. He moved his arm from under
it by turning on the comm and starting to run through
the record of Necron's public messages. "The new coloring bought me some cover. Didn't stay long."

"Did you find out anything about Manuel?" Maria
asked. There was a catch in her voice and Nohar
couldn't bring himself to say that their son had been
supplementing his income with petty theft. He sidestepped the issue.

"I found a coworker with a lead. Manuel may have
a ramcard with information these guys are looking
for."

"Like, what you have there?" Henderson asked.

"Another victim of the Bad Guys," Nohar said.

Beverly turned toward all of them from the kitchen
side of the room. "Why don't you all take a break
for dinner?"

Nohar ate dinner as he perused The Necron Avenger's collected works. Most were the typical hacker
montages of sound video and text that were spliced
together with little regard for form or sense. One article consisted of Mozart's *25th Symphony* conducted
by electric guitars and overlaid with images of the
Race—the one nonhuman species that wasn't created
on Earth. It culminated with news footage of the
bombing of Alcatraz.

That article was called "Requiem."

There was one called "Drips," more recent. This
was a collage of human generals and government offi-
cials spliced in with combat footage of the Pan-Asian
War, mostly moreau corpses. Spliced in with that were

scenes of human-supremacy groups preaching that the moreaus were so much genetic waste from the war, and should be disposed of like any hazardous material.

Another untitled piece was strictly sexual images run through slide-show fashion, intercut with subliminal images of needles and surgical procedure.

Nohar didn't know what to make of Necron's work, but there was a theme running through it—a near obsession with the moreau world that was at odds with what Nohar had seen of Oswald Samson. It might explain a pink owning a house in Compton.

The more of his work Nohar saw, the more he realized how paranoid and apocalyptic Necron's point of view was. There was a sense of intractable evil in the world Necron portrayed, a cycle of pain that led inevitably to disease and death.

The subtext—maybe it was even the point of all the messages—was that the disease and death were engineered by those who ran the country.

Necron made him uneasy. . . .

He was on his seventh message from the Necron Avenger when the comm went dead. Nohar looked up at the other three. Maria and Henderson were quietly talking to Beverly, finishing the last of their dinner. None of them had noticed anything going wrong.

Nohar had a bad feeling in the pit of his stomach. He got up from the comm and started moving to the front door, ducking under the pipes and around the three females.

"Nohar?" Beverly was the first one to notice him move, though she wasn't even facing him.

"Shh." Nohar kept moving to take position next to the door. He didn't have time to reach for his gun. Almost at the same time, the lights in the apartment went out and the door flew open.

"Nobody move!"

Nohar saw the arm belonging to the owner of that voice. It was pointing something into the room. Nohar didn't wait to see what it was. He grabbed the wrist, moving his leg so he could pull the speaker into his knee.

When his knee struck flesh, Nohar brought his other hand down on the back of the intruder's skull. The person flipped over his knee, and landed flat on his back. Whatever he'd been armed with went sailing into the room.

Nohar placed his foot on the intruder's throat, immobilizing him.

There was a pair of light-enhancing goggles on the guy's face, and Nohar tore them off, revealing the intruder's face. Nohar recognized him from his picture—

Looking up at him was Oswald Samson's son.

Now that he was face-to-face with the kid, he could see the oversized skull and the elongated fingers. The kid was a frank—a genetically engineered human.

Necron finally made sense to Nohar.

The kid coughed and spat, and managed to wheeze, "Where's my father?"

After it was clear that the kid was alone, Nohar sent Henderson out to fix what the kid had done to the power. Nohar restrained the kid with a belt and threw him on the couch. He retrieved the kid's weapon, a government-issue .45 automatic that probably belonged to his father.

Nohar shook his head and turned to the kid. The aggressiveness was gone. The kid seemed to deflate on the couch. Nohar saw him clearly in the dark, but frank or not, without the light-amplification gear his eyes probably hadn't adjusted to the dark.

"You were trying to do what?" Nohar asked the kid. He looked at the gun and thought of a wild shot hitting Maria, or Henderson, or Beverly and felt a lethal anger building. The adrenaline was still surging and hadn't found a true outlet yet. It was the kind of internal high that he could do anything on.

He leveled the Vind at the kid's forehead. "Explain. Now."

"I'm looking for my dad." His head tuned back and forth, as if he was trying to find Nohar.

"How did you get here?"

"Followed you."

There it was. This kid had come home to trashed house and missing father. When Nohar'd shown up, the kid had seen him and assumed he was one of the Bad Guys. He had even used the bleach to cover his scent. He'd probably been inside the house when Nohar had walked up to the door, and had slipped outside while Nohar was searching the place.

The lights came on again, and after a few moments the comm came back to life, still in the midst of playing one of Necron's messages. Nohar looked at the frank kid, no more than fourteen—for a human still a child—his eyes locked on the gun, and he could feel real fear begin to wash off of the kid in waves.

Nohar felt his anger fade somewhat. They were both in the same boat, and in the same position Nohar might have done exactly as this kid had. . . .

In fact he had done just that to Oxford.

Nohar lowered the gun. "The Necron Avenger, I presume."

The kid stared at him, and his eyes darted toward the comm. One of Necron's articles was playing the national anthem while panning across burned-out Moreytowns.

"The guys who took your father were looking for you."

Necron turned to face him. "I don't know what

you're talking about." He shook his head and stopped when his gaze landed on Maria. He stared at her for a long time, as if he recognized her.

"You know my son, don't you?" Maria asked.

It was in Necron's eyes. He knew all right. He saw the same familiarity that Nohar had only gotten from a bad picture. The coloring was different, but Manuel had Maria's face.

It should have hit me. I should have known *the second I saw that picture.*

Nohar crouched so he could look the kid in the eyes. "I found your house because I traced your posts. The name I came up with was Oswald." He reached over and grabbed the kid's shoulder, pulling him forward to look at him. Necron was now completely limp, near panic. "You used your dad's account, didn't you?"

He nodded slowly. "What's happening?"

"Manuel Limón, they want something he has." Nohar leaned forward. He knew just being close to a predatory moreau like him was intimidating to most humans. He was hoping to make Necron as cooperative as possible.

"Christ—"

"They've killed at least one person already."

Necron stared at him with a hollow look. Nohar was cruel enough to let him think the worst for a few seconds.

"Not your father. We have to get to Manuel before they do."

Henderson came in the door, and Beverly drew her aside, away from the drama on the couch. The kid jumped when the door opened. Nohar could tell that The Necron Avenger was close to breaking. He eased back and let go of the kid's shoulder.

Maria leaned forward in her chair, reaching a

cupped hand as if she was begging. In a way, she was. "Where is my son?"

"We were hiding him." The kid's voice came out in a breathless rush. "I promised—"

"We're his parents," Nohar said.

The kid was left speechless.

Nohar holstered his Vind and shook his head. "Helping us may be the only chance you have of seeing your father again."

There were a few more moments of silence, then it all came pouring out.

The kid's name was John Samson. His dad, Oswald, was involved in nonhuman immigration. When John was five or six, he'd been orphaned during a Pacific crossing in a cargo ship packed with too many franks and moreaus escaping Greater China. The mortality rate on that ship was close to sixty percent—and would have been higher if it hadn't been intercepted by the Coast Guard.

Oswald Samson had come across the orphan while processing the refugees and had decided to adopt him. The story came across in only a few terse sentences, but it was clear that John Samson remembered every bit of it.

He didn't even have a choice. His species had been engineered by Japan before the Chinese invasion, and one of the traits they'd been bred for was a photographic memory.

He and Manuel had met over the net. Some of his compositions seemed to echo Manuel's own worldview. That didn't surprise Nohar that much. Both kids had to feel similarly isolated, and had to have similar views on society as a whole.

Manuel was lost, as The Necron Avenger was lost. Manuel, like John Samson, watched the world pass by

him with a fatalism that seemed truly frightening. The
world was a burning building, a car wreck, an autopsy
that had no emotional content because there was no
connection between the watcher and the victims.

According to John, Manuel had no other close
friends. He had tried at school, at work, but no one
seemed to relate to the mule. He had even searched
out other mules, but most mules had bodies broken,
and brains damaged, and were too complete in their
own isolation. Manuel's curse was he did not *want* to
be alone.

John, the frank living in Moreytown, was the first
person Manuel had ever met who seemed to relate
to him.

The two of them had been talking over the comm
for two or three years. And, lately, they'd actually
been meeting in person. The data-trafficking had only
begun in the last few months, when John had let slip
that The Necron Avenger had some deep contacts in
the data underground that could move that kind of
merchandise.

They had moved about half a dozen pieces of such
merchandise, making a total of about thirteen grand
between them, when Manuel had showed up with the
last package—the one that was not supposed to
reach Compton.

"Everything was just like normal, until I hacked
what was on the card." John Samson shook his head.

"What was it?" Nohar asked. "What happened?"

John looked up at him, his eyes blank and dead.
"Fear is a natural thing, you know. Any rational person in this world has to be paranoid. There's no
choice." John shook a little, and screwed his eyes shut.
Nohar could sense the tension in John's posture. "No
paranoid hopes he's right."

"What was it?"

"Imagine your worst fears about the world confirmed. Imagine the vilest betrayal."

Nohar wanted to lean across and shake him. "What?"

"The Clinics—" His voice caught. John took a few deep breaths before he continued. "The Bensheim Clinics are intentionally infecting people with the Drips."

CHAPTER 17

John Samson's revelation was like accusing the Red Cross of spiking their blood cultures with hepatitis. It didn't make any sense. The Bensheim Clinics were an international charity that had been around almost as long as moreaus themselves—and they certainly didn't have a paramilitary force to cover up this kind of discovery.

At least, Nohar didn't think they did.

He spent over an hour grilling the kid about what was on that ramcard. Nohar got the information in minute detail. The kid remembered everything, he rattled off the data as if he was sitting in front of a comm screen reading it.

The ramcard was, at the very least, an explosive set of case studies on the spread of Herpes Rangoon in the United States. John Samson had read several charts listing the spread of the virus from one person through several other partners. In each case study the original vector for the disease was a female moreau impregnated at a Bensheim Clinic. In about half of the cases the fetus spontaneously aborted due to the virus, and in half of the remaining cases the fetus was born infected.

What made the files all the more damaging was the way the data was slanted to highlight those moreaus that infected the widest segment of the population, over the widest area.

What John couldn't give him was any explicit statement from the data that the Bensheim Clinics were intentionally responsible for the initial infections. It still could be accidental. As the bear in the waiting room told him, it was probably a logistical impossibility to test all of their stock. Though even if that was made public, and the ramcard was just tracking the problem, it was bad enough to probably spell the end of the Clinics.

But John Samson hadn't read all the data. There were several gigabytes on that card, too much to go through in the one sitting he had with the data. He had just read enough to set the natural paranoia going, and to believe that his and Manuel's lives had been in danger for being anywhere close to something like it.

That paranoia probably saved both of them.

"Where did you take Manuel?" Nohar asked.

"Safe hiding place," John said. "An old INS detention center on the border. I have my dad's access codes."

"That's safe?" Maria asked.

"The place has been abandoned for years." John looked up at Maria. "Sometimes, I think I'm the only one who remembers it."

Nohar freed the kid to take them all down to his vehicle. John Samson wasn't supposed to be old enough to drive, but he had followed Nohar in a decade-old van that made Nohar think of government institutions.

"There's a whole graveyard of trucks, vans, and cars abandoned by the Fed," John told him, as the four of them left Beverly's apartment building. Nohar believed what the kid said. Years of wind and weather had worn the van to a bone-gray. A thin layer of dust coated every window evenly, except where he had wiped clear the driver's side. The van still had government ID tags, and Nohar could still see the ghost of the word "Immigration" on the side of the van.

Henderson wheeled Maria out next to the van and stared at the vehicle. "It still runs?"

"That's why it took me over two weeks to get back here. Couldn't drive Manuel's car—they're probably looking for it. I had to work on getting this thing mobile."

Nohar nodded and walked to the rear and opened the back. The rear of the van was flanked by benches, separated from the driver's compartment by a wire mesh screen. It had obviously been used for hauling detainees around.

"Sorry you have to ride in back," Nohar told Maria. "Only place there's room."

"That's all right," Maria said. She grunted a few times as Nohar lifted her out of the chair and set her down on one of the benches. She felt way too light. All the muscle tone was gone. The sense of loss struck him again, the long path of years that could have gone in another direction.

Once Maria was settled, Nohar lifted the chair into the back. There were a few old elastic cords on the floor of the van, mixed with rats' nests and other debris. Nohar took one and secured the chair to the wire mesh separating the driver's compartment.

Once he had done that, John Samson started walking toward the front of the van. Nohar stepped out and shook his head. "No."

"What?" The kid turned around.

"You ride in back."

"Look we're on the same side—"

"You were waving a gun around, I don't trust you."

The kid looked at him and seemed to be gauging the probability of winning an argument with Nohar, or failing that, outrunning him. The kid had brains enough not to argue. He stepped in back with Maria, and sat down quietly.

When he did, Nohar grabbed another elastic cord and secured his arms behind him to a metal rod that was welded to the side of the van, seemingly just for that purpose.

He objected. "Hey, what're you doing?"

"You better hope," Nohar said, "that you gave accurate directions to this place, and my son is all right."

"What about my father?"

"That's my problem now." Nohar shut the rear door and walked Henderson up to the driver's side of the van. Henderson looked at him and said, "You're not driving?"

"I need to keep an eye on our boy back there."

Nohar opened the door for her, and after she stepped in, he handed her the .45 that John had been waving around. She stared at the gun.

"I'm going to have to come back to town." He needed to know for sure who the Bad Guys were. Until then, none of them were safe. "You'll need to keep an eye on him too. If he gives you any trouble, shoot him in the knee." Nohar shut the driver's door and got in on the other side of the van.

Nohar watched the abandoned red Python as the decrepit INS van pulled away. Changing vehicles was probably a good thing. He didn't want to get caught in a car someone else might've IDed. And who knew what warrants were out on that Oxford guy.

Once they headed out onto the highway, Nohar was lost in his thoughts, and he felt his gut twist.

There was nothing he wanted more right now than to see his son.

There was also nothing that frightened him more.

*   *   *

The ride took a few hours over the freeways of LA. Eventually, the traffic peeled away as they headed due east, toward Arizona. Buildings seemed to disappear into the desert as they left the fringes of civilization. The sun sank, and soon the old van drove along a tiny strip of the world carved out by its one working headlamp.

Nohar had the time to think of his son.

Seventeen.

At that age, Nohar had just stopped running with a local street gang and had started working for himself. He had started looking for people, a lot of folks got lost in Moreytown, and other folks would pay to find them. It eventually got to be a regular job. . . .

Nohar tried to reconstruct what it was like for him at seventeen. He had been physically adult for nearly ten years by then, and his brain was just growing into the body. He remembered his own isolation, a bequest from his father. He lived in an era that saw Datia as a hero, and he could never reconcile his own image of him with what the rest of the morey world saw. In the end, he was as surely isolated as Manuel was.

He hoped to God that he wasn't about to do to his son what Datia did to him. Though, in retrospect, it was hard to picture what Datia could have said to the young Nohar that would have fulfilled Nohar's expectations. How could anyone surmount the space of years that separated them?

Christ, it was probably too late for both of them.

The camp was unlit, so it was a complete surprise to Nohar when the gate sprang up in front of the van, caught in its headlight. It came at the end of a dirt track they'd followed off of the main road.

This was it.

The van stopped and Nohar got out, twisting the

kinks out of his neck which he'd been straining, looking back at the Necron Avenger every few minutes during the ride here. Henderson walked up next to him, staring through the sliding chain-link fence, into the darkness beyond.

"Like a prison," she said, her breath fogging in the cold night air.

The headlamp threw their shadows through the gate and across an empty field. At the other end of the field, Nohar could see the abstract shadows of a guard tower blocking out the stars. At its base was another fence, which seemed more substantial than the chain-link in front of him.

"Let's get Necron," Nohar said, walking back to the rear of the INS van.

He pulled open the doors and John Samson looked at him. "Thanks for remembering me. I can't feel my hands anymore."

Nohar shook his head and stepped in. He looked at Maria and asked, "How're you doing?"

"Fine," she said, but her posture showed differently. The ride hadn't been easy on her, and the pain showed on her face.

Nohar turned and untied John, feeling the same undirected anger he'd been feeling every time he realized how deeply Maria's genetics had betrayed her.

"Hey, watch it," John said, pulling his hands away when he was finally untied. He began rubbing his overlong fingers together. "They're sensitive."

Nohar growled slightly, and John jumped out.

Nohar followed, "You have the access codes for here?"

Necron nodded and walked up to one side of the gate. He looked at Henderson and said, "You should get back in the van, and drive it through to the main gate."

Henderson looked at Nohar as if looking for confirmation. Nohar nodded. She got in the van and closed the door.

John walked up to the side of the gate, the light from the van's headlamp exaggerating his frank features. With the shadows cast by the light, his head looked grotesquely swollen, and his fingers seemed to stretch impossibly toward the ground.

He stopped by a small metal box mounted on a pole. It had a recessed cover that swung open when he pressed it. Beneath it, an alphanumeric keypad lit up.

He looked across at Nohar. "The access code, '01082034.' " He spoke the numbers as he typed them on the keypad. "Remember it, it gets you through the perimeter." He grinned and shook his head as the gate started rolling aside. "Someone in the INS must be from Frisco."

Nohar didn't know exactly what John meant. He followed the van through the gate, and it didn't strike him until he, Necron, and the van were all through and the gate was closing behind them.

"01082034," January 8, 2034—the date of the Frisco Quake. It was 9.5 and did a lot of damage to LA even though it was centered around San Francisco.

Nohar grabbed Necron, and they followed the van, on foot, down to the main gate.

The complex was a mass of dull cinder-block buildings surrounding an even bleaker central section enclosed by barbed wire. Nohar only saw glimpses of what had been the holding facility, barracks lined up with less than two meters between buildings. Even with the barracks, in the flashes of light Nohar could see the remnants of plastic sheets that had sheltered people who hadn't fit inside the buildings. The plastic was torn and fluttered weakly in the wind.

Nohar and John had boarded the rear of the van, and Henderson followed the Necron Avenger's directions, driving to the north end of the complex, where the main administration building was.

The van's headlight swept across the front of the building, and Nohar saw that the door was opening.

Nohar's breath caught in his throat.

A tall feline stepped out of the door, blinking in the light. His coloring was mostly black, with hints of russet stripes that faded to near-invisibility.

Nohar forgot Necron, opened the rear door, and jumped out. Looking at Manuel, his words were frozen in his mouth. Somehow, he had thought he'd know what to say. Now, every rehearsed opening seemed to fail him.

It was Manuel who spoke first.

"Who the fuck are you?"

CHAPTER 18

The headlight shut off, and his son squinted at the van. "Sara? What's going on here? You shouldn't be here, it's dangerous." He had the same husky voice as his mother.

Nohar was shaking his head. "You don't know how dangerous, son." His voice was barely a whisper, and he didn't know if Manuel had heard it.

Manuel turned to him again and asked, "And who the fuck *are* you?"

I'm your father. For some reason the words wouldn't come. Instead, Nohar said, "My name's Nohar Rajasthan. Your mother hired me to find you."

"Oh, fuck—" Manuel didn't get to finish his statement, because Henderson had gotten out of the van and had run up and hugged Manuel.

Nohar noticed that his son seemed uncomfortable with the affection. But Manuel raised a hand and patted Henderson's shoulder. "You weren't supposed to be involved."

Henderson gave Manuel's ear a nip and said, "Thank God you're all right. I really thought that they got to you." She pushed herself away and looked back at the van. "I need to get Maria."

"Mom?" Manuel's voice started out as a whisper, but a thread of steel started to emerge as he said, "You brought my mother here?" He looked at John, who had just slipped out of the back. Nohar saw his son's claws extending and retracting, and he could sense a dangerous uncontrolled anger building in him. "Are you *insane*? Someone in her condition—"

Nohar stepped between the two of them. "I brought her."

"Are you trying to kill her? She hasn't been out of her apartment in—"

"It's all right, Manny . . ." Maria spoke, and the words cut into Nohar's heart. *Manny*.

Manny was a name Nohar hadn't heard in ages. Manny had raised him, from the time when his mother died, until Nohar had left home. Manny, Mandvi Gujerat, had been the medical officer on Datia's airlift, one of the few nontigers aboard. He had delivered Nohar, and had taken in the cub when his mother had died. Manny had been the only real father Nohar had ever had. Manny had been dead almost twenty years.

Manny had liked Maria, and Nohar wondered if his son's name was a coincidence.

"I was trying to keep you *all* out of this," Manny looked at Sara who was helping Maria into her chair.

"We didn't," John Samson said. "They got my father, damn it! I get back, my house is trashed, and tall, black, and hostile here is sniffing around the remains."

Manuel turned to John, staring at him.

"They haven't found you yet," Nohar said. "That makes this the safest place we've got."

Manuel whipped around and looked at Nohar. "We, who the fuck is 'we.' I didn't invite you to this party, Mr. Rajasthan."

Nohar looked at Maria. "You never told him my name."

Manuel looked back and forth between Maria and Nohar. "What're you talking about? Who *are* you?"

Nohar tried to say it, but the words just wouldn't come. After a few minutes all he managed was, "I'm

sorry. I didn't know you existed until a week ago."
He turned away, toward the dark cinder-block building that Manuel had come from. "I didn't know who
you were until yesterday."

Nohar shoved his hands in his pockets, feeling his
own isolation crushing down on him. He had lost everyone who had once been close to him, his mother,
Manny, Maria, Stephie—even Bobby probably only
thought of him as a diverting curiosity now, not a
friend. It was stupid to think that he'd achieve any
connection with his son, now, after seventeen years.
What would be the point?

Nohar let the others talk to Manuel. He heard his
son say, "Someone explain this shit to me before
things—"

"It's the card," John said. "It's hotter than we
expected."

Nohar pushed through into the building and
stopped listening.

That's not how it was supposed to happen.

The way it was supposed to happen—the son and
father meet for the first time, their eyes meet, and
there is supposed to be some paternal connect. They
should *know* that the same blood runs through their
veins. A bond like that shouldn't be erased by
time. . . .

It was the way his meeting with Datia should have
gone. He remembered wheedling a meeting with the
great morey leader, knowing that when their eyes met,
Datia would know and love him as his own son. The
way it went was wrenchingly familiar.

"Who the fuck are you?"

"Who the fuck do you think you are?"

"Why the fuck should anyone else care?"

It was stupid and silly. No one else cared. Why
should any moreau give a shit about his paternity? It

mattered as much as the specific tiger who donated the first strands of Nohar's genetic code. It was an irrelevancy.

"That's where you disappeared to." Henderson's voice came from behind Nohar. Nohar turned around and looked at her. There was concern in her voice. More concern than Nohar had a right to expect. She pushed the rest of the way through the plastic sheathing that half-blocked the doorway. "I thought you'd want to talk to Manuel?"

Fuck. Nohar opened his mouth, but he couldn't form the words. Everything was tied up in knots inside him. "I do," he said, "but . . ."

He couldn't finish the sentence, because Henderson pulled Manuel in after her. Manuel seemed to have the same expression of combined unease, anger, and confusion that must have been on Nohar's face. Henderson looked from Nohar to Manuel and back again.

"John's going to show us where we can set up house," Henderson said. "I'll just leave you two to talk things over. . . ."

She slipped back outside before either of them could object.

After a while Manuel said, "Ain't this a mess?"

Nohar nodded.

"So now what?" he asked. "Do I hug you, or do I try to punch that face in?"

"I don't know," Nohar said. He wanted to tell Manuel that he knew how he felt. But he knew too well how that would sound. He swallowed and forced out the words that Datia had never said, "You shouldn't give a shit about me. I shouldn't matter to you—"

"That's easy for you to say—"

"—but if you do care, I'm here for you."

Manuel seemed to be taken aback. "Fuck, you don't know anything about me."

Nohar shook his head. "I know enough."

"You don't know shit. I'm an outcast, an outlaw, you're the last thing I need. What I need is a ticket away from ground zero."

"Do you even know what you've stepped in?"

"Yeah. The Clinic's giving people the Drips. Not like there haven't been rumors—"

"We have pink commando squads running all over LA. They've blown up my house, tortured and killed Henderson's boss, tried to kidnap her, and carried out an armed assault on your mother's housing project—all because you disappeared with that card."

Manuel seemed to deflate a bit and walked back toward the doorway. "You think I planned all this?" He shook his head again. "It was just supposed to be a little easy money—"

"No such thing."

"We knew we had something nasty. We shut up here hoping to keep everyone out of it—"

"You didn't think anyone'd look for you."

"Hell, I thought people would look for us, but I didn't think that'd get people killed." Manuel leaned his head against the doorframe.

Nohar reached out and put a hand on Manuel's shoulder.

"If anything," Manuel said, "I'm the one no one should give a shit about. I caused all this."

Nohar squeezed his son's shoulder.

"Why should you care about some half-breed misfit?"

After a long time Nohar said, "Back when I was your age, there was a saying, 'species before nationality.' There's another half of that saying that people tend to forget."

Manuel turned to face him and Nohar lowered his hand. "What?" Manuel asked.

" 'Blood before all.' "

Manuel had inherited his mother's smile, and her tears. He grabbed Nohar's forearm with both of his and said, "So you're my father."

Nohar nodded, his voice failing him again.

"Damn," Manuel said. "I thought tigers had stripes."

There was a little nervous laughter. "Long story," Nohar said.

Nohar was impressed at their choice of places to hole up. The old federal buildings had been abandoned with piles of supplies and equipment. There was everything from cots to dried rations here. It had its own generators, still producing enough power to run the building and the security apparatus. In the room where John and Manuel made their home, there was a long desk with a set of inset comms linked to various parts of base operations and security, and behind it was a massive holo mapping out the whole complex. The map had several little digital readouts overlaid on what must have been a self-updating satellite image of the area.

The most distinctive feature was on the eastern side of the complex. There were acres of old government vehicles, parked between the inner and outer fences.

In a height of irony, the map told Nohar the official name of this place, "Camp Liberty."

Nohar helped bring out cots for the extra people, but as the night advanced toward midnight he decided he had to leave. They couldn't hole up here forever. The Bad Guys were still out there, and so was John's father. Someone had to go back to LA and try to deal with things.

Nohar had John copy the ramcard, which he said would take some time because of the encryption on the data. He gave it a few hours. Meanwhile he went out with Manuel to the vehicle graveyard.

"I don't know what you're looking for. The electronics on all these things are toast."

Nohar nodded as they walked past ranks of shadowed vehicles. Occasionally Nohar's flashlight would pick out a shadowed fender, a deflated tire. "I know, John told me how you spent a lot of time getting that vehicle running."

"Yeah—"

Nohar stopped at a small shack in the midst of the vehicles, playing his flashlight across the front of it. He hoped that it was what he had thought it was when he had seen it on the satellite map. Behind him, Manuel was still talking. "You know you can take the van. . . ."

Nohar shook his head. "It's the only thing that'll move all four of you."

The beam of the light played across cinder block and old tar paper. The front of the shack was a rolling metal garage door. Nohar walked up to the side of the building, and found a cover that opened to reveal a pair of buttons, green and red. Nohar depressed the green one.

"There's my car—"

There was a screech of old and ill-maintained machinery as the green button lit and the rolling steel door began to ease its way open. "No. People are looking for you, remember?"

The door opened all the way, and the lights came on in the small garage. There were dusty tools hanging on the walls, but what interested Nohar was in the back. He walked up to a set of pumps on the far wall and examined them. As he was checking to see if they worked, he found the question slipping out, "Did you ever wonder about me?"

"Fuck, what a question—what do you think? She barely talked about you, I didn't know your name until a half hour ago. Do you know how many times I've cursed you for this genetic meltdown I got laid with, for whatever happened between you and Mom."

"We broke up, she never told—"

"Yeah. I bet that was just because you were such a great guy."

Nohar choked back a knot of rage, and felt his claws digging into the cinder-block wall next to the pumps. "If she had told me—" Nohar whispered. He couldn't finish.

The ugly silence filled the room, broken only by the ticking metal of the overheated motor that had raised the door. For some reason, Nohar was becoming aware of the peculiarly individual scent of the motor, a smell of oil, dust, and old electricity that was somehow distinct from the smell he remembered from the locker at Saf-Stor.

"What are you here for, Rajasthan?" Manuel asked.

Why? Nohar thought. What does a blood tie mean to a creature such as him? As any morey? At least Manuel had one parent. Maria had been there for him. Nohar's own blood had abandoned him. His mother had been taken from him, and his father had never acknowledged any ties to his son as an individual.

"I'm here," Nohar said, "because I don't have anything else." He rapped his knuckles against the side of the pump making a hollow metallic ring, breaking the oppressive quiet. "There's still fuel here."

"What fuel?"

"Diesel," Nohar said. "The military was still using internal combustion vehicles during this place's heyday."

"Huh? We just saw a lot of your standard induction engines."

Nohar turned around and nodded. "Sure. Most of the vehicles here are civilian. But if this is here," Nohar tapped the pump, "I bet there're a few old National Guard vehicles here at least."

"Why you want something like that?"

"It'll be easier to get running. Sturdier machine." Nohar walked toward the front and waved Manuel over. "Come on."

Manuel followed him into the darkened auto graveyard.

It wasn't long before they were pushing a forty-year-old Hummer into the garage. It was painted in brown-and-tan camouflage, and still had the markings of a National Guard unit on it. The tires needed to be inflated, the oil changed, and a few cables and belts needed to be replaced due to dry rot. Most of what needed fixing was self-evident. The most difficult thing was starting it. There were spare parts for the vehicles in the garage, but it took them ten tries before they found a battery that would hold a charge.

It took two hours, but eventually the Hummer was there idling.

"I guess I'd better get going," Nohar said.

Manuel looked at the vehicle, full tank, actually running, and ran his hand over the hood. "I wish I had thought of this. Easier than trying to refurbish a fried inductor."

Nohar shook his head, "I'm probably the last generation that would remember these things. When I was a kid, there was still the occasional gas station on the corner. One or two I remember actually running."

Manuel turned to face Nohar, and the gulf of years between them was palpable. In a soft voice, Manuel asked, "Did you love Mom?"

Did I love her?

Nohar thought of that last message from Maria. The one where she had left him. He remembered how he had felt.

"Yes," he said.

Before the conversation could go any further, Nohar slipped into the Hummer and started backing out of the garage. He considered just driving away, but he sat and waited as Manuel closed up the small garage and jumped into the seat next to him.

He landed with a cloud of yellow dust. The grit seemed to cover everything, inside and out. Manuel didn't turn to face Nohar as he said. "Going to have to paint over those markings—thing stands out as it is."

Nohar nodded as he drove the Hummer back to the compound.

Manuel grabbed some spray paint and went over the Hummer while Nohar retrieved the copied ramcard. John was working at the comm, and when Nohar walked in, a shimmering rectangle popped out of one of the comm's data slots. John took it out and laid it in front of Nohar. Nohar stared at the rainbow-sheened ramcard as John said, "That's it. A copy anyway."

Nohar picked it up. Here was the thing that everyone was hunting for. It didn't look like much.

He made a cursory check to see that Maria and Henderson were all right, then he went back to the Hummer, which was now a collage of black-and-red spray paint.

When he reached the car, Manuel straightened up and asked, "Where're you going in this thing?"

"Back."

Manuel nodded. "Want to save the world?"

"Maria always said I was doing that." Nohar shook his head. "This is just self-preservation. The Bad Guys have your friend's father. He was INS. Only a matter of time before they figure out to look here."

Manuel had a fatalistic look on his face which told Nohar that he wasn't really surprised about that. "Need help out there?" he asked.

Nohar shook his head again. "We're better off if only one person's ass is in the line of fire. Stay here."

Manuel's look said that he wasn't too surprised by that either. "You coming back?"

"I don't know." Nohar looked down at the car, then across at the van. "If I'm not back in two days, get the hell out of here."

"Where?"

"South. Mexico."

"What about you? How're you going to find us?"

"I'll find you. It's what I do." He slipped into the driver's seat of the Hummer.

Manuel looked at him across the passenger seat; a cool desert wind blew through the open windows. For a moment the rest of the world seemed very remote, as if he and Manuel were the only living things left on the planet.

It seemed that some of that sense of isolation had reached Manuel. There was something very quiet, almost pleading, in his voice when he asked, "Why did you and Mom break up?"

Nohar sat there, letting the Hummer grind through a rough aged idle. He didn't have much of an answer for his son. *Why* did *they break up?*

"I wasn't there enough," Nohar said, the closest thing to an honest answer he could come up with.

Manuel looked at him as if he'd expected something more dramatic.

They stayed there looking at each other for a long time through the open window, the empty desert wind blowing past them.

After a while, Manuel exhaled. "This is all too sudden. I don't really know you—"

"I understand."

"I don't think I'm ready to be your son."

Nohar felt his heart sink. He turned away from his son and nodded. After all, what did he expect?

He heard Manuel walk around the front of the Hummer. At first he thought that Manuel was leaving, but after a moment he felt a hand on his shoulder.

He turned to see Manuel saying, "You seem okay, and you've done a lot for Mom, and Sara. So, *friends,* all right?"

Nohar looked at his son for a long time before he put his own hand on Manuel's.

"Friends," he said.

CHAPTER 19

Nohar drove back into LA. The suburbs passed by him like the circles of hell. He didn't reach the edges of Compton until about three in the morning. By then he was so exhausted that he just pulled off to the side of the road and slept where he was.

While he slept in the ancient Hummer, Nohar dreamed of his mother.

He is five again, sitting in the veterinary wing of the Cleveland Clinic. He is hunched over in a too-small chair. Whenever anyone comes near him, he growls. He is here to see his mother, and they aren't going to send him away.

Then the doctors and nurses are all gone. It is as if they have all abandoned the hospital.

He takes the chance and walks over to the big red door that leads to the feline ward. There are warnings plastered on the doors, but he doesn't read them.

The door opens on the smell of blood, feces, disinfectant, and death. He stands there, frozen in the doorway, his eyes unable to focus. He knows, somewhere in his head, that all the felines in this ward have died from a Pakistani-engineered variant of feline leukemia, a leftover from the Pan-Asian War. Everyone caught it from an improperly diagnosed jaguar.

Now it is different, the bodies lie in their beds, torn open. The ward is now a dead battlefield, the bodies

*scattered in the mud after a devastating attack. His
mother, near to term with her second pregnancy, is
facedown in the mud, clutching a rifle.*

*He hears gunfire in the distance, and walks through
the mud to the tree line marking the edge of the hill
the bodies cover. He pushes through the brush and sees
the war. A battle rages below him, on the streets of LA.
Black-uniformed humans fight heavily armed moreau
forces equipped as they'd been for the war. Ursines
carry body harnesses linked to thirty-millimeter anti-
tank rifles. Rats scurry through the urban landscape
wielding small submachine guns. Tigers, like him, like
his father, carry personal gatling miniguns that spray
three thousand rounds a minute into the human forces.*

*Above it all, flames race across the hills overlooking
the city.*

*At Nohar's feet is a weak bark. Nohar looks down
and sees one-eyed Elijah, the scarred brown dog with
the electronic voicebox.*

"What's happening?" Nohar asks.

*"man," Elijah says in his electronic monotone, "is
dissatisfied until he can destroy what he has created."*

The dawn sunlight woke him, the smell of smoke,
blood, and death from his dream following him into
wakefulness. His body ached, especially the base of
his tail, from sleeping in the car.

His first business was to find a public comm and
call Bobby back.

It took a moment for him to recognize Nohar when
Bobby answered his comm. But then recognition did
dawn, and he asked, "Nohar? Is that you?"

Nohar nodded. Dawn light was just reaching LA,
but where Bobby was it was nearly ten.

"What'd you do to yourself?"

Nohar thought he could ask the same question. Now

that he was over the shock of seeing Bobby on his feet, he could see how he had aged. He could see the wrinkles starting on his face. His hair was thinning and what was still there was beginning to gray. Looking at Bobby made him aware of how his joints ached from all the running around he'd done yesterday.

"What have you got on those numbers?" Nohar asked.

"Not as much as I hoped." Bobby shook his head. "Positioning data for a satellite. But there's nothing that officially occupies the area where your uplink was pointing—"

"There had to be something up there."

Bobby nodded. "It gets better. There is a satellite up there. Given time and location, my boys were able to find it. It's a Fed bird, and a black one."

"You sure?"

"My boys are sure, and I trust my boys. They tried getting into the thing's software, and they swear it was Fed defenses that locked them out. All we got on it is that it's in geosynchronous orbit over the central U.S., and that it's designed for extremely narrow-band transmissions. It's some agency's private communications center, private and secure."

"Any idea *what* agency?"

Bobby shook his head. "Could be anyone from the FBI to the IRS. My guess, though, would be the military. This is just a communications bird, not a spy satellite." Bobby leaned forward and asked. "What have you gotten into? I checked news reports on the coast, the cops are looking for you."

"If I knew, I wouldn't tell you—you've been dragged deep enough into this already."

Bobby shook his head. "You can't leave me like that, old friend. There's got to be something more I can do for you."

Nohar looked up and down the street. The sky was lightening, and with the dawn Nohar felt exposed. John Samson's paranoia was rubbing off on him. He felt as if he had spent too long standing in one place.

"Two things," Nohar said.

"Name them."

"Can your pet hackers get a list of people who did a specific search on the net?"

"That's not impossible."

"I need a list of people who've done a search for articles by a kid calling himself The Necron Avenger."

"That it?"

Nohar looked up and down the street again. The place was empty except for an occasional car. With the boarded-up buildings, this area of Compton looked like the aftermath of a full-spectrum war. It reminded Nohar of the pictures of African cities after the pandemic, after the gene-tech's microbes got out of hand.

"Do some research for me. The Bensheim Foundation and their Clinics. I need to know who runs what, especially in LA. I don't think I'll have time to hunt all that down myself."

"You got it." Bobby smiled. "You know, it's just like old times."

"Uh-huh. I'll call you back."

Nohar cut the connection, feeling older than ever. To his one-time best friend he was now nostalgia.

The Hummer—which only stalled out twice—got Nohar into Pasadena early enough for him to miss most of rush hour. Pasadena was pink territory, but nothing like Beverly Hills. Nohar didn't have to worry about cops stopping him just because he was nonhuman.

He was lucky, though, that no one stopped him because of the crate he was driving.

Nohar wasn't really sure what he was going to do eventually, but he was going to start by watching. He found a parking space in a garage that overlooked the main LA offices of the Bensheim Foundation in LA, the address where Manuel's ramcard was intended to go, and the place the van with the uplink was probably going home to.

The offices didn't stand out as much as the Clinic, probably because the building was nestled in among a series of similar structures which all seemed to have been built about the same time after the '34 quake.

Nohar chose his position before the start of business hours, so he could see the people coming here for work. He didn't know what he was looking for, but he knew that there was something here that would point to who was behind the Bad Guys.

If these people were going to such lengths to hide the information on that ramcard, that meant they were afraid of exposure. That meant that exposure was the one weapon Nohar had to end this nightmare—but he had to know what, and *who,* he was exposing.

His talk with Bobby confirmed for Nohar that whatever was going on went beyond the Bensheim Foundation. The Foundation didn't have paramilitary resources—at least they probably didn't—but Nohar was certain that they wouldn't be using a Fed satellite if the Fed wasn't somehow involved.

Nohar sat in the Hummer, on the top floor of the garage, and watched the entrance to the Foundation offices through his digital camera. It was a long and boring morning, watching the pinks move in and out of the building. He dutifully took pictures, low res so he wouldn't exhaust the camera's memory, just enough for identification purposes.

After about two hours, when it was nearing ten in the morning, Nohar finally got a break.

Walking out of the front of the building was a familiar face. It belonged to a tall black man with a jagged scar across his right cheek. It was the guy who had been first out of the helicopter at Pastoria Towers. The same bearing, the same arrogant hunter's stare. Nohar put down the camera when he saw that Scar was heading toward a dark Electroline van, twin of the one that had been watching Maria's apartment.

He pulled the Hummer out of its space and began peeling down the ramps of the garage. He only slowed to a normal speed—smelling what was left of the old brakes as he did so—when he reached the ramp out to the street.

He managed to pull out three car lengths behind the retreating van. Nohar slowed, matching the traffic flow, and wishing for a car less conspicuous than a spray-painted Hummer.

Fifteen minutes into tailing the van, the old instincts came back. He steered for blind spots in the van's rear view, using larger cars to run interference for him, hiding the all-too-conspicuous vehicle. It helped that the guy behind the wheel—whether or not he was aware of his garish shadow—wasn't doing anything to shake a tail. In LA traffic it would have been easy to get lost on the freeways.

Nohar stayed glued to Scar's van, down the Harbor Freeway, south, all the way to the coast.

He followed him off the freeway, until they reached the Long Beach Naval Station. . . .

When Nohar saw that, he just slowly drove by the guard shacks flanking the entrance. *"Shit,"* he whispered to himself as he watched the van pass through security in the rearview mirror.

* * *

Nohar drove into Long Beach and stopped at a public library kiosk to double-check what he already knew. The Long Beach Naval Station had been home to one of the country's top antiterrorism units during the last episode of rioting in LA. Apparently it had been a temporary assignment that had gradually become permanent.

That meant that the official news story about the attack on Pastoria Towers was probably right.

What scared Nohar was the fact that this all—everything that was happening—was a Fed operation. How could he fight against that kind of odds? The only reasonable option was to leave the country—and even that wouldn't put him and the others out of reach of this kind of operation.

He walked back to the Hummer, trying to think of what he could do.

They *had* run when the media arrived. The only real chance he had was publicity, widespread international publicity. That meant more than just Manuel's ramcard, that meant enough evidence of this Fed operation to punch it through the news filter of every comm on the planet.

There was little chance of him getting through the security at a military base, so he turned the Hummer back toward the highway and headed north, back toward Pasadena.

Nohar walked into the lobby of the Bensheim Foundation hoping that the pinks couldn't smell the tension around him. Luckily, moreaus weren't alien here, even in the Pasadena offices. The lobby guard didn't give him a second look, and Nohar saw a trio of female rabbits leave an elevator and head for the exit. From the way they were dressed, conservative, dark colors, lots of material, Nohar supposed they all worked here.

Nohar slipped into the vacated elevator, and the doors shut behind him. Out of the corner of his eye he noticed a security camera, so Nohar gave all his attention to the video display set into the wall of the elevator. It gave an office directory. He gave it a quick scan and highlighted the fifth floor—

The offices had their own on-site Clinic, and it was the least suspicious place for a moreau off the street to go. As the elevator rose, Nohar noted the other items on the directory. He scrolled through the items while looking as if he was fidgeting, tapping his claws on the screen.

Tenth floor, Systems and Building Maintenance. Ninth floor, Administration. Eighth floor, Accounting. Seventh and Sixth, PR and Community Relations. Fifth was the Clinic. Fourth was R&D and the Laboratories. Third was International. Second was Shipping and Receiving. First was Lobby and Building Security.

The strange thing was, this building was taller than ten stories. Nohar could remember that much from when he'd been watching it from the outside. He had this feeling confirmed as he looked at the display change floor numbers as the elevator rose.

Between the third and fourth floors there was a perceptible lag. Between every other pair of floors it took the number a little less than a second to change. Between three and four was almost three seconds.

Nohar could picture the side of the building. He had watched long enough to know that floor three was just as tall as the floors above and below it.

When the doors slid open, Nohar walked out into the hall leading to the Clinic itself. It was reminiscent of Compton, but this time the posters warning about sexually transmitted diseases seemed more ominous.

He made careful note of where the security cameras were located. Before he made it to the reception area, he slipped into the restrooms and entered a stall. He was improvising, and he wasn't quite sure what he was going to do—

What he did know was that he wanted to get a look at whatever was nestled between International and R&D. Nohar sat and thought of hiding until the building closed, but then he'd be dealing with active alarms and security that wasn't busy doing anything else.

He needed a distraction that would last long enough for him to get a good look around. If they were hiding a whole floor, how would he get to it? The elevator probably operated on some sort of code, so he couldn't use that. That left scaling the outside of the building, or the fire stairs.

That might be it.

Nohar left the bathroom and continued down the hall. He noted the presence of fire alarms and extinguishers. A false alarm was tempting, but there was little chance it would really empty the building before security discovered that there wasn't a fire. Besides, no one ever believes a fire alarm the first time it goes off. There's five to ten minutes before anyone believes it's the real thing, unless they smell the smoke themselves.

He needed another way to empty the building.

He walked into the reception area and took a clipboard form from the bored-looking human receptionist and walked around the desk. Instead of going to the waiting area, he walked to a set of public comms lining one wall around the corner from the entrance. He looked for security cameras watching the comms, and he seemed to be in luck. No cameras here, security was more interested in watching people come and go.

They'd eventually trace the call back here, and they'd have a video record of him all over the building, but at this point he didn't care. The only important thing was that they wouldn't connect him to this immediately. And all he needed was a little time.

Nohar slid in front of the clunky comm and ran his claws over the textured plastic. The rarely used keyboard was recessed beneath the screen, the keys had collected a lot of debris. He fed some money into the thing and switched off both the audio and video feed. Then he started a multiple destination message, composing at the keyboard. His message went to the Bensheim Foundation Administration, the police, and several news agencies.

The note was very simple. He claimed that the Outsiders—the same people who had taken credit for Alcatraz and Royd—had placed a bomb in the building and it was set to go off in ninety minutes.

They were good. It was only five minutes from his message—he had just walked into the waiting room and had sat down—when the klaxons of the fire alarms sounded, and the PA system came on telling everyone to evacuate the building in a calm fashion. They didn't mention a bomb, probably to avoid a panic.

That was fine as far as Nohar was concerned. He abandoned the clipboard and started out with the mass of male moreaus from the waiting room. Most headed for the elevator, but Nohar stayed with the ones who headed for the fire stairs.

The fire stairs wrapped around the inside of a concrete tube that did its best to amplify the klaxons, hurting Nohar's ears. The stairs were packed with people descending.

Nohar fitted himself into the crowd, hugging the wall. He continued down one floor, but at the next fire door he stopped, his back pressed to the wall, letting the people pass him. He stayed against the hinge side of the cinder-block wall, and waited.

Eventually, the fire door—which led to the anonymous floor between three and four—opened.

There wasn't a handle on the outside of the door, so Nohar grabbed the edge of it and pulled it all the way back toward him. Someone mumbled a "thanks" from the other side of the door.

Nohar stood there holding the door, waiting for someone to notice him. No one did. The moment the stairway seemed clear of everyone, Nohar slipped through the open fire door and into the secret heart of the Bensheim Foundation.

There wasn't anything that stood out immediately. Nothing to mark this place as something to be hidden. It was the same carpeted floor, same fluorescent lighting, same acoustical tile that Nohar had seen two floors above.

The fire door shut behind him, muffling the klaxons somewhat.

Nohar walked down the hall, passing ranks of offices, getting his bearings. At least it seemed that they had emptied this place as much as the rest of the building. Now he just had to figure out where to look. He had probably another fifteen minutes before the bomb squad brought their dogs and their chemical sniffers. . . .

Nohar turned the corner and was confronted with a much different hallway. The way was blocked by a heavy stainless-steel door that had the red biohazard trefoil etched into its surface. There was a portal in the door, and Nohar looked through it and saw a small chamber. Hanging on the walls were what looked to be human space suits.

Someone was working with some very dangerous stuff here.

Nohar backed up and took out his camera. He started taking pictures of the door and the room beyond.

He looked at the lock and decided there wasn't any time to try to open the door. Not that he wanted to go anywhere that required a full environmental suit.

Nohar backtracked from the door and ducked in each office, hoping to get lucky.

He did.

In the third office he found a comm unit running, in the midst of some sort of database search. Its owner hadn't logged out of the system, leaving Nohar with a comm that still had full access to everything.

Nohar slipped behind the comm and figured he had ten minutes to get it to tell him what was going on.

CHAPTER 20

Nohar took a ramcard out of his wallet, his record of The Necron Avenger's public net activity. He felt okay overwriting it; he didn't need that information anymore. He slipped the card into the comm's data slot and tried to call up a directory, a database, or some sort of menu.

Nohar managed to back up from the financial information he was looking at until he hit a menu listing the databases he could open. There were the typical titles, "Accounting," "Inventory," and "Personnel."

But there was a group of other databases with more cryptic names, "Bangkok," "Tangier," "Congo," and "Niger."

Nohar entered the Bangkok database and was confronted with a history of the Drips. Vectors, case studies, maps of outbreaks, pathology, demographics. Everything that anyone could possibly want to know about Herpes Bangkok, down to its genetic structure.

He already knew that they were tracking the Drips from the information Necron had given him, so he only scanned the information before backing up and trying another heading. His next try was "Tangier."

What he saw was a hepatitis variant. This wasn't a disease that was making the news. According to the database it was confined to the canines inhabiting the Hollywood Hills. Nohar thought back to one-eyed Elijah, and the other dogs, the ones who were falling

to some sickness. The people here were tracking that
disease. Looking at the information gathered here, it
was obvious that something odd was happening. Their
reports on transmission vectors were as detailed as the
ones for the Drips. The case studies of the disease's
progress were as complete—and this was for a community of moreaus that never saw the inside of a
hospital.

The genetic information was here, too. This time
Nohar paid a little more attention. He wasn't a scien-
tist, but he was beginning to get an ominous feeling
from the databases. They didn't seem to be the product of doctors interested in curing, or even attempting
to learn about a disease. The database seemed more
a critique of the virus. Scattered throughout were
words like "effective transmission," "efficient progres-
sion," and "optimum prognosis." As if they were rat-
ing the virus on how well it spread.

He scanned through the Tangier database, becoming more and more alarmed, until he came to a list of
concluding comments, one of which was absolutely
chilling.

"Hepatitis Tangier is not recommended due to an
unacceptably high chance of transmission to humans."

Nohar started downloading the database to his
ramcard. The comm flashed a warning to him, the
comm's voice lost under the sounds of the fire alarms.
"This is a secure database. Use is being logged. Do
you still wish to complete this operation?"

Nohar hit "Y" on the comm's keyboard. His finger
was shaking.

He had begun to realize that he wasn't looking
through a medical database. He was looking at a military one. He was looking at an analysis of biological
warfare agents.

He looked back at the Bangkok file, and found what

he had missed before. All the signs that he was looking at something someone had engineered in a lab.
More acceptable because the transmission rate to humans was nil. . . .

"Good lord," Nohar whispered to himself. He had
expected to find some signs of a dark experiment,
someone testing propagation of the herpes virus. He
had never expected to find out someone had engineered the disease in the first place.

"Congo," was a flu virus. It had apparently ripped
through the moreau population in The States about
two years ago. There had been a few fatalities, among
the very old and very young. Nohar skipped to the
conclusions—Congo had been abandoned because it
was unstable, prone to mutate.

The last one, "Niger," was the most recent file.
They had just completed the engineering of the organ-
ism. There were only two case studies, and there was
no question that the victims had been purposely infected. Both had died within a week of infection.

The virus attacked the connective tissue of the body,
and caused the internal organs to die off one by one.
The victims bled from every orifice, the blood filled
every cavity in their bodies. It refused to clot. And
near the end, the rabbit that had been infected was
vomiting up a black bloody mess that included the
lining of his stomach, throat, and tongue. By then the
file said the virus had undergone "extreme amplifica-
tion," which meant that every drop of that rabbit's
blood had enough virus in it to infect most of
Compton.

The bastards had engineered a variant of Ebola
Zaire. A variant that only affected moreaus. Somehow
they had found a common thread in the genetics of
all the moreaus that they could base their diseases on.
Nohar thought of Elijah again—

All of them, all moreaus, shared some genes with those first creations. Something about their virus needed that to spread.

The conclusions found that the virus wasn't lethal to humans.

Suddenly, his concerns for his own safety, even that of his son, seemed petty. He was suddenly looking at the possibility of a genocidal plague in the hands of people who might actually use it. Not just that, but in the hands of people who could use it most effectively. They had been doing these studies for years, studying the propagation of these viruses. If they wanted to use their Ebola Niger, they would introduce it at multiple points, in victims who would assure the maximum spread of the virus. No quarantine would be able to stop it. . . .

The ramcard popped out. He had copied all of the databases.

Nohar reached up for the card, looking up as he suddenly sensed another presence moving toward the office. The smell of humans was drifting toward him, and he could almost make out the sound of footsteps beneath the noise of the klaxons.

The owner of the footsteps knew exactly where he was going. A pink in a black uniform turned the corner of the office. He was armed with an M-303 caseless assault rifle. He leveled the oversized weapon at Nohar.

"Hold it right there!"

Nohar was already diving behind the desk as the guy let loose. The jackhammer of the rifle upstaged the klaxon as the office began shedding debris around Nohar. Paneling splintered, acoustical tile fell from the ceiling, fluorescent tubes shattered, and the comm exploded into a hundred fragments.

There was no room for negotiation with this guy.

Nohar felt a surge of adrenaline as he pulled out the Vind. He didn't have much time. His only advantage was the guy was firing wildly into the room, and had taken out the only light sources.

He waited for the gunfire to track into one corner of the room, then he sprang toward the opposite end, bringing the Vind to bear on the man silhouetted in the doorway. The guy caught the movement, and started to bring the rifle to bear, the bullets cutting a swath through the office paneling.

Nohar pumped off the two shots left in the Vind, one high, one low. The first caught the guy in the upper chest, the second in the left thigh. He wore body armor, but the first shot still knocked him backward. The second cut his leg out from under him, and he fell back into the hallway.

Nohar ran up and kicked the rifle away from the guy. He had managed to avoid killing the bastard, but Nohar couldn't bring himself to feel good about it. The hallway was rank with the smell of the blood that was pooling under the guy's legs, turning the blue carpet purplish-black.

"Go on," the guy said. His teeth were clenched against pain, and he sounded short of breath. "Kill me, that's what you're designed to do."

Nohar knelt over him, and saw that he was looking at a kid—at least in human terms. He wasn't better than nineteen or twenty. Still, Nohar held the empty Vind up to the kid's head and asked, "Who are you people? Is this a government operation?"

The kid spat at him.

Nohar didn't want to waste time. Everything was going to be converging on this office, the kid was just the first. He held the gun on the kid while he grabbed the M-303.

He was about to try another question, when he

heard a door open down the hall, by the fire stairs. The elevators were back there, too. The kid smiled, and Nohar wanted to smack him.

Nohar holstered his Vind and ran in the opposite direction, toward the giant biohazard door. Before he reached it, he ducked into another office. This one had a window overlooking the parking lot. He shouldered the M-303 and picked up an office chair. He used it to smash out the window.

Below him he could see the flashers of the police and fire departments, and the crowd of people circling the building. He was in trouble. He had spent too long at the comm. He had planned to slip out with the last of the evacuees; now he was surrounded by cops and about to be hit by an assault squad with automatic rifles.

He looked out through the window. The wind whipped at his face as he looked four stories down to the pavement. Too far to jump, he'd break bones for sure. And police were already running toward the building. The crowd was all looking in his direction now.

"Fuck," Nohar said, pulling himself out onto the small ledge under the window.

He extended the claws on his hands to get some purchase on the concrete, and it made his fingers feel as if they were being torn apart.

There was a similar ledge on the floor below, and he desperately needed to make it. There were the sounds of shouting and commotion behind and below him, as he faced the wall of the building. More important right now were the sounds of running feet coming down the hall toward the office he'd just left.

There was little choice now. Nohar reached down so his hands gripped the ledge he crouched on. Then he pushed his feet off the ledge. His body fell from

in front of the window, dropping from sight as the
gunman reached the entrance to the office. He jerked
to a stop that almost pulled his shoulders from their
sockets. He held on to the ledge, feeling as if his claws
would tear from his fingers. He fell against the window
below. He swung a foot back to kick out the glass.
He managed one solid kick, shattering the window.
He let go, allowing his forward momentum to carry
him into the blinds and the office beyond the broken
window. Glass bit into him as he rolled across the
floor at the foot of the window.

He got to his feet in a twin of the office above. He
ran for the door. Even though the adrenaline was firing through his body, sharpening everything, he could
feel where his body was screaming *enough*. His knee
felt as if he had blown it out again. Every joint in
both arms was on fire, especially the joints in his fingers. His claws felt as if they had locked in place.

He hobbled out of the office, through a forest of
cubicles, and tried to think of an escape route. The
more he thought of it, the less likely there was going
to be one. He was going to have to deal with the
security goons or the police. And it was looking more
and more as if the police were the lesser evil.

Nohar crashed through the door to the fire stairs.
He could hear a commotion a floor above. The security goons were hitting the stairs as well, trying to
catch up with him.

The flights were side-by-side, with little gap between
them. Nohar ran halfway down the flight and vaulted
over the railing, stumbling on the concrete of the next
lower flight. He almost fell headfirst into the landing,
but he kept moving. He could hear the footsteps of
the security goons above him.

The fire door on this floor was ajar, and Nohar
pulled it open and slipped inside. He found himself in

a large room, the walls piled high with packages and letters. There were several desks where packages were in the midst of being sorted.

Nohar stopped in front of one desk that was piled high with outgoing packages. He had no time, but he needed to get all the information off of him, he couldn't risk either the security goons or the police confiscating it.

He reached in, pulled out a handful of ramcard-sized packages. He dropped all but one with an address in Culver City that he'd remember. Opened the plastic as carefully as he could, though his rush left a jagged tear in the package. He slipped the incriminating ramcards inside—his copy of Manuel's find, and the ramcard he'd just copied—and ran the opening through the sealer mounted in the desk. The plastic fused with a hiss, sealing the ramcards inside. The package didn't look great, but if they weren't looking for it, it might get through.

Nohar shoved the package back into the pile and ran for the other side of the room. Behind him he could hear the security goons slip through the fire doors. For some reason, they didn't fire at him.

Nohar crashed through the door on the other side of the mailroom, and came face-to-face with a half-dozen policemen in heavy padded body armor. They carried long rods which they were pointing at several corners of the hallway, and one held the leash for a black unengineered dog who had been busy sniffing the base of the wall until Nohar had appeared in the hallway.

Nohar looked at the Bomb Squad guys, raised his hands, and said, "I surrender."

CHAPTER 21

The police weren't that gentle, especially with the rifle and the gun on him. All the while, Nohar kept telling himself it was better than being shot. Though, after that victory wore off, he found himself in a bit of a bind. The cops still wanted Nohar Rajasthan for questioning in the Royd murder, and they had a weapons charge on him at the very least, and it didn't take a signed confession for them to figure that he had something to do with the phoned-in bomb threat.

He was driven to the Pasadena station in the back of a much-too-small Dodge Havier, his hands held behind him by nylon strapping because the cops didn't have handcuffs big enough for him.

When they got him to the station, they cut the nylon off and dumped him in a holding cell. The cell was a concrete cube with a single steel door. The unpainted walls were swathed in graffiti, and the concrete bench was too low and too narrow for Nohar to sit on. Nohar stood there for what seemed like hours, trying to think himself out of this mess.

All he got out of it was the full effect of an adrenaline crash. In about half an hour he was crushed by fatigue, leaning against the cold walls, feeling his muscles cramp, every joint in his body hurting as if it were grinding broken bones together. His hands felt as if they would be locked into the same arthritic claws Maria was left with. He bled from enough places from broken glass and shrapnel that the cops had handled him with latex gloves. His body felt like one massive bruise.

Eventually, after about four hours, the cops came for him. This time they had handcuffs that fit.

They led him out of the holding cell, and Nohar tried to walk without limping. Three cops escorted him, and he could smell their tension. He knew if he made a suspicious move, he would probably get a bullet somewhere inconvenient.

He passed lines of desks, and as he passed, the pinks stopped what they were doing to crane their necks and watch the huge moreau walk by. There were a few whispered words between them, and Nohar could pick up an occasional word here or there.

"—there's the Fed case—"

"—shoot-out with the Beverly Hills cops—"

"—why a morey would do Royd like that, he was almost one of them—"

"—probably another psycho. Killing's in their genes you know—"

His escort dropped him in a windowless interview room—a featureless place with walls of acoustical tile. There were a few uncomfortable chairs, a metal table, and a mirror running the length of one wall. Nohar looked at the mirror and sat down facing it. There was little else he could do, and it felt good to finally get off his feet.

They kept him waiting for another hour. Long enough that, despite everything, Nohar began to doze off. He suspected they'd been watching him all during the wait, because the door slammed open just when he was nodding off.

Nohar glanced up at the door, didn't see anyone, and had to lower his gaze until he saw a short man. He was balding on top, and wore a small beard and mustache, as if the hair were slowly sliding down his head. He placed a portable comm on the table between them and looked at Nohar. Even standing, his eye level didn't reach above Nohar's chest.

"I'm Detective Gilbertez." His tone was disarming. "Are you comfortable? Can I get you anything?"

Nohar's first impulse was to say, "A lawyer," but he held back because he wanted to hear what this guy was going to say. He just shook his head and looked at Gilbertez and tried to read what was going on behind his impassive face.

"Fair enough," Gilbertez looked at his comm and flipped open the screen. "Nohar Rajasthan." He glanced up from the screen. "Don't feel as if you have to respond to me. Just listen." He looked back down at the comm, still talking. "Never changed your name. Old-fashioned, or did you just not care?"

Nohar followed Gilbertez's suggestion, and stayed quiet.

"Most of the moreaus we see through here are half your age—most shed the surname. Like the place-origin names the INS handed out, way back when, were some sort of slave name." He shook his head. Nohar wondered if he ever paused for a breath. "Says here that you were once licensed as a private investigator, but you let that lapse about ten years ago. What've you been doing since then?"

"Retired." The word felt heavy with irony after what he had gone through the past few days. He flexed his hands, they ached, especially at the base of his claws. It felt as if his fingers were still tearing at the concrete outside the Bensheim building.

Gilbertez appeared to ignore the irony in Nohar's voice. "Yeah, we have records from the State and the Fed. You've been on one of the homestead projects. Getting the nonhumans, especially the large predatory ones, out of an urban environment." Gilbertez looked up. "You know, for all the objections people made to that homestead project, from the hunting lobby to the Native Americans, I think it worked."

Nohar shook his head. This guy could change subjects on a dime.

"After they started that project the crime rate in their target neighborhood went down. They say it's just because the Fed moved the crime out, but the homestead areas haven't had any crime problems, nothing like the inner city. So what happened to your cabin?"

Gilbertez only paused long enough to look at Nohar's expression. Nohar didn't know why he should be surprised. Of course, if they hadn't known already, the first place the cops would have gone after seeing him at Royd's would've been his last known residence.

"Never mind, we'll get back to that. I take it you did a bit of hunting?"

"Have to eat," Nohar said. The shifts in this guy's conversation were giving him a headache. Gilbertez was wired, always moving, gesturing, talking. He had yet to sit down.

"Don't we all. And being that they gave you land without any income— Anyway, they found the buck you got last, all dressed up. Too bad the fire torched the carcass. Shame of a waste. Only had venison a few times in my life, but seeing those pictures made me want to cry. Which I guess brings us to Charles Royd."

Nohar didn't see the connection, but he let Gilbertez roll on under his own momentum.

Gilbertez started pacing in front of his comm. "Royd was another waste. Did a lot of good for this town for some asshole to torture him to death. He didn't go easy, you know—though I suppose you do, seeing the body and all. The Mayor, the DA, and the entire nonhuman population of this city want his murderer's head on a plate. Now I'm a nice guy, but I would really like to oblige them."

Gilbertez turned and leaned on the desk. With almost any other two people, the gesture would have him looming over his audience. As it was, he had to look up into Nohar's face. "Now I wonder if you feel the same way? We have the records from Royd's office, and you were up there, looking for him the same day. Weren't you?'

Nohar remained quiet.

"Then, after all that bullshit at Royd's residence, you turn up calling in bomb threats to the Bensheim Foundation. You've been very popular lately, and I suppose I should consider myself lucky that I've been the local boy assigned to this case." Gilbertez pushed away from the table. "You should consider yourself lucky you got me, too. I'm going for some coffee, want any?"

Nohar shook his head and watched Gilbertez pick up his comm and leave the room. *Just what that man needs, more coffee.*

Nohar sat and waited for the detective to return.

During the wait, it began to sink in that Gilbertez hadn't accused him of anything yet. Nohar couldn't help but think it was probably some sort of trap, but he began to wonder if he had gotten hold of a cop who might listen to his story.

Gilbertez returned with a cup of stale-smelling coffee. He set down his comm, leaving it closed on the desk. He gestured with his coffee and said. "You've had a little time to think. Do you want to contradict anything I've gone over?"

"I don't think I should say anything."

"Has anyone read you your rights?"

Nohar shook his head.

"Well I'm not going to. Everything we say here's going to be inadmissible. Now—you have any problem with what I've said so far?"

Nohar shook his head slowly, unsure of where this all was going.

"Let me tell you about my day. Middle of the afternoon—I haven't taken my lunch break yet—I find out we got hold of this tiger that everybody and their brother in Fedland is looking for. Case falls in my lap, and shortly after, so do a bunch of Fed agents talking about nonhuman terrorism. Now I could hand you over and have lunch, but I don't like overbearing Fed agents, so I send them to the local judge, who'll spend at least forty-eight hours to decide if any of the antiterrorism acts cover the crap you're accused of. Then I bone up on all the records we have of you, and what you seem to be involved in." Gilbertez drained the coffee.

"What Fed agency?"

"FBI. Though every black Agency claims to be the FBI when they interfere with a criminal investigation. If they were FBI, they were FBI through some special forces branch. One guy had a unit tattoo on his wrist and the other had a big scar on his face—"

Him again, "Black guy?"

"—Yeah, know him?"

Nohar shook his head.

"Suit yourself. What I got is a two-hour rundown on you, and I have a lot of questions—"

"Like?"

Gilbertez looked over at the mirror and said, "Like why someone torches their own house after going to the trouble of hunting down and dressing a buck deer. The story we have from the antiterrorist people at the FBI has you blowing the place to hide evidence of bomb-making equipment, or it blew up when one of the devices malfunctioned. Now they have the site, can't get local boys there, but they did loan us some holos of the scene, which was enough to get my curiosity going. I mean there's the carcass right in the middle of the ruins, and then there's all the bullet holes."

"Bullet holes?"

"Or some frigging huge termites in the trees around your house. I got one pic I blew up that has a pretty good view of a forty-five-cal hole in a cinder block that used to hold up your cabin." Gilbertez finished off his coffee. "Then we got this story that you're supposed to have killed Royd as some terrorist act. Set aside for the moment that I've never bought these Outsider people as moreaus—their targets, except for Alcatraz, have been humans who were working with nonhumans. Bankers who do business in Moreytown, folks who set up shop to market to moreaus, factories that have liberal hiring policies. The whole Outsider manifesto about species separation never carried much weight with me—"

"Who are they, then?"

"I suspect they're some radical humanist organization bent on creating hostility at any point where humans and nonhumans seem to work together. They claim to be moreaus just to make it worse for the nonhumans, calling down all these antiterrorism acts on them. Anyway, that's all beside the point. You're supposed to be involved in Royd's death, and then, three days after the guy's killed, you visit his office looking for him, then return to the house with the body. Just as you're in there, somebody calls the Beverly Hills cops to report an Outsider hit squad in Royd's house."

Gilbertez put down his cup and leaned toward Nohar. "So what's going on here?"

CHAPTER 22

In the end Nohar decided that he had little choice but to trust Gilbertez enough to tell him. It was galling telling this all to a pink, and a pink *cop* at that. But, at the moment, Gilbertez was the only angle he had for getting on top of this situation. Nohar gave the cop a sanitized version of what had happened—he left out the names, and avoided telling him where Manuel and the others were supposed to be hiding out.

Gilbertez let him talk, even though silence seemed out of character for him. He flipped open his comm and typed notes as Nohar spoke. Nohar had spent an hour telling Gilbertez everything he felt he could.

Afterward, Gilbertez stared at the comm and nodded to himself. "Well, what do you know now? Your story had an advantage over the Feds'—over most of the stories I hear in here—it fits the facts. That's good. Though you do sound like every other conspiracy-mongering nonhuman I've ever heard. Really too bad that you didn't get a chance to copy that database you sneaked into." Gilbertez gave him a knowing look, as if he *knew* that was one of the few points where Nohar had lied. "I'd like to see this ramcard you say started all this bullshit."

Nohar shook his head.

"If you don't tell me where these people are hiding out, it sort of limits my options here. I mean I got a suspect the Fed wants, and a wild shaggy-dog story

about one of the most respected charity organizations
dealing with nonhumans. I got to have more than just
that if I'm going to do anything with this. Now I don't
want to hand you over to these Fed guys, especially
if they aren't FBI, but I gotta have something a little solid."

"I can't tell you where—"

"I know, I know. I *am* trying to work with you.
Something sour's going on here—not that I necessarily
believe your doomsday scenario—and I'd like to know
what these Fed guys are up to. I need something more
than your story, though."

"What?"

"Maybe we could arrange a call with this hacker
friend of yours. The one who looked up that satellite
for you."

Nohar looked at him.

Gilbertez turned the comm around to face Nohar.

"Where the fuck are you?" Bobby said as his image
came into focus on the screen. He was sitting in a
darkened room, and what was left of his hair was
mussed and pointing out at odd angles.

From behind the comm Gilbertez shook his head.
Nohar guessed that Gilbertez's comm wasn't quite explicit when it came to identifying itself. "I need that
information."

"Christ, you know what time it is over here?"
Bobby reached off-screen for his glasses and a handheld computer. Bobby flipped open the small device,
and Nohar could see a soft-green display reflected in
his glasses. "Again, you got me wondering what you're
mixed up in."

"You—"

"—don't want to know, right." He glanced up from

the little computer and at the comm he was talking into. "You know that comm you're on isn't secure?"

Nohar looked at Gilbertez. "Didn't have much of a choice. Go on, what've you got?"

Bobby looked down at the handheld computer again. "We have a burst of net activity surrounding The Necron Avenger about six days ago. This wasn't some kid with his first computer either. Someone with access to a super-computer was looking for him. There're traces of this search everywhere on the net, and it all happened within the same five-minute period."

"Who was it?"

"We traced it as far back as a Fed node on the net, a naval gateway we can't get past. Whoever did the search did it through the Long Beach Naval Station."

"You mean the navy—"

Bobby shook his head. "All this means is that was the point they accessed the civilian part of the net. The search could have started anywhere in the Fed's net. Hell, it could have even originated outside the Fed net—they could have entered through some other gateway entirely, and have it routed through Long Beach. The fact is just that we can't backtrack it past there."

"What about the Bensheim Foundation?"

"That takes a little more explaining—"

As Gilbertez looked on, Bobby gave Nohar a rundown on the Bensheim Foundation. All the time Dr. Bensheim was alive it had been run by an independent board based in Geneva. After the founder's death, there was an internal struggle between the various arms of the organization and the board, ending with a multiple schism of the original Foundation. It split along international lines, so the Geneva Board still ran the Bensheim Foundation in Europe, but there were different Bensheim Foundations in the Far East, Africa, and in North America.

The Bensheim Foundation in North America struggled along by itself, near bankruptcy, for a couple of years until a corporate white knight came along to bail it out.

The white knight was named The Pacific Import Company.

"Why is that name familiar?" Nohar asked.

"Probably because of the congressional hearings back in '62 over alleged government control of a company called VanDyne Enterprises. All of it had to do with aliens, corporate shell games, captured extraterrestrial technology, and the habitat on Alcatraz."

"What does Pacific Import have to do with that?"

"VanDyne was a Race front. The Fed took it over through Pacific Imports. Pacific Imports is an open secret, most likely run by the CIA."

"The CIA runs the Bensheim Foundation?"

"Didn't say that. Pacific Imports could have funneled money from just about any covert arm of the Fed. And there was no other record of any involvement with the Bensheim Foundation. As far as I could discover, the Bensheim Foundation is still an independent entity. Their headquarters happen to be in LA, Pasadena."

Nohar's talk with Bobby helped convince Gilbertez that there was something to Nohar's story. Even so, Nohar didn't feel good about it. The last thing he wanted was a confirmation that it was the Fed that was engineering what he had seen in the Bensheim database.

Gilbertez took him back to a holding cell. As they walked through the station, emptier now that it was on the night shift, Gilbertez talked nonstop. "You

might have something here. I don't know, but I got
to check some things out myself. But if this does pan
out, you have to take me to these people who're sitting on this evidence you keep talking about. In the
meantime you should think about whether or not I'm
your friend. From your story you have reason to be
paranoid, but I think that just means you really want
me on your case rather than these Feds who're waiting
for me to turn you over."

Gilbertez opened the cell for him and removed Nohar's cuffs. Nohar rubbed his wrists as Gilbertez said,
"Think about it."

The door shut, leaving Nohar in the same cell with
only a concrete bench. As Gilbertez asked, Nohar
thought about it. He couldn't decide if he was for real,
or just a clever Fed plant trying to get the only real
information Nohar had, the location of Manuel and
the others. The location of the ramcards.

Even if he was legit, Nohar had no illusions about
any local agency standing up to the Fed on any level.
Gilbertez might get everything, but that didn't mean
he'd be able to do anything. Publicity was still their
only hope. When the Fed no longer had a secret to
protect, they might be safe.

He had to think of something.

Nohar lay down on the concrete floor of the holding
cell. It was the only place he could rest, and even
there he couldn't recline fully. He needed to get the
ramcards—the ones he sent to Culver City—into the
hands of a reporter. As far as he knew, even if Gilbertez was a Fed agent, no one knew that the database
ramcard existed.

All he needed was to contact a reporter on the outside, get one to pick up the ramcards. The database
spoke for itself, loudly enough that the pink news
would pick it up. The fact that the CIA—or who-

ever—was using biological warfare agents domesti-
cally, for whatever reason, would set off the alarms.
It would remind people too much of what had happened in Africa.

Nohar closed his eyes and tried to sleep. He
dreamed of his mother again. This time she wasn't
dying from Pakistani-engineered feline leukemia—this
time the Fed had injected her with Ebola Niger.

Gilbertez didn't return until early the next morning.
Nohar only knew the time from the sense of activity
beyond the holding cell door. Gilbertez was accompa-
nied by a uniformed cop, and he looked as if he hadn't
had any sleep. He tossed a pair of cuffs on the floor
next to Nohar.

"Put those on. You got to take me to these people
hiding out before all hell breaks loose around here."

Nohar looked up at Gilbertez and tried to get some
clue as to what he was feeling. It wasn't hard to pick
up the scent of fear. Something had really disturbed
him. The uniformed cop was wary, but Gilbertez was
really scared.

"What's going on?"

"Somehow they got a judge. Someone's walking
downstairs with transfer orders for you. We have to
be on our way before those Fed agents show up, or
I'll *have* to hand you over." Gilbertez glanced at the
watch on his wrist for emphasis. "We don't have much
time. If we don't get a case put together fast, you're
going to disappear into the Federal machinery. You
don't want that to happen while you're still an accused terrorist."

Nohar stood up, holding the handcuffs. The uniform
took a few steps back. "Are these necessary?"

"You're still a suspect. Play along, and we can get
out of here smoothly."

Nohar put the cuffs on his wrists as loosely as their size would allow. "And him?" Nohar gestured to the uniformed cop with both hands.

"A concession to regulations. Suspects are escorted by at least two police officers. This has to be by the book, or anything that gets turned up'll be tainted. You don't need to worry about Ortega. I know his uncle."

The uniform nodded, but the set of his expression did not inspire much trust in Nohar. He couldn't help feeling as if this whole situation was some sort of setup.

Gilbertez and Ortega hustled him out of the holding cell and took him past the elevators and toward the fire stairs. They certainly gave the impression that they were sneaking out. Nohar kept an eye out for security cameras, and didn't know whether to be reassured or dismayed by the fact that all the cameras they passed were inactive or pointing the wrong way.

They led him up the fire stairs to the rooftop parking area. In the rear, past the banks of black-and-white aircars, was an unmarked Plymouth Pegasus. Its sleek lines were at odds with the forced aerodynamics of the cop cars. The police cars were heavy-duty bubbles, where the Pegasus was a cream-colored arrowhead.

Gilbertez led them straight to the Pegasus.

Hackles rose on Nohar's neck as they approached the car. A car like the Pegasus was out of line for someone on a detective's salary. That meant someone had provided the car. Nohar didn't think the LAPD was in the habit of handing out sports cars as unmarked vehicles. He could see Beverly Hills detectives tooling around in a Pegasus; a Pasadena cop, no.

But Gilbertez pulled out a remote, pressed his

thumb into the sensor, and the gull-wing doors swung open to accommodate them.

"Nohar better sit up front, more room there. You get in back, Ortega." Ortega glanced at Nohar, and again his expression was less than reassuring.

Nohar slid into the passenger seat in front of Ortega, and he couldn't help thinking that it gave the cop a perfect shot at the back of his head as he wedged himself in the tiny space in the front of the Pegasus.

The fact was, there wasn't any way they could've fit Nohar in the back anyway.

Gilbertez slid into the driver's seat and fired up the fans, and the Pegasus sluggishly rose. It was obviously overloaded with Nohar in it, and Nohar tried to avoid looking down as Gilbertez slid away from the garage and out over Pasadena.

The way tension was rolling off of Gilbertez, Nohar almost expected a troop of Fed agents to run out on the roof and attempt to shoot them out of the sky.

The Pegasus climbed, and Nohar watched the headsup display, a green vector map of the airspace corridors. A few lines in the display were a warning orange because the Pegasus was hugging the bottom of its legal flying space.

Strangely, Gilbertez was quiet through the whole ascent. It seemed unnatural to Nohar—the man seemed to run on nervous energy.

Nohar looked across at Gilbertez and asked, "So what did you find out?"

"Huh?" Gilbertez slid the Pegasus into the civilian air corridor above Pasadena. The Hollywood sign slid by the passenger window as the aircar turned for an approach on downtown Los Angeles.

"You said you were going to check things out. Did you find out anything more about these people?"

Gilbertez glanced back at Ortega before he answered. "No, nothing more than you told me."

You're lying. Nohar could feel it. He wanted to look back at Ortega himself, but there was no way he could move his head in the small space provided by the Pegasus. *I bet you don't have any clue who Ortega's uncle is.*

"Okay," Gilbertez said. "Where are we going?"

Nohar started talking, uncomfortably aware of Ortega's presence behind him.

CHAPTER 23

The aircar banked over the Santa Monica Mountains and Nohar could see the surface of the Hollywood Reservoir shimmering green in the dawn light. "Down there?" Nohar heard Ortega say, the first words he had spoken in Nohar's presence. It wasn't a voice that inspired trust.

"Yes," Nohar lied.

Gilbertez was nervous. Nohar could feel it, but the mood didn't make it into his voice. "This was where you ditched Royd's car. The police and the Fed have combed this place with a fine-toothed comb."

"That's why I picked it. Why look somewhere you've already searched thoroughly?"

No one expressed any further doubts. Nohar knew that his story stretched belief, but he hoped that it was plausible enough to get them clear on the ground.

"Land near the harvesting pylons," Nohar said. He peered through the window, trying to make out details on the ground. There was a fuzzy patch in a clearing and he pointed toward it. "There."

Gilbertez obligingly aimed the Pegasus for a landing in that clearing. He looked across at him and said, "Are you sure?"

Nohar nodded, wondering exactly what was going to happen when they landed and found nobody there.

*　　*　　*

The Pegasus put down in a clearing about twenty meters from the tree line. Opposite the trees was the edge of the reservoir, alive with shimmering engineered algae and the rotating booms. Near the edge of the water sat a squat little cinder-block building. It was windowless, and only had a single steel door.

Gilbertez got out first, then Nohar. He stood looking over at the building, shaking his head. "They're in there?"

It did look bigger when we were in the air. Nohar nodded. "Let me show you."

Nohar took a few steps toward the structure.

Ortega's voice came from behind them. "Why don't you stop right there?"

Nohar turned around, slowly. Gilbertez was already facing Ortega. He didn't seem very surprised by seeing his uniformed cop holding a gun on them.

Ortega held his automatic, covering both of them. Nohar noticed that he'd waited until he'd walked far enough away from the car. There was now no way that he could clear the distance between them before Ortega fired.

"I don't think there's anything in there," Ortega said.

"Why don't we just look—"

"We will." Ortega pulled a card-sized radio from his pocket, flipped it open. "As soon as my backup arrives." Not too surprisingly, the radio Ortega started talking into wasn't police issue.

Nohar glanced across at Gilbertez and said, "He's not talking about LAPD."

Gilbertez shook his head.

"This was all a setup," Nohar said.

"Only so much I could do with a gun to my head."

Nohar looked back at Ortega, watching him, waiting for his attention to shift. "You found out more than you told me." *Come on, start talking, Gilbertez. It's what you're good at.*

"I made the mistake of checking up on the credentials of the two Feds who showed up for you. Didn't have fingerprints, but I had their pictures from when I scanned their ID. Now the ID turns out to be legit, there are two FBI agents with those names and ID numbers—" Gilbertez turned to look at Nohar, "—but the FBI says that they're on assignment in Orlando, Florida."

"So they're not FBI agents?"

Gilbertez looked back at Ortega, who was putting away his radio. "It gets better. I ran their pictures through a half-dozen criminal databases, including Interpol. The one with the scar is a native of South Africa, named Tabara Krisoijn. He's a mercenary wanted by a half-dozen countries from the UAS north."

"They'll be here in a few minutes. Just keep talking." Ortega had a nasty grin.

"What's he wanted for?" Nohar asked, hoping for something in the conversation to agitate or distract Ortega. From the look of Ortega standing there and holding the gun, Nohar doubted that he was going to let that happen. He was too damn confident having the upper hand like this.

"It amounts to terrorism under the guise of antiterrorism. He's worked for a number of governments within the UAS, the Islamic Axis, and even Europe, but the folks he's hired to hunt down are usually outside the nation's borders—civilians, too."

Nohar nodded. Ortega was unmoved. That probably meant that he didn't care what information he had. And *that* meant that he was probably not meant to survive whatever was going to happen.

Nohar kept thinking of how he found Royd. . . .

Gilbertez was still talking. "The other guy is in the terrorist database for involvement in extreme humanist activities. He's ex-Navy, ex-Special Forces. Name's Frank Trinity."

Nohar's attention was caught by a familiar scent. The algae covered every scent in the area like a shroud, but he could still make out a vaguely canine subtext to the air. He listened carefully, tuning out Gilbertez, who was going on about Trinity's history in the military.

Beyond Gilbertez's voice, and beyond the constant whir of the pylons behind him, Nohar could hear rustling in the woods. Four or five large animals pushing their way through the brush.

". . . this guy." Gilbertez gestured at Ortega. "I don't know who he is, other than he works for the same people. The only thing I found out about the antiterrorism unit at Long Beach was that it was supposed to be decommissioned by Congress a few years ago."

Ortega spat, for the first time reacting to what Gilbertez was saying. "Those shitheads on the Hill didn't know what they were doing."

Nohar jumped on Ortega's reaction. "You're part of that unit?"

Ortega gave Nohar a stony expression. "I don't talk to fucking animals."

"You are part of it, aren't you?" Gilbertez asked, seeming to clue in on what Nohar was doing.

Keep him distracted.

"You make me sick, you know that? Sticking your neck out for a furball like this pile of garbage." Ortega shifted the gun a little toward Gilbertez.

"There's a murder here, and this furball didn't do it."

Ortega shook his head. "Fuck Royd. He was no

better than these engineered *things*. Killing him didn't
mean any more than killing one of them."

"Is the Fed behind this?" Gilbertez asked. Nohar
didn't know if Gilbertez could see the mixed Rottweiler slip out of the woods behind Ortega. It was
Blackie, from Elijah's pack.

Ortega chuckled. "This government doesn't have
the *balls*." There were three or four dogs behind him
now, approaching with a deliberateness that was out
of sync with their appearance. "They set up an operation to take care of a threat, and they didn't have the
will to see it through."

"What threat?" Gilbertez had to see the dogs now.
Nohar was impressed with his ability to stay focused
on Ortega.

"If you can't see the threat, you're part of it. Nothing worse than a traitor to your own species." Ortega
raised the automatic and leveled it at Gilbertez. "You
know, we don't even need you anymore."

It was the distraction that Nohar had been waiting
for. He dove for Ortega. Gilbertez ducked. And
Blackie came out of nowhere to seize Ortega's wrist.
He fired a wild shot, then Nohar had his arms over
the bogus cop's head, and the handcuff chain around
his neck.

Blackie shook Ortega's wrist until the gun fell. Gilbertez took a step to recover the gun, but Blackie
placed a possessive paw on the weapon and growled
at him.

Ortega stopped struggling, and Nohar dropped his
limp body to the ground. He checked his neck for
a pulse.

"Is he still alive?" Gilbertez asked.

"Yes." Nohar was unnerved to realize that there
was slight disappointment in his answer. He fished

around for a few minutes until he found some hand-cuff keys on Ortega.

Gilbertez kept turning, looking at the pack of dogs that surrounded them.

Nohar fumbled with the handcuffs until he got them open. He flipped Ortega over and handcuffed his hands behind him. Nohar had to close them all the way to get them to fit.

"What are they doing?"

"Watching us." Nohar carefully reached for the gun, and this time Blackie backed away from him. "Be careful. They have no love of humans."

"What are they doing *here?*"

"we return the help that no-har gives us." Elijah's electronic monotone came from the rear of the pack. The others parted to let Elijah's brown form through. He focused his good eye on Gilbertez. "more men come. we watch men approach, land. see no-har threatened."

Nohar nodded as he began manhandling Ortega back to the Pegasus. Gilbertez looked toward Nohar. "What are you doing?"

"We both have to get out of here before Ortega's backup arrives. We only have a few minutes." They had less than that. Nohar was beginning to hear the resonant hum of approaching aircraft.

"They have a tracking device on the Pegasus," Gilbertez objected.

"You aren't taking the Pegasus." Nohar's mind was leaping ahead, coming up with some sort of workable plan. He turned to Elijah. "Can you get this man down to the city? He's going to help me expose the men who gave you the sickness."

"this man." Elijah's monotone spoke. The whole pack started in on a chorus of staccato barking.

Gilbertez backed away from the sudden canine debate. "What are you talking about?"

Nohar wedged Ortega in the passenger seat. "Ortega's people infected them with an engineered form of hepatitis."

"I'm going to help you—how?"

"I'll fly decoy in this thing. You get back to Hollywood and get a cab to Culver City."

"Culver City?"

Nohar wedged himself into the driver's seat in the Pegasus. Now that his hands were free, he could ram the seat back as far as it would go. If he'd had the time, he would have liked to rip out the seat and sit in the back seat, that would give him just about enough leg room.

"A Doctor Brian Reynolds is getting a package from the Bensheim Foundation. Inside it are two ramcards, information detailing everything they're responsible for."

"But I need a warrant—"

"Don't *arrest* anyone. Get it to the media. The ramcards, and the story I told you. If this is a rogue operation, that will be enough to shut these people down."

Nohar fired up the fans on the Pegasus, and the grass ripped around the pack's feet as the engine powered up.

"we will escort this man." Elijah's electronic voice was barely audible over the sound of the Pegasus' fans. He turned his good eye to Nohar.

Gilbertez looked from the brown dog to the closing doors of the Pegasus, as if events were moving too fast for him. "What about—" the closing door cut off the rest of Gilbertez's question.

Nohar shook his head as much as the cramped space would allow. "No time."

The Pegasus lifted off from the clearing and Nohar kept an eye on the rear video as the pack led Gilbertez back into the woods. That was it, then. He had made his decision. He was the decoy. His job was to distract these people long enough for Gilbertez to get the information to the media.

He couldn't help regretting the fact that this meant that he was probably never going to see his son again. But his son was probably better off without him. . . .

He eased the Pegasus into the civilian air corridor, the vector display on the headsup flashing yellow, orange, and red at him. He had only flown an aircar twice in his life—and once was into the reservoir beneath him—and he wasn't terribly good at it, especially in a sports car that was overburdened with his weight. His presence shifted the aircar's whole center of gravity, and the nose kept dipping on him.

He cleared the trees, and the proximity radar began beeping all sorts of warnings at him. He looked for the radar display, but before he found it on the dash, a huge shadow shot over the top of the Pegasus. A matte-black helicopter flew across the Pegasus' path, barely ten meters above him. He had to pull the aircar all the way to the right and down to avoid a collision.

At that point, Nohar ignored air corridors, gaining altitude, or even leveling out the Pegasus. All that mattered was speed, and being pointed away from the helicopter.

He shot north, the belly of the aircar almost brushing the tree line, and flew right under another black helicopter, just like the one that had been at the assault on Pastoria Towers. *Might even be the same one.*

The two helicopters flanked him, easily matching the Pegasus' top speed.

The mountains dropped away and Nohar could see Burbank ahead of him. He had the feeling that he would never make it there. A pair of red dots appeared on the windshield and made vibrating independent journeys across the headsup display, across the hood of the car, ending at each of the forward fans.

The Pegasus shook as two shots, fifty-cal or better, pounded into the forward fans of the Pegasus. The air in front of Nohar was alive now with flying chunks of fiberglass. Part of the fan housing smashed into the windshield, fragmenting the headsup into a million emerald-and-ruby pieces. The front of the car dropped while the rear stayed under power.

The Pegasus did a somersault.

Nohar tried to control the crash, cutting power to the rear fans. Trees tore at the car, the left side of the Pegasus smashing against the side of a tree and bouncing off. Branches crashed through the windows as the aircar tore through the cover. Nohar had barely shallowed out the angle of descent as the aircar plowed into the ground, throwing up showers of topsoil and setting off the airbags. Nohar felt the car roll once before he lost consciousness.

CHAPTER 24

The first sensation that Nohar was aware of was agonizing pain in his left arm. His awareness filled out, cataloging each pain as it came to him. His neck, the base of his tail, every joint in his legs, even the muscles in his jaw ached.

Water splashed across his face. He sneezed and opened his eyes. He expected to see the wreckage of the Pegasus around him. The last thing he remembered was the airbag deploying.

He didn't see the Pegasus when he opened his eyes.

His upper body was taped to a heavy chair. He couldn't see much, because a bright light was focused on his eyes. What he could see of the room was a concrete floor, and he could smell the must and damp, as though they were in a basement. There were two people here. He could smell their confidence. The fear and tension he smelled was his own.

"Time to finish." The voice had a faint accent. It took a while before Nohar recognized it as Afrikaans. The speaker moved near Nohar, close enough for Nohar to make out his face past the light. He was a light-skinned black man, with a large scar on his right cheek.

"Krisoijn," Nohar whispered. It even hurt to talk.

The man reached out and grabbed his face, clenching Nohar's jaw shut. Nohar was too weak to resist, and his neck hurt too much for him to turn away.

Krisoijn's muscles stood out like steel cables on his arm.

"You'll only speak now to answer my questions." Krisoijn leaned in. "You fancy yourself a hunter—but man is still the most dangerous predator on this planet. Your ancestors only survived because man permitted them to live. Your kind exists now only because man permits them to live. You only live now because I permit you to live. Do we understand each other?" He withdrew his hand.

Nohar wanted to rage at the man, but he knew that there was little point in antagonizing him. He consoled himself with the thought that Gilbertez was talking to some reporters even as Krisoijn was talking to him.

It didn't last.

"I mean it when I say it's over." Krisoijn waved over the other man in the room. Nohar recognized the scent before he saw the man.

"Too bad about Ortega, but we all have to make sacrifices when the species is at stake." With every word Gilbertez spoke, Nohar felt his gut sink. Gilbertez held up a ramcard that shimmered like a rainbow in the spotlight. "You saved us a lot of trouble tracking this down. The session was logged, so we knew you copied the databases. They'd been tearing the Pasadena building apart looking for where you stashed it." Gilbertez placed the card on a cart on top of its twin.

They both lay next to a makeshift electronic device covered with silver-gray duct tape. It took Nohar a moment to realize that it was Elijah's voicebox. Gilbertez noticed Nohar looking. "Too bad we had to deal with them like that, but you had to let slip about Tangier, didn't you? That's one of the keys to the whole project, you know, engineer a virus that twigs on just the few proteins that are common to all moreaus, on the genes you inherited from the first few dogs. Had to start with them. If that tidbit got out, it could unravel everything. The rumors about the Drips are bad enough."

Krisoijn reached out and pulled Nohar's head to face him. "I am leaving you in Gilbertez's capable hands. I know you're thinking that you're strong enough to stay quiet—or maybe you're hoping that you'll die before you tell us anything more. I know that's what you'll be hoping for. It's a vain hope."

Krisoijn let go of Nohar's head and walked out of the room. Nohar heard a door shutting him in with Gilbertez. Nohar turned to face Gilbertez and said, "You?"

"Surprised? I find that gratifying." Gilbertez walked over to another cart and rolled it near Nohar's chair. Nohar saw the spotlight glint off the metal of surgical knives and a set of needles. "It's nice that we're not going to be pressed for time here, like we were with Royd. You've been a pain in the ass, and I'm going to enjoy this."

Gilbertez looked at the cart and looked at Nohar. Somehow his tense movements, and constant chattering were taking on a whole new sinister cast.

"It was all a setup." Nohar's voice came out in a groan.

"That's what you first suspected, wasn't it? I had to bring all my talents to bear to get you over that first impression. That was work. Trying to sympathize with a moreau, that was effort. My first hope was to talk out of you what we wanted. You were a little too cagey, so we absconded with you. When you led us to a dead end, Ortega pulled his trump. Between us we were supposed to overpower him, and do it a bit too late. The dogs were a bit of a wildcard that almost screwed everything up."

"You wanted me to tell you where Manuel is," Nohar said. "I'm not going to."

"Yes, that was the idea. But that's sort of moot now." Gilbertez picked up an air hypo and checked the charge in it. "You see, we managed to piece it together, once we knew that we didn't have the real Necron Avenger. You told us our quarry was still at large, and with Manuel and the data. We just had to press on Oswald Samson a little to get him to talk about his adopted son—"

Nohar stared at Gilbertez.

"Oh, you think less of Oswald now," he smiled. "Don't. No one can hold up under a professional interrogation." Gilbertez turned to face Nohar, his expression telling him that he was enjoying the process of revelation. "We got enough from him before he died to get a picture of The Necron Avenger. From there it was just a short step to double-check the Government net and find old INS sites that've seen recent net activity. Krisoijn's on his way to clean that up now."

No . . .

He had screwed up. Failed in the worst possible way.

Gilbertez pushed up Nohar's right sleeve and pressed the hypo into the exposed part of his uninjured arm. Nohar started to struggle. It seemed useless. The chair was steel and anchored to the concrete floor. He was held down to the chair by straps across his chest and upper arms. His forearms were strapped to the arms of the chair. Even his thighs were held down by a belt strapping him down to the seat. Only his lower legs had any freedom of movement.

Pain flared in his left arm and Nohar stopped struggling.

Gilbertez smiled. "I've just injected you with a synthetic drug. It doesn't even have a street name yet. It's a cousin to flush, it has hallucinogenic and stimulant qualities. The important thing for you is to realize that its main effect is to sharpen perceptions."

Nohar felt as if the world were suddenly trying to tear open his brain. Gilbertez's voice was painfully loud. The spotlight seared his eyes, even through closed lids. Worst was the pain in his arm, magnified a hundredfold.

"Most important for you," Gilbertez's booming voice said, "is the perception of pain."

Nohar clenched his jaw and whispered, *"Why?"*

" 'Why' what, my friend? Why the project? Or why are you strapped to that chair?" Nohar didn't answer. His jaw was clenched tight enough for his own fangs to bite into his gums. That pain, even amplified, was nothing compared to the feeling as Gilbertez unstrapped his wounded arm. "The project," Gilbertez continued, "is the ultimate solution to a problem the government saw during the last riots here. The riots, and the nonhuman population, were becoming a threat to national security. This antiterrorist unit here—it never even had a proper name—was formed to meet that threat, and it recruited men who saw the threat. The operation grew to a point that, when our government arbitrarily decided to ignore the threat, we didn't abandon the fight. The threat is still here, in this country, and there is only one way to eliminate it."

Gilbertez bent his arm upward and Nohar roared. The sound tore at him as if it were ripping the skin out of his throat. "I'm afraid it's broken. That'll do for a start." Gilbertez held Nohar's arm, and Nohar could feel the adrenaline surge of combat. He could feel the chemical rush as it flowed through his system. His nerves screamed.

"As to why you're strapped here— You were very cagey with your information. Even though we have that ramcard you copied, the ramcard stolen from Compton, and the location of Manuel Limón, we can't be sure what else you might be hiding. So I'm going to go over it with you a few times." Gilbertez turned Nohar's wrist, and the broken bones in the forearm grated against each other.

Nohar roared again. The conscious part of his mind wanted to start talking, give Gilbertez what he wanted to gain some respite from the pain. But the adrenaline was in control now. The thinking part of his brain was already pushed aside by the Beast created by the gene-techs.

His good arm balled his hand into a fist, and the tension in his own muscles felt as if it could break the bones in that arm. He opened his eyes, and the world stood out in a relief so sharp that the edges of every object were painful to see. He could smell Gilbertez, smell the fleeting traces of Krisoijn and the three other men who must have strapped him here. He could hear Gilbertez's heartbeat, and the breathing of the guard outside the door. He could feel the grain on the leather strap on his wrist, and he could feel the slight change in tension as the bolts holding the arm in place began giving way.

Gilbertez was still talking, but the part of Nohar's brain that listened was shut off, drowned in the tide of chemicals. The Beast had always been there, but Gilbertez's injection actually seemed to strengthen it. . . .

Gilbertez moved Nohar's arm again. Pain shot through Nohar. He arched his back and roared again. His arm strained against the chair and the room echoed with shearing metal. Nohar's right arm came free with a ten-kilo piece of the chair strapped to his wrist. The belt holding down his chest and forearms was anchored to that part of the chair, and it fell away as he raised his arm.

Gilbertez turned, letting go of his other arm. He was backing away, but the world had slowed for Nohar. Gilbertez barely took a step before Nohar's arm connected.

Nohar's fist, with ten kilos of extra weight attached to it, slammed into the side of Gilbertez's head. Gilbertez's head snapped back, and he flew out of the spotlight. Nohar could hear him thud limply against one of the concrete walls.

He was still strapped to the chair, but now half the chair was dangling off his right arm. His left arm didn't want to move, but he brought the buckle on his right wrist in reach of his hand so he could peel it off.

He'd just gotten it when he heard the door begin to open. He grabbed the arm of the chair with his newly freed right hand. When the guard stepped into the room, Nohar threw the jagged wreckage of the chair at about where the man's head should be. Nohar still couldn't see past the spotlight, but he heard the sound of a sickeningly soft impact, and of a body striking the floor.

He tore away the remaining restraints on his legs and sprang out of the chair, clutching his broken arm to his chest. Once he stood, he punched the spotlight, Glass fell into the suddenly darkened room and Nohar could smell burned fur and blood. He paid little mind; adrenaline and Gilbertez's drug still raced through his blood, coating everything with a razored immediacy.

The room shot into monochrome focus when the light died. Gilbertez was crumpled on the ground, his neck bent at better than a forty-five-degree angle. He didn't breathe. Nohar marked him as dead the moment he saw him.

The guard lay in the doorway, still alive, making choking noises as he clutched his throat. Arterial blood was collecting in a pool under him.

Nohar stepped up to the cart where Elijah's voice-box sat. Next to it were the ramcards, gray in the darkness. Nohar grabbed them and slipped them into a pocket.

On the way out, he bent and took the choking guard's sidearm.

CHAPTER 25

The door led out into a hallway with the same cinder-block walls, and the same concrete floor. Naked fluorescent tubes lit the hall with a vibrating white glare. Overhead pipes hugged the ceiling, low enough that Nohar had to duck as he ran down the corridor. He passed security cameras, and he could hear an alarm going off somewhere.

He made it to one end of the corridor and had to stuff the guard's automatic in his pocket so that he could open the door to the stairway. He still clutched his broken arm to his chest.

As soon as the door opened, he could catch the scent of at least three humans coming down. Their steps echoed in the stairwell. Nohar slipped inside before the door was open fully and pulled out the gun. The first man turned the corner a flight above him, just as Nohar flicked off the safety.

Nohar saw him, a kid dressed in a Marine uniform. Nohar was running on screaming instinct, and it didn't register that the pink facing him was a kid, or a Marine. What Nohar saw at the top of the stairs was an enemy with a rifle.

The kid's posture stood out in relief, like a neon sign advertising his intent. Nohar didn't hesitate.

Nohar's stolen sidearm was a submachine gun disguised as a pistol. One pull of the trigger sent five shots into the rifle-wielding Marine. Every shot hit, and the kid never had time to react. He hit the wall behind him, splattering blood, then he fell face first down into the stairs, rolling toward Nohar.

Nohar started up the stairs before the Marine had fallen halfway. He had to jump over the body, and he managed it without thinking of anything but the two enemies that were still up there.

Nohar was moving faster than he had a right to go, and his nervous system was screaming at twice the speed his body was moving. The world seemed suspended in gelatin around him. As he dove around the corner of the landing, he ducked low, almost to the ground. The two other Marines had heard the gunfire, and had barely enough time to bear their weapons. Their aim was a meter off.

The bullets from their machine rifles tore parts of the cinder block away from the wall above Nohar, showering him in a cloud of dust and concrete shrapnel. He had already had his gun pointed where he wanted the bullets to go. The automatic emptied itself of the remainder of its ammunition as the shots tore up the stairway, through both Marines. The gun was empty before Nohar's dive hit the ground.

Neither Marine got up from the crumpled heap they formed in the stairwell.

He had landed on his broken arm, and he pushed himself upright with an inarticulate roar. The pain was intense enough for his vision to black out and for his stomach to heave. But it didn't stop him moving. The pain seemed to sharpen his perceptions even further. All of the thinking part of his brain was now devoted to tactics, getting him out of here alive.

Nohar tossed the empty automatic down the stairs.

The enemy was converging on this point. He had to get out of here before they blocked off his escape. He ran up the stairs and grabbed one of the machine rifles. It was awkward, and probably dangerous one-handed, but he didn't have time to fiddle with a holster.

Nohar ran up the stairwell. He had to keep moving, keep the enemy reactive. The moment they had the chance to think, to plan, he would be crushed by sheer numbers.

He needed to know where he was, find a point of escape.

He passed two more doors as he ascended. They were marked with numbers that decreased as he went upward. Nohar didn't stop until he reached the next door. It was marked with a zero.

He had to put down the rifle to open the door, and every nerve in his body primed itself for an attack while he was vulnerable. He managed to get through the door without being ambushed.

The door led to a massive, dark chamber broiling with dry heat, and filled with the deafening resonance of dozens of giant fans. Under the high ceiling, ranks of massive metal boxes led away from the door. Above the humming machinery, massive fans fed huge vents in the ceiling.

Air-conditioning for an immense underground complex. The units were probably here to hide the heat signature from a spy satellite, the fans above dispersing the heat to dozens of widely separated points on the surface. It meant that he was a floor or two away from the surface himself.

As the door shut, he could sense the closing noose of troops behind him. He could hear movement above and below, even over the resonance of the air-conditioning units.

Nohar looked up to the massive vents in the ceiling. They were being fed by slow-moving fans about three meters across. The vents had to lead to the surface.

Nohar tossed his rifle on top of one of the huge air-conditioning units. He grabbed as high as he could reach with his good arm and pulled himself up, pushing on the sides of the unit with his feet. He managed to lever himself up on top of it. Beneath him, under a wire mesh screen that dented inward with his weight, a ferociously spinning blower shot near-searing hot air into him. It was like lying on top of an oven. He rolled off and stood. As huge as the unit was, there was still enough clearance between it and the ceiling for him to stand upright under the vent above.

The vent, and the fan feeding it, was protected by a set of metal bars. Nohar reached up and grabbed the center bar, putting all of his weight into pulling it free. It came loose so easily that he almost tumbled from his perch.

The fan in the vent moved slowly, but not slowly enough for him to climb into the vent while it was still moving. The fan was mounted above a metal strut, and beneath that, the motor was exposed. Nohar could see the metal sheath that fed the power cables into the fan. He grabbed it and yanked. After the second try the cables came free with a shower of blue sparks.

The fan slowed to a stop and Nohar pushed the rifle up into a horizontal pipe that fed into the side of the vent above. Then he grabbed the strut bracing the dormant fan and hooked his feet through the grating that he had pulled off the vent.

Pulling himself up was agonizing, especially with the extra weight on his feet. One-handed he managed to chin himself up to the strut. Even then, he had to raise the elbow of his broken arm up on top of the strut to give him the leverage to pull himself the rest of the way up.

Pain clouding his vision, doubled up across the strut under the fan, he managed to reach down for the grate. He managed to keep hold of it with his feet, and he got hold of the center bar so he could pull it shut behind him. He was even able to wedge back into place the way he had found it.

He wished he could start the fan again, but there was no way to do it safely from above, even if he could reattach the wires he had yanked free.

He couldn't stay where he was. He stood, precariously balanced on the strut between two fan blades. The side vent where he had pushed the rifle was too small for him. So he had only one direction to go.

Nohar looked up, but the vent above was shrouded in gloom that even his good night vision couldn't penetrate. The rifle had a shoulder strap, and he slung it on his back. The strap was too short, and it hung wrong, but he couldn't afford to leave his only weapon.

He turned around until he found a ladder set into the wall of the vent.

Slowly he began the painful ascent.

To his telescoped sense of time it seemed it took hours for him to reach a horizontal vent he could fit through. The ladder was designed for pinks and his feet could barely find purchase on it. He also had to use the elbow of his broken arm to keep his balance every time he reached for a higher rung. Once he twisted the broken arm, blacked out from the pain, and nearly fell.

His ears were numb from the echo of the blowers beneath him, and even with the fan disabled, the heat was burning and almost unbearable. His eyes watered, and his fur itched, and all he could smell was the dry scent of heated sheet metal.

He might have missed the passage if the ladder he was climbing didn't end there. He reached for another rung, and his arm met empty space. He managed to pull himself into a horizontal vent about half the diameter of the vertical one. He crawled forward, his digitigrade legs slipping into a horizontal gait, limping on one foreleg.

Twice, now that he wasn't in immediately physical danger, the adrenaline-fueled Beast left him in a state of collapse in the vent, blacking out from pain and exhaustion. Each time it took a severe effort of will to keep going.

It took an eternity for him to move down that darkened tunnel. Eventually, his progress was stopped. A carbon-black barrier walled off any further advance. The thing was louvered and spongy, and felt as if it was formed on a metal framework. Combination of heat dissipation and security. To keep people like him from wandering around the ventilation system.

Nohar moved back until he was well clear of the barrier. Then he unslung the rifle and made sure it was on full auto. Then he emptied half the clip into the blockage. The sound was deafening in the enclosed space and his nose was seared with the smell of the gunfire. This rifle wasn't caseless, and burning hot cartridges bounced all around him.

In front of him, the black material tore away from a network of copper pipes. The pipes leaked cold water into the vent, and Nohar could suddenly smell salt.

Nohar edged back up to the barrier. It was damaged enough that he could form an opening he could squeeze through. He bent two broken pipes back to the walls of the vent, and he forced the remaining horizontal pipes to bend up enough to allow him to crawl through on his stomach. It was a tight fit, and he had to leave the rifle behind until he made it through. Then he pulled it after him.

Time was precious again. They might have missed his entry into the vent, but between the gunfire and the damage he had just caused, they were sure to know where he was now. He probably had only a matter of minutes to make it outside.

Fortunately, the reason for the heat barrier was that he was within twenty meters of a vent to the outside. He only had to crawl a short way until the vent emptied into a concrete chamber that was topped by a square grate that looked up at the sky. Under the grate there was enough clearance to stand upright. The grate was heavy, iron, and padlocked shut. He didn't know what was out there, but he could see the edges of the landscaping camouflaging the vent outlet.

Nohar didn't want to start shooting, alerting whoever was above, but he had to break the lock.

He raised the butt of the rifle and slammed it into the lock. It took him five tries, and a split in the composite stock of the weapon, before the padlock popped open.

He slung the rifle and started pushing the grate up. It was hinged at the base, and it was heavy. It took all of his strength to push it up with enough force that it arced over into the bushes.

Nohar scrambled up out of the vent and crouched behind the bushes to get his bearings. He could hear alarms, and people running. He looked around and saw low military structures, and a lot of armed Marines running toward the building nearest him.

Opposite the Marines was a concrete landing pad on which sat two of the black helicopters he had seen too much of lately. The twinned rotors on the one nearest him were starting to move. He could see a pilot seated, and the door in the side was hanging open.

The copter had probably been all set to leave when the alarms sounded.

Nohar sprang from his cover and ran for the helicopter. He heard commotion behind him, and a few seconds later he heard the sounds of gunfire. A few bullets tore into the asphalt as he ran, but the shooters were far enough away that the sight was completely disconnected from the sound.

The pilot must have seen him, because the door on the helicopter started closing. It was too late. Nohar managed to dive into the body of the aircraft before the door had closed completely. He landed on his bad arm, and he roared in pain and dropped the rifle.

The pilot stood, scrambling to get out his sidearm.

Nohar grabbed the rifle and put a shot into the front windscreen. The broken stock hammered into his shoulder, but he managed to keep hold of the gun. The area where it struck the armored glass starred and rippled in rainbow colors where the bullet was suspended.

"Take off now!"

The pilot sat back down, and Nohar heard the obliging whine of the rotors picking up speed.

Nohar looked around him. The rear of the copter was in disarray, as if its inhabitants had had to leave in a hurry. *Probably bugged out to hunt me down,* Nohar thought.

The copter rose, and the adrenaline high finally began fading from his system. He couldn't ignore the pain in his arm anymore; it was slamming him like a jackhammer.

Now that he was aware of the future beyond the next thirty seconds, he began to think of Krisoijn.

CHAPTER 26

The helicopter levered itself into the sky.

"Toss the gun back here," Nohar said.

After a few seconds, the pilot's sidearm slid along the floor next to him. Nohar dropped the rifle and picked up the pilot's automatic, checking to be sure it was loaded and the safety was off. He lay there for several minutes, the pain from his injuries racing through him in shuddering waves. He wanted to collapse. He couldn't allow himself to do that.

With agonizing slowness, one-handed, Nohar pulled himself up off the floor of the helicopter. It took him three tries before he could manage it. He made it to the front of the helicopter, and through the broken windscreen, he could see the skyline of Los Angeles scroll by as the helicopter banked over Long Beach.

"East," Nohar told the pilot. He collapsed into the seat next to the pink. It was too small and he was hunched over, giving him a chance to feel the bones grinding in his forearm every time the helicopter changed attitude.

The pilot looked across at him. "What the fuck do you think you're doing?"

"What matters is what you think I'll do if you don't do what I say." Nohar had to aim the gun across his chest, to point at the pilot's head. "East, where the other helicopter was going."

"I can't do that."

Nohar put another shot, past the pilot's face and into the side window. The bullet was suspended in the armored window, throwing rainbows across the surface of the broken glass. Nohar leaned toward the pilot. "I don't like defeatist attitudes."

Nohar could smell the fear emanating from the pilot. He was another kid, barely twenty. Nohar remembered the kid on the stairs. He couldn't get that image out of his mind.

It was a good thing pinks were rotten at picking up emotional cues, or he'd know that Nohar wasn't going to kill him. Nohar could tell he had the kid on the edge, so he pressed while he had the advantage.

"There's at least one helicopter that had a lead on us. It's fully loaded. You're not. That means you can catch up."

"You don't understand what you're asking—"

"One more word, and I put a bullet through your cheek."

The pilot shut up.

"I can read your radar. Follow him as fast as this crate can go."

The helicopter banked west, and the pilot didn't say another word. Nohar watched for signs that the pilot was holding back on the acceleration. He knew less about helicopters than he did about aircars, but from the looks of the displays in front of the pilot, the speed on this thing was maxed out. Looking out the windows at the angle of the coastline told him they were traveling in the right direction.

Once the towers of LA drifted behind them, Nohar lowered his weapon. He glanced down at the console in front of them.

"You're not going to see them on that," the pilot said.

Nohar looked up.

"Go ahead, shoot me. Even if they were within short-range radar contact, they'll only show if their FOF transponder's on."

"How much of a lead?"

He could see the pilot debating with himself over his cooperation. "Fifteen minutes."

"Distance?"

"Ninety to one-fifty klicks."

Nohar didn't know whether to curse the distance, or be thankful that Krisoijn hadn't reached his destination yet.

The pilot looked at Nohar. "You know, I'm worthless as a hostage. They're not going to hesitate shooting us down."

"Then get moving."

Nohar looked down at the console. His vision was blurry with fatigue and pain. He switched the automatic to his other hand, clutched to his chest. He hoped the captive pilot wouldn't try anything while he held the gun in his broken arm.

Nohar began flipping switches on the helicopter's comm.

"What are you doing?"

"How do you get a civilian channel on this thing?"

The pilot looked at what he was doing. "They'll be able to monitor everything you say on that."

"As long as the person I call can read me."

"The first dial to 'CIV,' the second to 'DAT,' and the third to 'TRN/RCV.' "

Nohar did as the pilot said. After going through an on-screen menu he managed to get the familiar blue AT&T test pattern logo. He was never happier to see that image.

He slipped a ramcard—the one he had copied from the Bensheim database—into the comm's data slot.

"What are you doing?" the pilot asked. He still

smelled of fear, but he had recovered enough for
Nohar to trade the automatic back to his good hand.
It hurt to move his broken arm toward the console,
but he could move his fingers enough to operate the
comm.

"What are *you* doing?" Nohar said.

"What?"

"What is the mission of that military cabal you
work for?"

The pilot looked at Nohar as if he was nuts.

"What do you think is going on here?" Nohar said.

"You obviously escaped from detention . . ."

Nohar would have laughed if his arm didn't hurt so
much. He began typing in Pacific Rim Media.

"Why was I being detained?"

"I don't know." The pilot paused. "You obviously
are a morey terrorist—"

"Why else would I hijack you, right?"

The pilot nodded.

"You don't have any idea what their agenda is?"

"Whose agenda?"

"The people you work for."

"The Marines?"

Nohar shook his head as a receptionist came on-
line to take his call. The man on the other end of the
comm was an immaculate Asian gentleman who was
just imperfect enough to be flesh and blood and not
a computer facsimile.

Nohar knew he was a real person when he saw the
expression of shock at the sight of his caller. Nohar
didn't know if the handgun was in the frame, but the
man could certainly see the ragged blood-spattered
clothes and the broken arm.

"Pacific Rim Media." The man announced it in such
a way that Nohar knew in his secret heart he hoped
the response would be, "Oops, wrong number." The

man never even gave Nohar the obligatory, "May I help you?"

"Not the Marines," Nohar said.

"What?" said the man on the other end of the comm. The man's movements were jerky with interference. Nohar stared into the screen. "Connect me with Stephanie Weir." The receptionist looked unsure, so he added, "Tell her it's Nohar calling. She'll talk to me."

"Just a moment." The receptionist's face showed the relief he felt, putting Nohar on hold.

Nohar hoped he was right, and Stephie would talk to him.

"What are you doing?" the pilot asked.

"You'll see it on the news, if we live."

He shook his head and stared out the distorted windscreen. The eastern half of Los Angeles slid underneath them. Aircars passed above them as they flew illegally low over the suburbs. The helicopter had maxed out at about two-fifty klicks an hour.

"Making demands to the media won't help. They still won't negotiate with you. If you gave up, they might not shoot. . . ."

"No demands," Nohar said. "No negotiation."

Stephie's face replaced the Pacific Rim test pattern and she started off on him before the video had fully resolved. "What the hell do you think you're doing, calling me at work like th—" When the video was fully on-line, Stephie stopped talking and just stared.

"Get a blank ramcard ready to download."

"What happened? Where are you—"

"Do it."

Nohar saw Stephie fumble around her desk, eventually sliding a ramcard into her comm. "What's going on?"

"Something for your news division." Nohar pressed

the button for a burst transmit of the ramcard's contents to Stephie. Once the data started shooting through the comm network, Nohar said. "Make copies of this. Transmit at least one overseas. They're monitoring this comm."

Stephie shook her head. "What is this?"

"A rogue military operation. An antiterrorist action gone out of control. That card you're downloading is a database detailing domestic biological warfare experiments, using the North American Bensheim Foundation as a front."

"What?" The word came from Stephie and the pilot, they had almost the same expression. The display on the screen showed the card almost downloaded to Stephie's comm.

"No time. The database has enough for the story." The display started flashing that the transfer was complete. Nohar swapped out the card, painfully with his broken arm, and slipped in the other one.

"Get moving once this thing downloads. You aren't safe until all this information is public."

"But—"

The second card, the one that started all of this, didn't take nearly as long to transmit. It was over before Stephie could ask him any more questions.

Nohar cut the connection. He hoped that he hadn't just condemned her like he had condemned Elijah.

"We're being ordered to land," the pilot told him, holding a hand up to his headset.

"That isn't going to happen."

"Look at the radar," the pilot said. He flipped a switch so Nohar could hear the audio he was listening to.

". . . repeat, you are being ordered to land. Acknowledge, or you will be forced down . . ."

Nohar glanced at the radar. There were two blips

following them, both had the letters marking an active transponder. They were closing fast.

"Those are two Vipers. Fully armed attack copters. This is a troop carrier. Which do you think's faster?"

Nohar gripped the gun tightly. "Landing isn't an option." In the background the commands from the Vipers continued in a monotonous litany.

"Don't you understand? They are going to shoot us down if you don't let me land."

No, they would've already. For a moment Nohar wondered why they were still airborne—they were well within missile range. Then he looked down at the suburbs sliding by below them. They were waiting for them to clear the civilian population. . . .

"Hug the freeway," Nohar told him.

"What?"

"Get over the freeway, as low as you can without hitting any cars."

The pilot hesitated a moment, then he banked the helicopter down toward the Riverside Freeway. The Santa Ana Mountains filled the front of the windscreen as the copter dove toward Anaheim. As Nohar's stomach dropped out, he looked in the rear video and saw the Vipers on their tail. The black copter he was in resembled a grotesque beetle under its counter-rotating props, the two Vipers were as narrow and lithe as dragonflies. Even at this distance Nohar could see their stubby wings, there to carry weaponry that couldn't be attached to the Viper's narrow fuselage.

"We're aiming right toward March Air Force Base—"

Nohar didn't respond. He watched as the mountains slid by the helicopter. Below them, traffic sped by in a blur, rolling along an endless ribbon of concrete. It felt as if Nohar could reach down and slap the roofs of the cars as they shot by beneath them. Air Force base or not, as long as they were so close to traffic, the pursuers wouldn't dare shoot them down.

The problem was going to come when they ran out of traffic. The freeway they were on would take them to I-10, which would take them all the way to the Arizona border, where the camps were. At some point, over the desert, they would have to turn south, giving the Vipers a clear shot at them.

Nohar didn't know what he was going to do then. He hoped to catch up with Krisoijn before then.

The copter blew past March on the northern turn up toward San Bernadino and I-10.

"We're headed toward Norton now."

"Just take Ten east." Nohar stared at the radar, where other blips were joining the Vipers. They were far away, but from the speed he could tell that he was looking at a pair of conventional aircraft taking off from March, fighters. . . .

Shit!

The pilot looked at Nohar as he took the turn onto I-10. The traffic was lighter, and the population of Greater Los Angeles was now mostly behind them. Ahead lay mountains, desert, and a clear field of fire.

"We have to put down," the pilot said. "I can radio that we'll put down at Norton Air Force Base—"

Nohar shook his head; all he could think of was Maria. "How close are we to them?"

"What? The other helicopter?" The pilot shook his head. "There's still at least seventy-five klicks between us."

Nohar gripped the gun and pressed it into the pilot's head. "We're supposed to be faster—"

"The jog north, following the freeway, it eats up time."

They'd never catch up with them at this rate.

The board in front of the pilot started coming alive with red lights and buzzers.

"What's happening?"

Over the speaker Nohar heard the tinny voice of one of the Vipers, "You are ordered to land *now*. This is your final warning."

"One of the Vipers has a radar lock on us." The pilot turned toward him. "We have to land *right now!*"

Nohar tasted copper on his breath, and felt the rush of his pulse in his ears and in his wounded arm. "No." The word was almost a whisper.

"Fuck this," he said. "Shoot me, then."

The copter tilted and ducked toward a clear spot beside the highway. Nohar gripped the gun, but it was pointless to shoot, even if he could. There wasn't any way they could escape the pursuit.

The pilot yelled into the radio, "Hold your fire, I'm landing."

The alarms didn't go away, but the missile didn't come.

They were almost on the ground when a new voice overwhelmed the channel the Vipers were using. "Two unidentified attack helicopters, disarm your weapons now! Desist pursuit and accompany us to March Air Force Base."

The pilot's expression changed.

"What is it?" Nohar asked.

"The fighters . . ." The pilot shook his head as if he couldn't understand what was happening.

Nohar heard the Vipers talking back, "We are on an authorized antiterrorist mission. We have been ordered to stop that helicopter—"

The fighters called back, "You are following illegal orders. You are to accompany us or be fired upon."

There was a long pause before the Viper said, "We require confirmation from our command—"

The Viper didn't even finish getting the whole phrase out. Another voice, weaker with distance, broke in on the channel. "Black four and Black five, your mission is aborted. Repeat, your mission is aborted. Follow the fighters to March Air Force Base as you've been instructed."

"We need to hear from Colonel Shuster—" said one of the Vipers. "This is a matter of national security."

"This is *General* Thomas Charland, and Colonel Shuster is under arrest pending a court-martial."

There were a few more exchanges, and the pilot's face grew more incredulous as he listened. On the radar, Nohar could see the blips of the fighters looping around to escort the two attack copters.

"Colonel   Shuster,"   the   pilot   whispered. "Arrested?"

There was only one way Nohar figured that could happen so quickly. The command at Long Beach had been monitoring his transmission to Stephie. General Charland must have decided to cut his losses.

"What's happening?" The pilot whispered.

"Don't land," Nohar said. "Follow Krisoijn."

"Why—"

"Your general decided that the project was blown."

"What project?" The color drained from the pilot's face. "Not that bullshit you were talking about."

"Move this thing."

The pilot looked at Nohar's gun, and banked the helicopter southeast, accelerating toward Arizona. "Biological warfare?" The words were almost inaudible. Nohar could sense the pilot's fear again. This time the fear wasn't because of him.

The kid had just realized that what Nohar had told Stephie might be true. Of course no one had ever told him what the unit at Long Beach was doing. As far as the pilot could tell, Nohar was just another violent morey with a conspiracy theory.

That was until his superiors reacted. The pilot knew as well as Nohar did that the only explanation for the recall was that someone had monitored Nohar's comm transmission, and had responded to it.

General Charland had to be in command, running the show. That was the only way he could have reacted so quickly to the leak of the biowar database. There was probably a plan set in place, with predesigned evidence, preselected fall guys. There was probably a script waiting for this Colonel Shuster laying out exactly what he would say to the Congressional investigating committee when they subpoenaed him. There would probably be stories of how an internal investigation had been onto these folks all along, and just about to hand out indictments when the news broke.

General Charland had just decided to "discover" the conspiracy and arrest its ringleaders before the news started making headlines. His ass was going to be covered.

"Will they recall him?" Nohar asked.

"Who?"

"Krisoijn, the other helicopter."

The pilot shook his head. "He's supposed to be radio silent. It might not even be on."

This General Charland, Nohar had too good a picture of that Machiavellian bastard already, might shout orders, but it was too easy for Nohar to believe that they'd let Krisoijn go through with his objective, just so there'd be an example of what a loose cannon he was. It would help distract attention from the officers in charge of this mess.

"We're going to catch up with him," Nohar said.

The pilot didn't contradict him.

CHAPTER 27

With the pursuit gone, the helicopter sped across the desert, in a straight line for Camp Liberty and the Arizona border. The pilot didn't talk much anymore, but he flew the copter where Nohar wanted it to go.

While southwestern sand and rock blew by underneath them, Nohar used the comm. He called a half-dozen media outlets, spreading the information on what was going on as widely as possible. Half of them treated him like a psychotic, the other half humored him long enough to download the database on the ramcard. He told everyone who would listen about the coming attack on Camp Liberty, down to the location.

One of the people who seemed to listen was Enrique Bartolo from *Eye on LA*, the reporter that Henderson had called at Pastoria.

Nohar was on his seventh call when the pilot said, "There they are."

Nohar looked up through the bullet-scarred windscreen and saw a dot hanging over the horizon. The black dot seemed to grow as Nohar watched. His rotten day vision couldn't make out any details, but the coloring and the position were right.

"How long before we reach the base?"

"Five minutes."

"Can we beat them there?"

"Barely."

Nohar watched the fuzzy black dot of the other helicopter. It grew, but much too slowly. The difference in the helicopter's load made only a slight difference in speed.

If they could reach the place first, he could get everyone out.

If . . .

Suddenly, the fuzzy black form of the helicopter rose and banked to the left. "What are they doing?"

The pilot shook his head. "They know I'm compromised."

"How?"

The pilot turned toward him. "Someone looked back. You kind of stand out."

"Fuck—" There wasn't any way they could have missed him in the copilot's seat. Even if they'd missed him, the bullet in the windscreen was a giveaway.

The other copter was sliding close, too close. Nohar could see the copter lining up with them on the left and above. He started to make out the landing gear and the massive side door. It was sliding open as Nohar watched.

"Can you get more speed out of this thing?"

The pilot shook his head, more out of stress than negation, and dipped the nose of the copter. The machine started tilting toward the desert floor, just as Nohar began to hear gunfire over the sound of the rotors. It sounded distant, almost fake.

The smell of panic filled the cockpit as the bottom dropped out of Nohar's stomach. The copter fell toward the desert floor. At the last minute the pilot pulled up and the copter shot by about ten meters above the ground. Rocks and cactus seemed to reach up almost far enough to grab them out of the sky, and sand billowed in a cloud behind them.

"Fuck," the pilot said, "They're above and behind—"

The dive had added about fifteen or twenty klicks to their speed. They started banking, back and forth, evading the copter behind them, and large rock formations that sprang up ahead of them.

Nohar heard more gunfire behind them. The sound still seemed distant, but this time he heard something pounding the outside of their helicopter.

"Shit," the pilot said, pulling the copter up into a climb. The desert fell away and was replaced by sky. Just as the horizon slid under his feet, Nohar saw sunlight reflected from something on the horizon.

A window. It had to be a window in the distance.

More gunfire, and an explosion rocked the helicopter. The cabin filled with the smell of ozone and fried ceramics. The rotors began making ugly rhythmic knocking noises, and half the lights in front of the pilot began flashing red.

"What—" Nohar started.

"The primary inductor blew. I have to put her down."

The copter was shaking itself apart now. All over the console, things buzzed for the pilot's attention. The knocking and the shaking were getting worse. "Losing alignment on the rotors—" He said it through clenched teeth, and Nohar didn't know if the pilot was talking to him or not.

The nose of the copter dipped.

The gunfire continued, as if they couldn't tell that the helicopter was in trouble.

Nohar dropped the gun and tried to pull the safety harness around himself. It didn't fit, and he had trouble doing it one-handed. He roared as the attempt jostled his busted arm, sending fiery waves of agony through that half of his body as the bones ground together.

They were barely fifteen meters above the ground

when he got one strap fastened. They were slowing, but not enough. The helicopter was trying to shake itself apart as it shot over the four-meter-high perimeter fence.

Suddenly, below them, the desert floor was covered by ranks of vehicles. An endless parking lot spread out below them. In front of them, in the distance, was the fence and the low buildings of Camp Liberty.

The pilot tried to bring the nose up, tried to slow. But the helicopter began pitching against him.

More gunfire, and this time he heard a sickening screech of abused metal. The two rotors had gotten out of sync enough to touch. Nohar saw a shower of ferociously turning metal erupt from above the helicopter and tear into the cars below. The copter was now completely dead to the pilot's control. It nosed straight down into the ranks of parked vehicles.

An INS van flipped up and smashed against the nose of the helicopter. Nohar was thrown against the single safety strap holding him into the seat. His head struck the armored windscreen, which was the only thing between his face and a jagged mass of twisted fiberglass and metal. The van slid with the helicopter, its body tearing through the desert floor and screeching like the damned.

The copter pushed the van about thirty meters before it stopped moving.

The body of the helicopter fell back, tilting the nose up, away from the damaged van. The rear of the helicopter slammed to the ground with a screech of twisted metal.

The pain in Nohar's arm was so intense that he had to look down to assure himself that it wasn't a stump. His breath came in ragged gasps, and he could smell his own blood leaking from gashes in his forehead.

The pilot was in better shape. He looked as if his

nose was broken, but he didn't seem injured other-
wise. He was shaking his head and saying, "My God,
we made it."

Nohar wasn't so sure.

He unhooked the harness that was still attached to
him, and picked up the gun. As he stood, he could
feel the line of bruises across his midsection where the
harness had bit. His legs buckled and he had to sit
and breathe for a few moments before he could
stand again.

"Any weapons on board?" he said between ragged
gasps for breath.

The pilot looked at him with disbelief in his eyes.
"Do you know how lucky we are to be standing? You
can't be thinking . . . ?"

Nohar raised the gun at the pilot.

"You want to commit suicide, be my guest." He
gestured toward the end of the compartment. "There's
a heavy machine gun that belongs to a mount in the
door."

Nohar pocketed the automatic and found the
weapon the pilot was talking about. The thing was
nearly two meters long and fed from a belt. It was a
fifty-cal at least. It was obviously intended for a door
gunner, the only support on the frame was a ratchet
meant to slide into a preset mount.

"This is it?"

The pilot looked at him and nodded.

Beggars can't be choosers.

Nohar picked up the belts of ammo and draped
them over his shoulders. The weight bore down on
him, lighting fires in his old shoulder injury as well as
his broken arm. For the first time in ages, Nohar tried
to force the Beast to come out. He tried to conjure
the adrenaline and the engineered combat machine

that lived in his genes. He was so close to the edge, he couldn't tell if his biochemistry responded.

After standing and sucking in breaths for nearly a full minute, psyching himself up for the insanity he was about to step into, he managed to lift the fifty-kilo weapon one-handed.

Carrying it balanced, one-handed, was awkward.

"Open the door," Nohar said.

The pilot nodded, and the doors in front of him began to open with a rattling hydraulic wheeze.

Once the other helicopter passed from above them, Nohar stumbled out. He ran, each breath feeling as if it were tearing burning holes in his lungs. He loped past the wreckage of dozens of abandoned government vehicles, many now sporting fifty-caliber bullet holes. To his right, over the edge of the compound ahead of him, the other helicopter was banking, preparing to land.

Nohar ran for the compound thinking twinned thoughts, that the pilot was right when he said that he was committing suicide, and that in there were Maria and his son.

In the daylight, Nohar could now see the whole complex. It must have covered a hundred square kilometers. He was heading toward the inner fence that separated the vehicles from the compound and could just glimpse the dozens of buildings through the small vents in the heavy steel fence. The place shimmered in the daytime heat, like a mirage. Nohar ran through the heat, and it felt as if he were slogging through mud.

He made it to the fence about the time the other copter was dropping troops at the southern end of the compound.

Nohar realized that the commandos had no idea where Manuel and the others were in there. That was his only chance. Nohar ran along the fence line and found an access gate. He had to drop the machine gun to flip open the keypad access. For a few moments he almost blanked on the access code that John had given him.

Then he remembered earthquakes—

"01082034"

It slid open for him.

Nohar grabbed the gun and ran inside. The small pedestrian gate was next to a much larger gate that was designed for vehicle access. The gate was plastered with red signs that said "Access Forbidden" in about twenty different languages.

Between the pedestrian gate and the large vehicle gate was a small guard shack that offered some cover. Nohar dove into it and forced the barrel of the machine gun through the window facing the Bad Guys' helicopter. The window shattered, and Nohar braced the gun on the guard shack's desk.

The ratchet of the gun wedged in a control panel, and the barriers on this side of the vehicle gate began raising and lowering.

Nohar concentrated on getting the belt of ammo off of him and feeding it into the weapon. He ducked down behind the machine gun and sighted on the helicopter. It was still unloading, three or four pinks were rappelling from lines dangling from its sides.

Nohar let the copter have it.

The sound was deafening. Each sledgehammer shot shook the guard shack and slammed the ill-braced weapon into Nohar's bad shoulder. The small room filled with the smell of gunsmoke and heated brass. The barrel wanted to travel, but somehow Nohar kept pulling the weapon back on target. He could see sparks flying off of the side of the helicopter. And he tracked the shots until he was firing into the door.

The dangling pinks dropped so quickly that Nohar couldn't tell if it was panic or free fall. Two others fell out of the side door, unattached, tumbling to the ground.

The helicopter banked and started pulling up and away to the left, empty rappel lines still attached to it.

Nohar tracked upward toward the twin rotors.

By then the helicopter had turned and brought its own fifty-cal to bear on the guardhouse. Nohar caught the hint of a muzzle flash and ducked under the console. The little building shook as the copter strafed it. It offered cover, but no protection. The slugs carved through it like paper. Nohar could only hope that they didn't have a steep enough angle to get a good shot at the floor.

The building shook with each impact, and electronic debris showered him from the console as it was torn apart by gunfire.

The gunfire suddenly became erratic. He could still hear the fifty-cal jackhammering in the distance, but the shack no longer shook with the impact. Nohar didn't risk a look out until the gunfire ceased completely.

When he looked out he could still see the enemy copter. It was banking to the left, but the steepness of the turn told Nohar that it was uncontrolled. The fifty-cal was almost pointing to the ground as the copter tried to pull an impossible inside turn.

Nohar's shots inside must've taken out part of the navigational controls.

The copter tried to spiral upward, turning so steeply that its rotors were almost perpendicular to the ground. At that point there was no way the pilot could maintain stability. The nose pitched down and the whole thing corkscrewed into the ground, out of Nohar's view behind the buildings. Though he couldn't see it, Nohar heard the impact and the secondary explosions of the inductors letting go.

He struggled to his feet. Each time it was becoming more of a trial. Pain was no longer localized in his arm. He felt bruised in his abdomen, the old wounds to his knee and shoulder, the cuts on his face, and a half-dozen places where pieces of the guard shack had cut into his flesh. Breathing was pain.

But he couldn't stop.

He looked down at the machine gun. There were a half-dozen shots left on the belt. With a shaking hand, he removed the empty part of the belt from the other side of the gun. Then he grabbed it, the heat of the barrel searing his knuckles when they brushed it, and started after the commandos.

CHAPTER 28

In the daylight, the camp seemed like a waiting room for hell. Heat rippled off of every surface. The smells were of metal and hot asphalt. The buildings were whitewashed cinder block the color of bleached bone. The few windows were boarded over with gray plastic construction panels. Everything was dry, functional, and dead.

Nohar limped along the asphalt strip between buildings, listening, concentrating on odors, trying to sense how close he was to the Bad Guys.

He was heading toward the south end of the compound, toward the Bad Guys and away from Manuel and the others. He was hoping to harass the attackers enough that Manuel and the others might have time to escape.

All he needed to do was buy time. The next helicopters were going to be news crews. Then it would be over.

Nohar didn't know how much time *he* had. His broken arm was clutched to his chest in a twisted parody of Maria's arthritis. He had to strip off his jacket and shirt because of the heat. His new black coloring made things even worse. His breath would come only in coppery gasps, and the fifty-cal machine gun felt as if it was about to tear his good arm out of its socket with every step he took.

The Bad Guys were quiet. For a while it seemed as

though he were the only living thing moving between the whitewashed buildings. The only things he heard were the dry wind and his own breath. The sense of isolation was so complete that he almost missed the first commando.

He was just about to turn a corner, heading toward the southern end of the compound, when he realized he smelled tension and exertion that wasn't his own. He paused long enough to hear two sets of footsteps, running lightly. The sound would have been quiet enough to miss beneath the noise of his own breathing if not for the tearing sound of the soles adhering to the asphalt.

Nohar had just stopped at the corner of the building when one of the commandos sprang around at him. He was ducking around the corner to cover the intersection. Nohar was right there. The man's submachine gun was up, but it was covering the street. It was a miscalculation, because the guy had to back up and turn to cover Nohar. Nohar didn't give him that chance.

The fifty-cal had a barrel that was nearly half the length of the distance separating them. Nohar jumped from the wall, pivoted on his good leg as if he were throwing a shot put, and swung the gun up so the barrel slammed into the man's chin.

The guy dropped like a sack of wet flour.

He had a partner.

As the weight of the fifty-cal still carried Nohar in a circle, the other one sprang up while Nohar's back was to the corner. Nohar could feel the man's presence, even before the first wild shot went off.

Nohar didn't let the new guy get a second shot. He swung the fifty-cal back in an arc, slamming the stock into the new guy's upper body. The impact shook Nohar's shoulder, sending daggers of pain through the joint. He heard another wild shot, and he smelled gunsmoke and the char of something ricocheting off of cinder block.

He also heard the body strike the asphalt.

Nohar turned back toward the downed commandos, carried partway by the pull of the swinging machine gun. Both were out of it for the foreseeable future, unconscious. The lower part of Number One's face, and Number Two's neck, were both turning a violent shade of purple.

Nohar dropped the fifty-cal. The sound was like another helicopter crashing into the ground. He couldn't carry the thing any farther.

He checked the intersection to be certain that there weren't more Bad Guys about to drop on him, and then he bent and grabbed one commando's gun. He had to fight a wave of nausea and vertigo as he bent over. The only reason he didn't vomit from the pain was because his stomach was completely empty. He stayed bent over, vision blacking out, for a few long moments before he could retrieve a weapon.

When Nohar straightened, he looked at what he'd picked up. These guys weren't prepped for stealth. Instead of the covert Black Widows, these submachine guns were matte-black Glock 23s, a common enough weapon for antiterrorist forces, as well as terrorists. The lightness of the weapon was a relief after the machine gun. It almost disappeared in his hand. The barrel on the thing barely extended beyond the trigger guard, just enough to prevent someone from accidentally shooting off a finger.

Nohar checked once more to assure himself that the two downed commandos weren't getting up, then he started a quiet halting run in the direction from which they had come.

                        *   *   *

The next set of Bad Guys, he heard in time.

Nohar was padding next to one of the dull cinder-
block buildings, his shoes lost somewhere with his shirt
and jacket. He heard movement from the other side
of one of the gray panels boarding over the windows.
He could hear whispered voices, though the words
were unintelligible. He had time to force his mind
away from his injuries, time to steel himself for a
confrontation.

Nohar circled around until he found the entrance
to the building. It was another panel of gray, leaning
loosely against a hole in the cinder block twice as high
as the windows. Nohar pushed it aside for a moment
with the Glock, listening. When he was sure the movement was deeper within the building, he slipped inside.

After the blinding-white desert exterior, the inside
of the building was midnight black. Nohar had to stare
into the darkness for a few moments before his eyes
adjusted to the monochrome gloom.

The first detail that Nohar could make out was an
IV drip bottle hanging from a stand in the corner. The
sight was like a lump of ice in his gut. He turned
slowly and saw a stretcher, a desk, a cart carrying a
few items of monitoring equipment.

He had stumbled into the camp's infirmary.

The sounds came from down a corridor to the rear
of the room where he stood. Nohar walked across the
linoleum floor, his steps stirring small clouds of dust
that made his nose itch. Naked fluorescent tubes hung
dead from a corrugated metal ceiling. The corridor
was flanked by drywall, the whitewash not quite covering the joints.

He passed two open doorways and checked briefly
into each one, making sure they were as empty as his
other senses told him they were. One was an operating

theater, the overhead light dangling like a spider about to feed on the table beneath. The other was a small ward with a half-dozen bedframes, mattresses gone.

Nohar moved down the corridor, hackles rising as he closed on the commandos. In his mind he was already picturing hospitals, like the one where his mother had died. He could imagine them filled with moreaus dying of an engineered plague. He could imagine the virus spreading through the hospital until the corridors were coated with infected blood and a stay there was a death sentence. He could imagine the pink doctors wading through the gore, unconcerned and uninfected, disposing of bodies. . . .

The copper taste of blood in his mouth wasn't exertion or fatigue anymore; it was anger. The humans who had created Nohar's kind would never accept them.

Man is dissatisfied until he can destroy what he has created.

At the end of the corridor hung a pair of swinging doors. There were two windows of dirty plastic that looked into the room beyond. Even before Nohar had reached it, he could hear that was where the Bad Guys were. He could make out two of them from their voices and the sound of their footsteps. One was about five meters from the door to the right, the other was two meters away and to the left.

Nohar swallowed and shouldered through the door and leveled the Glock at the nearest commando and fired high, above the body armor. The man took a slug in the back of the neck and fell face first into a pile of old boxes. Nohar swung the Glock over to where the other was and found himself facing a stack of more boxes—

Fuck!

Nohar ducked to the side just as the other one flung

himself around the obstructing boxes and started firing. Nohar swung his Glock around to fire at the same time. Nohar was faster, but he was falling backward and his aim was off. He felt something slam into his thigh as his own shots slammed into the commando's chest and neck.

The guy fell back through the swinging doors as Nohar hit the ground.

Nohar groaned. A bullet had torn into the meat of his left thigh, and it felt as if someone was drilling a hole in his leg with a dull bit. For a moment or two, the new insult flared greater in his awareness than his broken arm. Somehow, though, the anger seemed to feed on the pain, growing stronger with it. He lay there, feeling blood spread beneath him and the rage ignite within him.

He shouldn't have been able to move at all, he had been running so long on the verge of collapse.

But slowly, his broken body fought for each movement with a flare of pain. His breath shuddered and his limbs shook. He dropped the gun. But Nohar made it to his feet.

His leg wasn't broken. It bore his weight, the wound burning with the fire of torn muscle. Nohar forced the leg to move despite the pain. He moved deliberately, as if a sudden motion might split his skin and send his insides spilling on the ground in front of him. He bent down, feeling waves of nausea again, and grabbed the Glock from the man who'd gotten shot in the back of the neck. It lay on top of a pile of boxes, easier to reach than the one he had dropped on the floor.

Limping, Nohar pushed his way out of the building. He stopped in the lobby to tear some remnants from his pants to tie around the leg wound with one shaking hand.

*   *   *

Nohar made it all the way back to the wreckage of Krisoijn's helicopter. He stood at the edge of a debris field and stared. Unlike the one he'd flown in, this helicopter had been aimed straight down into a building. It looked as if the rotors had torn into its body and had ripped it apart. There were pieces of helicopter scattered for fifty meters in every direction.

Nohar could see two bodies. One was out on the asphalt, the rappelling cord wrapped around him, his head turned ninety degrees from the rest of his body. Nearer the wreckage was a victim of the helicopter's rotor. The blades had torn him nearly in half.

But there wasn't a sign of Krisoijn or any living Bad Guys.

Nohar didn't believe he had taken out all of them, and that meant that they had slipped by each other as Nohar made his way south. As Nohar turned around to catch up with the enemy, he heard the rapid hammer of a Glock echo in the distance. He started a limping run toward the source of the gunfire.

In addition to the rattle of the Glocks, he could hear the cough of a forty-five automatic. Nohar felt a sinking feeling.

He had left Necron's forty-five with Henderson.

He ran with a bobbing gait, pushing his burning leg harder than it wanted to go, his broken arm clutched to his chest as if it were fused to his body. He could feel tacky warmth seeping down his left leg, matting the fur beneath the makeshift bandage. The edges of his vision had turned black and every breath was an effort. He lost track of how many times he stumbled; his thoughts were losing any linear cohesion under the physical assault to his body.

Nohar ran down the center of the complex's main roadway, focused only on moving toward the small cluster of buildings where he'd heard the gunfire. Nohar knew where the shots must be coming from. It was the only thought that seemed to remain clear and focused through the red haze of pain.

The sounds were from a low undistinguished structure that squatted at the northern end of the main strip of asphalt. The main administration building.

There was a period of time that seemed to black out from his memory, and the next thing Nohar was aware of, he was leaning against the nose of the INS van that Henderson had driven them all here in. He stood on the cracked apron surrounding the administration building.

The gunfire had ceased. The silence was a sickening hole in the pit of Nohar's stomach.

The two swinging doors, metal and chicken-wire glass, showed two bullet holes near the top. Nohar could see lights in the hallway beyond the doors, and barely stopped to look through the glass. His consciousness had shrunk to a singularity that contained only the awareness of combat. His body was moving long after it should have stopped.

Nohar opened the door with his bad arm, unwilling to drop the Glock even for a moment. It felt as if a knife were slashing through his arm from the inside. He could feel bone grinding and muscle tearing. His jaw clenched shut, keeping him from crying out.

Even so, they must have heard him, because a pair of human forms turned the corner to face Nohar down the length of the hall. Nohar didn't hesitate. He sprayed the Glock, firing through the window at the two men. Fragments of glass bit into his skin, through the fur. He emptied the clip, and when the Glock was finished firing, Nohar realized that the deafening sound was his own roar.

Both of the men lay heaped at the end of the corridor.

Nohar stepped into the building, tossing away the empty gun and pulling out the pilot's sidearm. The air was rank with the smell of blood, human and feline.

Some of the feline blood wasn't his own.

The sounds coming from Nohar's throat had lost their resemblance to speech. He loped along the corridor, listening and trying to make out the scent of the enemy. There was no mistaking the smell of humans here. There had been five of them.

Three now.

Nohar stopped by the bodies, crouching, concentrating on where they had come from. His breaths were ragged and quick, and the pain in his arm and his leg had begun to tighten on his chest. Every sensation filtered through the pain, fragmenting everything into a series of disconnected moments. Through it only one thought managed to retain its focus, a hard kernel of anger that told him to kill the enemy.

Kill the men.

Kill the humans. . . .

Nohar moved through the building, the twists of the halls lost to him. He barely perceived the halls he passed through. What drew him was the scent of man, and the scent of blood.

Footsteps came toward him, and he faded into the shadow of a nearby doorway. The pilot's gun fell to the ground, forgotten.

When the commando ran past Nohar, toward his downed fellows and the sound of gunfire, Nohar reached his intact arm out of the doorway, his claws fully extended. He caught the man in the midsection, and the man's weapon went flying down the corridor. Nohar had time to see the man's eyes widen, before he kicked out with his good leg, tearing from the groin down, and throwing him into the opposite wall. The effort dropped Nohar onto the ground as his left leg collapsed, but he rolled and pushed himself upright with his good hand. His hand slipped a few times in the man's blood, but he managed to struggle upright.

Nohar left the man to slowly go into shock as he limped toward the last two enemies.

The scent of blood became stronger as he approached the heart of the building. Human and feline, and other scents merged into an all-encompassing odor of death. Nohar knew he smelled his own death, and his son's, and especially that of the humans who had brought this down—

Nohar sprang through a doorway, and into the maw of death itself.

The first one was right beside the doorway, guarding it. Nohar knew exactly where he was from the sound of his breathing and the smell of his sweat. Nohar turned, his good hand reaching the man's throat, the claws biting into the trachea. He was nowhere near quick enough. The man's weapon fired once as Nohar pulled the man's neck free. The shot slammed into Nohar's abdomen, Nohar stumbled back into the room, feeling a fire in his gut worse than anything he felt in his arm or leg. He could feel blood sheeting across his stomach, and down his back.

His back hit the wall of the room, and fragmented images—pieces of the scene in front of him—began sinking into his consciousness.

The Necron Avenger, John Samson, lay on the floor unmoving.

Near the doorway, at Nohar's feet, lay Sarah Henderson. Necron's automatic had spilled from her hand, and her eyes stared upward, glassy and unmoving. She had taken a half-dozen shots, one right in the chest. Nohar was standing in a pool of her blood. Maria's wheelchair was behind a large desk with an inset comm. Her face was swollen where someone had struck her, probably breaking the cheekbone. But she still breathed.

Standing behind that desk, facing him, was his son.

"Manuel." Nohar's voice was a ragged whisper. He spoke as if the flesh had been scoured from his throat.

Nohar tried to take a step forward, but an Afrikaans voice said, "Don't move."

Krisoijn stood behind Nohar's son, holding a gun to his temple.

CHAPTER 29

Nohar froze, and that gave time for his brain to start working again. He had screwed up. He had let anger override everything else. Now here he was with his guts leaking out everywhere, his body racked by so many insults that he couldn't distinguish separate sources for the pain. The pain was an omnipresent haze that he sucked in with each breath. Every few heartbeats his vision would black out for a moment as another wave of agony broke over him.

He shouldn't have been able to stand, but, seeing Manuel, he managed to.

Seeing Manuel had an almost supernatural force. He could see everything that he had missed before. Maria's bone structure, the shadows of his own coloring. Manuel's eyes could have been born directly from Nohar's mother.

"Nohar?" Manuel had the same husky voice as his mother. He tried to take a step forward, but Krisoijn held him back.

"No one moves," Krisoijn said. "This is messy enough already."

Nohar shook his head and forced the words out, "It's over. Long Beach, the Clinic, it's all exposed. . . ."

Krisoijn laughed.

Nohar stared. "He knows," Manuel said. He reached onto the console and tossed a ramcard over at Nohar's feet. "He doesn't even care about this anymore."

Nohar looked down at the card, glinting rainbows in Henderson's blood.

"Why?" The question felt as if it tore the flesh from inside his stomach. He was beginning to feel dizzy and light-headed. "Why go through with this—" He felt his knees giving way. He dropped next to Henderson's body. His good hand caught himself on her stomach. Her flesh was blood-soaked deadweight.

"You, Nohar." Krisoijn said. "I wanted to see you die."

"You got what you wanted," Manuel said. His voice was quick and strained, showing the pull of adrenaline. Nohar recognized it. "Why don't you go meet your plane—"

Nohar stared into Henderson's unmoving eyes, feeling his life pump out of the hole in his stomach with every heartbeat. "Plane . . ." Nohar whispered. He barely heard the word himself beneath the sound of his heartbeat.

"You cannot attack such a threat on a single front." Krisoijn was distant, the Afrikaans accent just cutting through Nohar's pulse. "Your escape from Gilbertez compromised this operation. The whole enterprise had to be terminated. You've done us damage, but you haven't come close to stopping our effort."

The operation at Long Beach was only a small part of something much larger. Nohar didn't know if Manuel realized it, but the fact that Krisoijn had even hinted at that meant he didn't intend to leave anyone alive. The bastard knew the media were coming, but he planned for them to find an inexplicable bloodbath where his own corpse was absent. The soldiers he had brought in with him, the bodies scattered around this abandoned place, they probably hadn't known that much.

Nohar forced himself to look up at Krisoijn. The man's eyes were dead, black, and showed little trace of any emotion. Nohar looked at Manuel and saw the fury burning in him, mirroring his own. Nohar could see the tense muscles, the strain of reining in all the instincts to flee or fight. "I'm sorry," Nohar said to Manuel. He was apologizing for his failure, the entire string of events that had begun with denying him a father, and ended with him impotent, bleeding on the ground only three meters from his son.

Krisoijn spoke. "We are the dominant species on this planet, and we will not tolerate a threat to our existence."

Nohar knew that he was about to shoot. He had to do something. He tightened his stomach muscles, and held his broken arm to the wound, pushing himself up against Henderson's body. "You murdering bastard. There's no reason for this."

"No reason?" Krisoijn said, his voice raising. For the first time there seemed some emotion in his voice. Nohar struggled to his feet as Krisoijn spoke. "Do you have any idea what you engineered monstrosities did to my homeland? A whole generation of my family was lost during the war, and in the revolution that followed all of my brothers and sisters—all of them— were killed. I took a machete to the face, and barely survived myself. I was six years old."

Nohar tried to focus. To fix the room in his brain, to connect the impressions through the fog of pain he walked through. His son and Krisoijn stood behind the central control panel, in front of the giant holo map of the complex. On the map, lights blinked, show- ing the status of the compound. There were two flashing red lights where the two helicopters had gone down.

Maria was in a corner, sitting in her wheelchair, still unconscious. He could hear her breathing, ragged but steady. Two guns lay on the floor. The dead human's Glock lay on the floor near his body by the wall opposite Nohar. Less than a meter away from Nohar was the forty-five that Henderson had been using. Beyond that, in front of the console was John Samson, face down. . . .

For the first time Nohar realized that there was no blood coming from John Samson's body. His clothes were splattered with blood, but from all appearances it was Henderson's. And, if he concentrated, Nohar could hear him breathing. It wasn't the slow rhythmic respiration of someone who had lost consciousness.

"He didn't kill your family," Nohar said, waving his good arm at Manuel. "Let him go."

Krisoijn shook his head. "Every one of you is a danger to the species." He cocked his head toward the door. "How many people have you killed today?"

Nohar took a step forward. "You had my son."

Krisoijn pressed the Glock into Manuel's head and said, "I'll make you a deal. You give me back one of my brothers, and you can have him."

Nohar staggered forward another step, and his foot was next to the forty-five. Nohar stared at Krisoijn, keeping his attention. "How many men have you killed, Krisoijn?"

"In defense of the species."

"Royd, Samson, how many others?" Nohar shook his head. It was cruel, but he was hoping that word of his father's death might prod John into action. "You're just another fanatic. Just like my father."

"Do not compare me to an animal." As Krisoijn spoke, Nohar's foot kicked the gun gently. It slid across the linoleum and stopped next to John Samson's head.

"Both of you wrapped up in your own righteousness," Nohar said. "*They* wronged you, and *they* must pay. Datia saw humanity as the enemy, you see the nonhumans—it's just revenge."

"You are a danger to the survival of the species—"

"And you don't hesitate to engineer the same kind of weapons that devastated your homeland. Your brothers died in the revolution. Which one of the plagues killed your parents?"

John realized a gun was in reach. He inched his hand toward it. His effort was too slow, especially since Nohar could see plainly that he was on the floor out of Krisoijn's view behind the console. Samson obviously didn't realize that, and he moved cautiously.

"I think this has gone far enough," Krisoijn said. Nohar could see the tensing of the muscles in his arm as he prepared to squeeze the trigger.

"If you shoot him, what's going to keep me from tearing out your throat?" Nohar tried to take all of his resolve and put it into his voice.

"You'll be dead before you cross the table." Krisoijn's voice was confident, but Nohar could see the hesitation in his arm.

Samson's hand touched the butt of the forty-five.

"I know you," Nohar said. "My family was killed by the enemy, too. My mother died carrying my only siblings, from a virus designed in some human lab. My father was shot down by pinks in the National Guard."

"You don't know me!"

"We know each other, Krisoijn." Nohar stared straight into Krisoijn's eyes as he listened to Samson moving. "You know what drives me. If you put a bullet into my son's head, you *know* that nothing will stop me from tearing your heart out."

Krisoijn was backing away from Manuel, the Glock trained on Manuel's head. "Maybe so," Krisoijn said, reaching the wall and edging toward the door. He was angling around the console to bring both of them under the stare of the submachine gun. "Maybe I have to kill you first—"

Krisoijn's gun moved, just a little, toward Nohar. Samson had been paying attention. He rolled out from behind the console, aiming up at Krisoijn. The automatic fired twice before it clicked on an empty chamber.

The Glock fired as Manuel ducked. Krisoijn fell back toward the wall, the two bullets lodged in his body armor.

Nohar leaped at him.

The jump at Krisoijn felt as if it tore his intestines loose from his abdomen. His broken arm wouldn't move, so Nohar shouldered into Krisoijn's gun arm. The Glock kept firing, blowing holes in the holo map, throwing sparks across the room.

When Nohar's full weight connected, the drywall gave way and they blew through into the neighboring room, a massive chamber divided into office cubicles.

They stopped moving forward when Krisoijn slammed into a cubicle wall. The Glock had stopped firing. Nohar heard the trigger click a few times before Krisoijn brought it down on the side of his skull.

The impact caused Nohar's vision to black out, and he stumbled back on his wounded leg.

Blood clouded his vision, it took most of his strength to yell back through the hole in the wall. "Manuel, get Maria and John out of here—"

His words were cut short by a stabbing pain beneath his ribs. His vision cleared enough to see Krisoijn's hand removing a knife from his side. He slashed again, but Nohar managed to block the thrust with his good arm.

Krisoijn faced him with almost a feral grin as he waved the knife between them. He'd tossed away the empty Glock. "I don't need a gun to finish you off."

Krisoijn swung again, and Nohar blocked the thrust with his good arm. This time he felt the blade take a part of his bicep with it. He could feel his strength ebbing. Pain and fatigue were pulling him down with iron bands. There was no way he could hold off Krisoijn for any length of time. Defending himself was pointless as near to the edge as he was.

"Me, maybe . . ." Nohar said.

Krisoijn must have seen the resignation in Nohar's eyes, because he grinned even wider. He dove with a fatal thrust toward Nohar's neck.

". . . but not my son," Nohar raised his hand for a block, and the blade passed through the palm and out the back. The pain of the knife stabbing through tendon and bone was distant—everything seemed distant, as if he was watching at a remove.

Krisoijn's expression changed when Nohar's hand grabbed his own. Nohar's hand enveloped Krisoijn's in a crushing grip that drove the knife even deeper.

Nohar pulled back, dragging Krisoijn toward him.

Krisoijn beat at Nohar's hand with his free hand, but Nohar barely felt it as he bit into Krisoijn's wrist. The man screamed as Nohar's fangs sank into his arm. Nohar twisted Krisoijn's hand until he felt the bones separate and Krisoijn dropped to his knees.

Krisoijn fell to the ground holding a stump of a right arm. Nohar's right hand slowly, painfully, unclenched, letting go of Krisoijn's hand. The hand fell, and the knife slowly slid out of the wound to fall next to it.

Krisoijn got to his feet, clutching his bleeding arm to his stomach.

Nohar felt his legs give way. He fell, unable to raise either hand to protect himself. He landed on his left side, barely turning to avoid falling on his broken arm.

The world was turning gray. Even the pain seemed distant, felt through a gauzy haze. He couldn't find the strength to move any more.

He stared upward, at the corrugated steel of the ceiling, sensing that he was dying.

Dying wasn't good enough for Krisoijn. He stepped into Nohar's field of vision, holding the knife in his left hand. He knelt, putting a knee on Nohar's chest. Nohar didn't feel his weight, he didn't feel much of anything anymore.

Krisoijn raised the blade, and Nohar waited for it to bite into his neck.

Before the blade descended, Krisoijn turned to look away from Nohar. A look of surprise crossed his face. Then a spray of bullets took away most of that expression above the lower jaw. He fell, his scar the only recognizable piece of his face left.

Nohar turned toward the wall they had broken through, and saw Manuel standing there holding a Glock.

The one the last Bad Guy dropped, Nohar thought.

He might have smiled before he lost consciousness.

It might have been hours later, but Nohar managed a small episode of lucidity. He opened his eyes enough to see the faces of some pink EMTs manhandling him into another helicopter. He was assaulted by the sounds of dozens of people crowding too close. He saw flashes of sunlight off of vid cameras, past the guys carrying him.

Fuck, hate hospitals.

He turned his head and saw the IV bag above his head. He was strapped down, immobile. He could feel burning tightness in his leg, his arm, his hand, and especially in his stomach—which had the weird feeling of having been melted away. He was light-headed and everything seemed far away.

Painkillers, he thought, his brain refusing to put together complete sentences.

He was still trying to figure out why he wasn't back home at his cabin.

"You're going to be all right, you hear me?"

Nohar turned to see a familiar-looking face. *Knew his mother.* Nohar managed a friendly expression, through the drugged haze. He tried to say something, but his vocal cords didn't seem connected to him any more.

"You hear me?"

Yes . . .

"You're a hero, Dad. You know that?"

Dad. He wondered at the word for a few seconds, then decided he liked it. *Manuel,* the name came to him finally.

Manuel reached out and touched his shoulder before the EMTs hauled him into the helicopter.

"A hero," Manuel shouted above the rising sound of the rotors.

Nohar shook his head.

No, Nohar thought of his father. *Not a hero.*

He looked at his son, feeling his head clear for a moment. "We're going to be fine." He managed to whisper. "Both of us."

Manuel nodded, though Nohar didn't know if he could hear him above the noise of the helicopter. Then the doors slid shut on him, and they were taking off.

Was it enough? Nohar wondered as he closed his eyes.

It was better than his own father.

It would have to do.